AN AMATEUR SLEUTH'S GUIDE TO MURDER
"Plan a cozy day by the fire with a cup of tea, snuggle in, and enjoy. The day will be over before you know it. And there may even be time to make Lynn's Yummy Murderous Mac and Cheese for dinner."
—Nancy Coco, author of the Candy-Coated mystery series

FIVE FURRY FAMILIARS
"A fun read for those who enjoy tales of witches and magic."
—*Kirkus Reviews*

THREE TAINTED TEAS
"A kitchen witch reluctantly takes over as planner for a cursed wedding. . . . This witchy tale is a hoot."
—*Kirkus Reviews*

ONE POISON PIE
"*One Poison Pie* deliciously blends charm and magic with a dash of mystery and a sprinkle of romance. Mia Malone is a zesty protagonist who relies on her wits to solve the crime, and the enchanting cast of characters that populate Magic Springs are a delight."
—Daryl Wood Gerber, Agatha winner and nationally best-selling author of the Cookbook Nook Mysteries and Fairy Garden Mysteries

"A witchy cooking cozy for fans of the supernatural and good eating."
—*Kirkus Reviews*

A FIELD GUIDE TO HOMICIDE
"The best entry in this character-driven series mixes a well-plotted mystery with a romance that rings true to life."
—*Kirkus Reviews*

"Informative as well as entertaining, *A Field Guide to Homicide* is the perfect book for cozy mystery lovers who entertain thoughts of writing novels themselves. . . . This is, without a doubt, one of the best Cat Latimer novels to date."
—*Criminal Element*

"Cat is a great heroine with a lot of spirit that readers will enjoy solving the mystery [with]."
—*Parkersburg News & Sentinel*

SCONED TO DEATH
"The most intriguing aspect of this story is the writers' retreat itself. Although the writers themselves are not suspect, they add freshness and new relationships to the series. Fans of Lucy Arlington's 'Novel Idea' mysteries may want to enter the writing world from another angle."
—*Library Journal*

OF MURDER AND MEN
"A Colorado widow discovers that everything she knew about her husband's death is wrong. . . . Interesting plot and quirky characters."
—*Kirkus Reviews*

A STORY TO KILL
"Well-crafted . . . Cat and crew prove to be engaging characters, and Cahoon does a stellar job of keeping them—and the reader—guessing."
—*Mystery Scene*

"Lynn Cahoon has hit the golden trifecta—murder, intrigue, and a really hot handyman. Better get your flashlight handy, *A Story to Kill* will keep you reading all night."
—Laura Bradford, author of the Amish Mysteries

TOURIST TRAP MYSTERIES
"Lynn Cahoon's popular Tourist Trap series is set all around the charming coastal town of South Cove, California, but the heroine, Jill Gardner, owns a delightful bookstore/coffee shop so a lot of the scenes take place there. This is one of my go-to cozy mystery series, bookish or not, and I'm always eager to get my hands on the next book!"
—*Hope By the Book*

"Murder, dirty politics, pirate lore, and a hot police detective: *Guidebook to Murder* has it all! A cozy lover's dream come true."
—Susan McBride, author of the Debutante Dropout Mysteries

"This was a good read, and I love the author's style, which was warm and friendly. . . . I can't wait to read the next book in this wonderfully appealing series."
—*Dru's Book Musings*

"I am happy to admit that some of my expectations were met while other aspects of the story exceeded my own imagination. . . . This mystery novel was light, fun, and kept me thoroughly engaged. I only wish it was longer."
—*The Young Folks*

"*If the Shoe Kills* is entertaining, and I would be happy to visit Jill and the residents of South Cove again."
—*MysteryPlease.com*

"In *If the Shoe Kills,* author Lynn Cahoon gave me exactly what I wanted. She crafted a well-told small-town murder that kept me guessing who the murderer was until the end. I will definitely have to take a trip back to South Cove and maybe even visit tales of Jill Gardner's past in the previous two Tourist Trap Mystery books. I do love a holiday mystery! And with this book, so will you."
—*ArtBooksCoffee.com*

Books by Lynn Cahoon

The Tourist Trap Mystery Series
Guidebook to Murder * Mission to Murder * If the Shoe
Kills * Dressed to Kill * Killer Run * Murder on Wheels * Tea
Cups and Carnage * Hospitality and Homicide * Killer Party *
Memories and Murder * Murder in Waiting * Picture Perfect
Frame * Wedding Bell Blues * A Vacation to Die For * Songs
of Wine and Murder * Olive You to Death * Vows of Murder
Novellas
Rockets' Dead Glare * A Deadly Brew * Santa Puppy *
Corned Beef and Casualties * Mother's Day Mayhem * A Very
Mummy Holiday * Murder in a Tourist Town

The Kitchen Witch Mystery Series
One Poison Pie * Two Wicked Desserts * Three Tainted Teas *
Four Charming Spells * Five Furry Familiars * Six Stunning
Sirens * Seven Secret Spellcasters
Novellas
Chili Cauldron Curse * Murder 101 * Have a Holly, Haunted
Holiday * Two Christmas Mittens

The Cat Latimer Mystery Series
A Story to Kill * Fatality by Firelight * Of Murder and Men *
Slay in Character * Sconed to Death * A Field Guide to
Homicide

The Farm to Fork Mystery Series
Who Moved My Goat Cheese? * Killer Green Tomatoes * One
Potato, Two Potato, Dead * Deep Fried Revenge * Killer
Comfort Food * A Fatal Family Feast
Novellas
Have a Deadly New Year * Penned In * A Pumpkin Spice
Killing * A Basketful of Murder

The Survivors' Book Club Mystery Series
Tuesday Night Survivors' Club * Secrets in the Stacks * Death
in the Romance Aisle * Reading Between the Lies * Dying to
Read

The Bainbridge Island Mystery Series
An Amateur Sleuth's Guide to Murder

Seven Secret Spellcasters

LYNN CAHOON

Kensington Publishing Corp.
kensingtonbooks.com

KENSINGTON BOOKS are published by

Kensington Publishing Corp.
900 Third Avenue
New York, NY 10022

All Kensington titles, imprints, and distributed lines are available at special quantity discounts for bulk purchases for sales promotion, premiums, fund-raising, educational, or institutional use. Special book excerpts or customized printings can also be created to fit specific needs. For details, write or phone the office of the Kensington Sales Manager: Attn.: Sales Department. Kensington Publishing Corp., 900 Third Avenue, New York, NY 10022. Phone: 1-800-221-2647.

KENSINGTON and the KENSINGTON COZIES teapot logo Reg US Pat. & TM Off.

First Kensington Paperback Edition: August 2025
ISBN: 978-1-4967-5283-3

ISBN: 978-1-4967-5284-0 (ebook)

10 9 8 7 6 5 4 3 2 1

Printed in the United States of America

The authorized representative in the EU for product safety and compliance is eucomply OU, Parnu mnt 139b-14, Apt 123
Tallinn, Berlin 11317, hello@eucompliancepartner.com

To Megan Kelly, for all the support and book talk over the years.

Seven Secret Spellcasters

CHAPTER 1

Mia Malone sat in her catering director's office at the Magic Springs Lodge, reading the new catering proposal specifications again. Trying to understand them was a whole other task. On the one hand, the Lodge's loosening of Frank Hines's policies from when her former boss ruled the hotel was a good thing. It meant that Mia's Morsel's, her catering company, would be able to at least send proposals to a local board that would make decisions on who would be awarded the contract. On the other hand, the specifications were so detailed that Mia didn't think her company would qualify to even compete. Even with the extensive community contacts of her current manager, Abigail Majors.

Blake Sandburg, Mia's new boss at the Lodge, wanted bids from catering companies that had at least fifty employees, had a nondiscrimination policy in place for staff, and would sign an NDA for each assignment. The minimum-employee policy alone would rule out any catering company in the local area, and most Boise-based companies didn't want the three-hour-each-way drive for a local event. She guessed that Twin Falls companies might apply, but they mostly hated coming up the mountain, especially for evening events. Mia thought her new boss might have to change her criteria.

Blake was all business. Her meetings ran fast with a preset agenda. If you had something to bring up, you sent the request to her email no later than two business days before the weekly meeting. Or the item was put on the agenda for the next week.

Frank liked to play with the staff's minds. Blake didn't want anyone to be surprised or have to think on their feet. Working for Frank had been a nightmare, but Mia wasn't sure working for Blake was going to be much different.

James Holder, the head chef at the Lodge and kitchen manager, stuck his head into her office. "Want some butternut-squash soup for lunch? I accidentally made too much when I was testing a recipe for next week. I'm serving freshly baked bread with it. Come into my office, and we can plot a mutiny while we're eating."

The kitchen and James, as the chef, had been given new rules as well. Menus were to be standardized with only limited menu changes that allowed them to save money on ordering in bulk. This also meant that James was limited in what he could order from Majors Grocery in town. A problem she'd heard about not only from James, but also from the store owner and her boyfriend, Trent Majors. She'd told Trent to file a complaint with the corporate office, not her. She'd told his mother, Abigail, the same thing when she complained about the catering rules that were excluding Mia's Morsels. She wasn't fighting anyone's battles but her own.

Mia knew there was more to the story than the loss of the Lodge's business adding to Trent's recent bad mood. His dog, Cerby, was at his hellhound training at the McMann werewolf camp in the deep woods north of Magic Springs. Trent got updates every evening from Cerby's trainer. And, from what she'd heard, Cerby was acting out due to experiencing homesickness.

The cages they'd seen when she went up to the camp with Trent last week to drop off Cerby had been huge and indestructible, with iron bars. She'd made Trent leave Cerby's favorite blue-and-white print blanket and stuffed dragon with him, even though his other classmates didn't seem to need anything from home. The cage next to Cerby had held the biggest Rottweiler Mia had ever seen. And she was positive that the "cat" in the next cage was a mountain lion.

Cerby, now a year-old Maltese, looked like he'd been misplaced in the residential camp. When they'd taken him up for testing, even the werewolf who'd completed his intake had been skeptical until the five-pound Maltese had levitated the six-foot-tall trainer and held him there until Trent convinced Cerby that the man had a treat in his pocket.

As Mia closed her computer and tucked the printout of the application process into her tote, her phone rang. It was Trent. "Hey, James, I'll meet you there in a couple of minutes. I need to take this."

"Tell Trent hi," James said as he left her office, closing the door behind him.

She answered and followed his directions as she sat back in her chair. "James says hi. What's going on?"

"Why do you think something has to be going on for your boyfriend to call in the middle of the day on a Wednesday?" His warm voice held a twinge of humor.

"Nothing's wrong? I guess I'm just on edge. I'm so glad I'm off tomorrow before the Friday event. I'm not sure I can get all of Blake's pre-event checklists done before she wants me to start on the debriefing checklists. The woman loves her reports. Paper. Not a verbal check-in at the meeting or an email. She wants a hard copy on her desk no later than Monday morning at ten a.m. This is a routine, monthly dinner for the Magic Springs Men's Club. What happens when I do a big event?" She sighed, then realized she'd been venting for a while. "Sorry, so why did you call?"

"Are you still getting off at two today, like you planned?" He waited for her to confirm, then continued. "Good, because we need to go pick up Cerby. Max McMann, his trainer, thinks he's not ready for hellhound training. Maybe in a few months. He said they might need to do an individualized program for him."

"Uh-oh, what did he do?" Mia hadn't liked the idea of sending the dog away for a residential training program in the first place. Cerby didn't like being away from Trent. When he'd stayed with Mia while Trent was fishing with his dad, he dreamed of dragons. And what Cerby dreamed, he shared with Mia. Even that distraction hadn't kept him from missing Trent. He slept with her on her bed. Not in an outdoor cage.

"Max wouldn't tell me, but there was laughter from the other guys when he called. He said we'd find out when we got to the camp." He said something to some-one else. "Look, I've got to go if I'm taking off. I'll pick you up at the school at two fifteen?"

"Sounds good. I'm missing my Cerby cuddles." She hung up and tucked her phone into the back pocket of her jeans. It was funny how quickly the little hellhound had become part of her life as well as Trent's. She'd eat a quick lunch with James, get all the gossip, then come back and finish the midweek report.

Tomorrow, Grans was coming over to help her set up the new potions lab. Abigail had agreed—no, insisted—on helping them stock the shelves. After she took the coven's national council test on Monday, Mia's training as a kitchen witch would be complete. Her grandmother had scheduled a transfer of powers the night before Halloween. Just in case she decided to join the coven at the party they were having the next eve-ning. She thought it unlikely, but her grandmother had insisted she leave the option available.

Mia wasn't a joiner. She found her groups of friends more naturally in her activities. Okay, she admitted to herself, her friends were all work friends. But really close work friends.

The October calendar kept filling up with must-dos, but at least now, Cerby would be home with them. She'd missed the little guy more than she'd realized she would. Maybe she was reacting to Christina Adams, her former employee and almost sister-in-law, in the process of moving to Oregon. She wasn't gone just on a vacation. Christina was leasing an apartment and at-tending the mandatory training for her new job that started the second week of November.

Change was happening all over Magic Springs, and
Mia wasn't liking it one bit. She knocked on the open
door to James's office, and he waved her inside. He
was on the phone. "Yes, Blake, I know I haven't turned
in my proposed menu changes for November, but you
also changed my supply chain and I'm scrambling to
make sure I can locally source the product for the holidays."

He bounced his head back and forth as he listened to
her response. "Well, yes, that would help tremendously.
I'd love to use my normal suppliers for the holiday season. As soon as I confirm they can still supply us after
I told them we weren't going to be using them anymore, I'll turn in those new menus."

Mia tried to stifle a laugh.

"Of course, I understand this is a onetime exception.
I'll be looking for new suppliers who meet your criteria
right after I confirm the menu changes and get that on
your desk." James grinned at Mia. "One step at a time,
Blake."

Mia lifted one of the covers on a tray in front of her.
The soup smelled divine—and it even had a hint of
cinnamon. Her mouth watered.

"I've got to go now," James said as he hung up. He
took the cover off the other tray revealing two bowls
and a plate of warm rolls with a generous side of butter. "You can tell Trent he's welcome when you see him
tonight. I got us a reprieve from Bossy Blake. I never
thought I'd say this, but I'm kind of missing Frank."

"Bite your tongue. At least Blake isn't actively trying to get rid of me. At least not that I know of. Have
you heard anything?" Mia took the cloth napkin and

put it on her lap, then she took a spoonful of the soup. She closed her eyes and groaned. "Yummy."

"No wonder Trent keeps you around. You're very sensual." He smiled at her as he took a sip of the soup. "And you have great taste. This is yummy. But no, I haven't heard that our Bossy Blakie wants to fire anyone, especially not you. You earned the weekly star for turning in all your paperwork last week on time. Tell me your magic."

Mia almost choked on her soup. James didn't know her secret—that she was a kitchen witch—and she preferred that no one at the Lodge ever find out. She wiped her face with the napkin. "No magic, just hard work."

"You always were a stickler for the details of the job. I can't believe Frank thought this place would even run without you." Then James went on to tell her all the gossip, including the fact that Frank was now managing a fast-food restaurant in Billings, Montana. "Of course, it is a chain franchise."

Mia laughed at her friend's jokes and kept up her end up of the conversation, but as soon as she'd finished her lunch, she excused herself to get back to work. "Trent and I are going for a drive up to Wolf Creek Mountain this afternoon. Before the weather changes."

"I bet he wants to scope out some hunting places for his dad. I can't believe that man has such a huge guide business. He's always got at least one of his clients staying at the Lodge during their hunting trips. I guess it makes the trip upper end if they don't have to sleep in a rustic cabin or on the ground." James stood and walked to his office door. "But don't let me keep you. I know you want to get ahead on those reports, Miss Follows All the Rules."

"That's all I do anymore, reports," Mia grumbled as she headed out the door. "Thanks for lunch. It's the perfect soup for a chilly fall day."

"I thought so as well," James said as he stood watching her from the doorway. "I know you have a secret, and I'm going to find out what it is. No one can get all of Blake's reports done without a little help."

Mia wished she used magic to help her get the tedious work done, but Grans had warned her for years that a kitchen witch never used their powers for personal gain. She felt her power in the dishes she cooked, and she had an innate ability to make flavors sing in her cooking. But making meals was rarely for her. It was to take care of others—either family or her community. That was her real magic. Feeding others.

By the time she got home, Trent was already at the school waiting for her. Mia's Morsels was shut down on Wednesdays since Abigail had changed the delivery schedule after Christina had given notice. Abigail and the new hire, Finley Shiley, now cooked on Mondays and delivered on Tuesdays. Unless they had an event that weekend, the business location was closed on Wednesdays and then open for drop-ins and classes on Thursdays through Saturdays. Tomorrow, Mia didn't have a class to teach, but she needed to prep for the next one on Autumn Soups. She had an existing class lesson in the file, but she wanted to adjust and add to the recipes she offered. That way, students could take a class several times without getting bored.

Trent sat on the steps to the old academy, leaning against the front door.

She locked up her older-than-dirt Honda and went to meet him. "Do you mind if I run upstairs to change and check on Mr. Darcy? Now that Dorian has left his body, he gets lonely when no one's around."

"And he can't open a door or a portal to go outside without Dorian's magic. It must be frustrating to go back to being just a cat." He stood and gave her a quick kiss. "We have some time. I told them I'd be there before six. That's feeding time, and they don't like having extra people around the hellhounds then."

"Mr. Darcy's not just a cat, he's my familiar. But yeah, I think he got used to having Dorian's magic around, as well as someone to play with all the time." She unlocked the door, and they went inside. The school was quiet and cool. Most of the time, the place was filled with noise and energy. With Christina leaving, and her fiancé, Levi Majors, Trent's brother, going with her, Mia's life had quieted down a lot. Trent walked with her as they went up the stairs to the third floor. "Gloria, she's not as sociable with Mr. Darcy as he'd like. I hear them talking about me at times, but I think she mostly sleeps when the school is quiet."

"Have you thought about my offer?" He held his hand out for her keys and unlocked the apartment door. It was probably overkill to have locks on the front door, the kitchen door, and the apartment door, but as they were still finding secret passages into the school, Mia liked being a little security-focused.

She heard Gloria's laugh at her thought.

Trent looked at her when he opened the door. "What's she giggling about?"

At odd times, Trent could hear her kitchen witch doll. Mia thought it was mostly when Gloria wanted him to hear her. "She thinks my assumption about security is funny. I know, Gloria, if someone wanted to get inside, locks wouldn't keep them out."

"But locks will keep humans out, especially the kids who used to use this place as party central," Trent called out to the doll. He closed the door and looked at Mia. "You're ignoring my other question."

"I'm not. There are a lot of moving parts right now." Mr. Darcy was on his back legs reaching up to her. Mia picked him up and headed to her bedroom to change. "Hey, buddy, Trent and I have to leave for a few hours to go get Cerby from camp. We'll be home and make dinner soon, and I'll be here all day tomorrow, okay?"

Mr. Darcy jumped on the bed, then hurried out of the bedroom to go see Trent. He didn't think her schedule was okay, so he was going to ignore her now. He'd be mad when she got home, but there was nothing she could do about it unless she got another pet. Or accept Trent's invitation.

Before moving in with Trent, they needed to have a long talk about logistics. On the one hand, Mr. Darcy would have Cerby during the day if they moved in together. But she wasn't sure if that was a good idea or not. Mia slipped out of her business casual clothes and into jeans with a T-shirt and her leather jacket. She was pulling on her socks and boots when her phone buzzed with a text.

Tell Mr. Darcy that I'll bring Muffy with me tomorrow. I feel his distress even over at my house.

Mia keyed a quick thanks to her grandmother and tucked her phone into her jeans pocket. When she got into the kitchen, Mr. Darcy was eating the canned food that Trent had dished up for him. Trent had opened a soda and was scrolling through his emails on his phone.

"Mr. Darcy, Gran says she's bringing Muffy over tomorrow, so stop being such a baby. You'll see Cerby tonight." Mia grabbed a bottle of water from the fridge and stood in front of Trent, who was still staring at his screen. "I'm ready."

He glanced up at her and smiled. "I can see that. I took out hamburger meat for tacos and put it in the fridge if that's okay. I'll cook when we get back."

"Sounds great, thanks." Mia started thinking about what she had to go with the tacos. "I can make Spanish rice and maybe homemade salsa and tortillas. I've been working on a recipe."

Trent was still sitting and reading something on his phone.

"What's going on? Work issues?" She took a sip of her water.

He tucked the phone away and stood. "No. But it's a good thing that we're going to get Cerby. An inspector from the National Office of Magical Creatures is coming to Magic Springs next week to interview me and examine Cerby. Someone from the coven has inquired why a witch who had rescinded his powers was given a hellhound from the Goddess."

"That's not good. You need to call your mom." Mia grabbed her keys and purse.

"You call her on the way to Wolf Creek. I need to focus on the drive." He waited for her to lock the door, then they started downstairs. "I gave Mr. Darcy some clean water too. He seemed to be annoyed at what he had."

"That's because Dorian would turn on the kitchen tap for him. He likes his water cold and fresh. I might have to get one of those fountains that keeps water running all the time. I never thought I'd say I miss the days when my cat was sharing his body with a witch's earth-bound spirit." Mia turned on the outside lights since it would be dark when they got back and left the foyer light on as well. She didn't like the school to appeared dark. The building attracted trouble when it was dark and unattended. If she moved in with Trent, she'd have to find someone to rent the upstairs apartment. Someone she trusted. That was one of the reasons she hadn't yet given him an answer.

Besides, she was setting up her potions lab here. What would she do, come over to the school to do her kitchen witch work? Maybe it would be a good thing to separate work and life. Which made her think about the fact that her grandmother had been less than forthcoming about what her responsibilities would be when she took over the role.

As she said, too many moving parts.

When they got to Wolf Creek, Mia realized why the werewolves who ran the training camp had suggested a more individualized plan of training for Cerby. Unlike the first time she'd visited, the place was lit up in pale-pink fairy lights with what looked like a carnival set up in the forest. Mia could see the Ferris wheel circulating

in the background. Cerby had been doing some redec-
orating.

Trent stared into the tree behind Cerby's cage. "Is
that what I think it is?"

Mia nodded. She'd seen the image when Cerby had
stayed over and shared his dream. "I think he brought
his dragon to life so he wouldn't be lonely."

A bright purple dragon about the size of a large
wolfhound sat on a branch of a tree behind Cerby's
cage. Cerby wasn't watching the dragon; he had opened
his cage and was dragging his blanket and stuffed lamb
out of the oversized cage and toward the truck.

Cerby knew they'd come to take him home. Him and
his new friend.

CHAPTER 2

Mia pulled out a bacon, egg, butternut squash, and potato casserole from the oven early the next morning. Abigail had made sure that the rest of breakfast, which included muffins, orange juice, and fruit salad, was on Mia's small kitchen table, along with plates and silverware. Mia could feel the excitement from Gloria as the doll watched the gathering. True to her kitchen witch roots, Gloria loved watching people eat.

Grans had arrived with Muffy and a suitcase. Trent's letter from the coven leadership had called together what Mia liked to call her "mini coven." Trent was filling everyone's coffee cups and making sure there were enough chairs. His parents were there, including his father, Thomas, who had tucked into the table on the window side of the room. He was currently watching the baby dragon sleep in the oak tree in the backyard. The only people missing were Christina and Levi, and they were in Oregon, setting up their new lives. But Trent had talked to Levi last night as they drove home from the training facility.

"How in the world did you get him back from Wolf Creek?" Thomas asked. "I mean, without someone seeing him."

"We told Cerby that the dragon had to turn invisible. He told Buddy to stay close but not to show himself." Trent nodded to Mia. "Everything on the table?"

"Looks like it." She put a serving spoon in the casserole, then pointed to the fridge. "Grab that home-made ketchup and salsa and put it on the table. I can dish up the casserole here and pass out the plates if that works."

"The dragon's name is Buddy?" Thomas asked.

"I think it's Bryghananth but Cerby calls him Buddy," Trent answered as he sat at the table.

"Perfect." Abigail set the plates on the counter next to the stove. "I'll hand them out. Mary Alice, sit down, and we'll get the breakfast going."

The system worked well, but Mia couldn't count the number of meals they'd had up here. And the kitchen couldn't hold any more people. If Levi and Christina were here, they would have been squeezed in. Maybe moving to Trent's house wasn't a bad idea.

As if he'd heard her thoughts, he winked at her. She frowned. *If you're in my head, you'd better get out and stay out.*

A surprised look passed over Trent's face, proving that he had been listening to her thoughts. He took the plate his mom handed him and said, "I'm sorry."

"We are going to talk about this," Mia said as she dished up the last plate for herself.

Thomas looked from her to Trent. "Did I miss something?"

Grans waved Mia down with her fork. "I guess we have one more lesson I need to tell you about. The good thing is, it seems like the two of you are bonding well."

Abigail laughed, then focused on the meal. "Remind me to explain this to Christina as well."

"It works with humans?" Now Mia wanted to talk about the telekinetic bond she'd discovered.

"I'm not sure what you all are talking about but we need to focus on Alfred Howard's arrival," Thomas said, trying to bring the conversation back to Trent's letter. "Can I say it's a bad time for a dragon to be hanging around? Maybe you should have left Buddy at the camp for a few weeks."

Now Cerby woke up from his nap and growled at Thomas.

He'd been sleeping next to Muffy on the floor near the window seat where Mr. Darcy had been curled up. Now all three animals were staring at Thomas like he'd taken the last treat and thrown it away.

"Dad, Cerby and Buddy have bonded. You can't break up a pair. You should know that." Trent reached back and rubbed Cerby on the top of his head. "But you're right on both counts. We need to set up a game plan for this investigator. It's a bad time for us to have a dragon. I don't think there's been one in the area for years."

Mia shook her head. "When was anyone going to tell me that dragons are real?"

"Well, since we haven't had one in Idaho since the nineteen fifties, the subject wasn't relevant to your training," Grans mused, tapping a finger on her chin. "This does remind me that I need to add you to the archives access so you can do research. I'm sure the library still has an open access point. They never close those off like they should."

Mia's left eyelid started twitching. She closed her eyes and took a deep breath. Every time she thought she had a handle on this being-a-kitchen-witch role, something else was added to the mix. Like Trent reading her mind. And the archives. And, well, dragons. She stood and refilled her coffee cup. It was a good thing she didn't have to work today. It was going to be challenging enough on Friday to pretend that the world was normal and without magic.

"Mia, don't worry about Trent and the investigator. We'll handle it. I know you've got a catering event tomorrow, and we need to formalize your graduation as well as the Halloween party. And your transfer night." Abigail pulled her planner from her purse. "When are you taking the exam again?"

"She's scheduled for Monday. Howard's showing up on Tuesday. The transfer ceremony is next Thursday, and of course, the coven's Halloween party is the next day. Maybe Mia should consider taking off time from the Lodge for the next few weeks." Grans leaned over and watched Abigail make notes in her planner. "And we need to set up the archive access no later than

Saturday. She might need it before her exams. And it might take a few tries to get right. One more thing, too, Robert and I are having an engagement party in a week or so. It will be held at the Lodge. I've told that woman I insist that Mia's Morsel's cater the party desserts. I guess Robert has enough pull to get that done."

"Blake hasn't said a word to me about it." Mia's heart started racing. She stood and grabbed her planner. "Grans, I'm not sure we can get everything done in time."

"Well, then it's a good thing you have a few extra hands for the next two weeks," a voice answered from the living room. Christina and Levi stood with their bags in the hallway. Christina rushed over to Mia and kissed her on the cheek. "Don't worry about it. We'll get it all done."

"I thought you were training?" Mia squeezed her friend into a hug. She hadn't realized how much she'd missed seeing her.

"After Trent's call last night, I negotiated a later start date. I'll need to be there by December first. And, since we're home now, I'm having my engagement party in November too."

Levi hugged his mother. "To be perfectly clear, the princess is having two parties. One here, and one in Boise at that fancy hotel where Isaac works. It was a compromise. And if you want it, her brother said you could cater the one in Magic Springs. He said he owed you one."

Mia didn't think her eyelid was ever going to stop twitching.

"Oh, good, there's still food left." Levi grabbed two plates from the cupboard. "I'm starving."

"You're always starving," Trent said as he stood to grab two more chairs out of the storage closet.

"We need to get back to planning what we're doing about Howard's visit," Thomas grumbled as he looked out at the oak tree where Buddy was putting out a small fire on the branch where he was perched. He rubbed his forehead.

Christina sat in Trent's spot and took the plate of food Abigail had handed her, moving Trent's plate toward Mia. She followed Thomas's gaze as she asked, "Who is Howard, and . . . is that a purple dragon?"

They got Christina caught up on Cerby's new friend. Levi had forgotten to mention Buddy to her after Trent called last night. He'd told her he needed to come back to Magic Springs for a week or so. The Majors family was going to need to put on a show for the magic inspector when he arrived, so it would be better if the brother who was supposed to have the powers was here in case something happened.

Mia didn't think anyone was going to be fooled. Coven canon said that in a generation, only one child would wield the family's magic. It was perfectly fine for Abigail and Levi to both have power. They could even add Thomas to the fun. But Trent was one step too many. He'd given up his power to Levi in a formal ceremony overseen by the coven, but his power hadn't left him like it should have. And now, Trent had a Goddess-delivered familiar, Cerby. Levi hadn't even found his familiar yet.

Life was going to be interesting around here for the next few weeks. Her phone rang, but after glancing at the display, she let it go to voice mail. If the Lodge had been calling, she would have jumped on the excuse to leave and go to work. Instead, the call was from Sabrina, the coven membership chair. Probably asking, again, if Mia was going to join the coven on Halloween.

At least Abigail was dealing with all of the coven's requests and questions on the Halloween party.

"You need to be focusing, not letting your mind wander," Grans chided her. "Abigail's been trying to instruct you on the different powers from the herbs, powders, and potions as we're setting up your lab, and you're worried about the coven."

"The girl's got a lot on her plate." Abigail tried to come to Mia's rescue. "Besides, I'm going to leave my potions cookbook with her just in case. I think I've got all her supplies in containers and labeled."

"As will I, but that's not the point." Grans turned to Abigail. "Mia needs to bond with the room. And she can't do that without understanding how it's being set up."

"Thanks for trying, Abigail, but Grans is right. I wasn't fully here. I need to practice being more in the moment. If I'm at work, I'm worrying about Mia's Morsels. If I'm home, I'm worried about work." Mia turned her phone completely off. "Maybe that will help." She picked up her pen and checked to see where she'd stopped paying attention. "Tell me again about the third shelf?"

"It's where your aromatics will be stored. There's a precise order to the bottles, which allows you to focus on the spell and not reading bottles and containers. I know it might seem old-fashioned, but we have our rituals to ensure that we are successful with our potions. No use remaking the wheel when it's already been discovered." Abigail listed off the contents of the bottles one by one. "Next summer I'll teach you how to dry and store your herbs."

Grans raised an eyebrow.

"With Mary Alice's permission, of course." Abigail hurriedly added as she glanced at her watch. "Oh, I need to run downstairs. We're Zooming with Christina's mother about the receptions."

"Tell Mother Adams I said hi." Mia grinned. That would probably set off the matriarch of the Adams family, and Mia didn't even have to be there. Knowing how to push a person's buttons was an exact science. One that she used with her ex-fiancé's family often. Well, except Christina. Mia had claimed her as found family as soon as the engagement had been called off.

"I thought you had untied the knots between you and the Adams family," Grans asked as Abigail hurried out of the room.

"Except when it comes to Christina, I have. I don't like the way Christina's mother pushes her around. I thought when Isaac married Jessica, she'd be Mother Adams's new project. But this wedding to Levi has the woman wound up like a spring, waiting to explode."

Mia opened a door and found her storeroom already set up, with cleaning supplies even. Grans had outdone herself. "I've been practicing the calming spell and focusing on Mother Adams as much as possible. It seems to be making her more anxious. Am I doing it wrong?"

"Probably not. But some people can't be fixed. Roxanne Adams is one of those people. I did the same spell on her for years when you started getting serious about Isaac. Nothing helped." Grans stepped over to where a desk and chair sat, surrounded on two sides by wall-to-ceiling bookshelves. "I've also set you up an office in here. You can add a computer, but I liked keeping track of my spells and progress in a handwritten journal, as did my ancestors. I bought you a new journal to use. The ones from the past, well, they're all here, on the shelves. Years of history of kitchen witches, all the way back through the Salem trials. The few written materials they had from before were destroyed so no one would find them. It was a dark time."

Mia walked over and ran a finger over the spines of the journals. Sparks of random magic followed her touch. "They're beautiful. The entire lab is perfect. Are you sure you want to turn this over to me? Won't you be sad?"

Grans looked at her, confused. "Oh, I'm not giving up my power. We never adopted that tradition. I'll be a kitchen witch until I die. Then my power and whatever spells we haven't already transferred into your grimoire will transfer to you. The transfer ceremony is power from the Goddess to you."

Mia thought about what her grandmother had told

her. "Maybe that's what happened in Levi and Trent's ceremony. The Goddess added power—she didn't take it from one witch and give it to the other."

Grans went over and pulled a book off the other side of the bookshelves. "I wonder if we can prove that in some way? As it is, if the coven finds out Trent has power, they will attempt to strip him of it. And the process isn't pretty. If we can prove that this is the Goddess's blessing, the coven can't work against it."

"Isn't Cerby that proof?" Mia went over to look at the books on the other shelves. These were published editions and included all the fairy tales she'd been reading to help her acclimate to her new magical role. "The Goddess gave him to Trent."

"You're right! I think you might have solved your boyfriend's problem. I need to find a previous case, though. One that the National Council will accept as a model. We might be able to fix this as soon as Mr. Howard shows up in Magic Springs." Grans sank into the chair with a groan. "And with that, I think we're done for the day. Go help Abigail. I can feel her angst all the way up here. Mother Adams has claimed another victim. I'll work here."

Mia hurried downstairs, leaving Muffy and Mr. Darcy in the potions lab with Grans. She'd come back to move them all back into the apartment for lunch. She might have to bring Grans's meal down to the lab, though. When her grandmother started researching, she didn't stop until she'd found an answer.

She hit the last stair and was turning toward the reception area when she realized that Grans hadn't told her about Trent's ability to read her mind. And her newly found ability to send him messages. "Another day," she said, looking back toward the stairs. She hoped her grandmother had enough days to tell Mia all the things she needed to know. She hated learning from experience unless she was cooking a new recipe.

She sent good wishes up to the Goddess for Grans's good health. Then she listened to see if she could find Abigail and the others. Cerby walked out of the kitchen and ran toward her. The others had been found. She picked the little Maltese up, giving him cuddles as she turned toward the kitchen.

Before she could take two steps toward the kitchen, someone knocked on the door. She glanced at Cerby. "It's Grand Central Station around here today."

He barked in agreement.

Mia hoped it wasn't a neighbor letting her know a purple dragon was flying around her backyard. She thought Buddy was in stealth mode, but Christina had seen him. On the other hand, Christina, by being part of Mia's world for so long, wasn't exactly human anymore. Or maybe she wasn't only human. She had accessed a bit of her natural ability to her extraordinary powers. A fact that Mia thought might have made her so good at cooking and had brought her to the top of her college class as well.

Christina hadn't used magic consciously. It had been more in her self-confidence and attitude. She'd been outstanding because she believed she could. And the magic of her friends had supported her.

When she opened the door, a short man dressed in a green suit greeted her.

"Good morning, Miss Malone. I was wondering if I could have a word with Trent Majors. I understand he's here with his mother and brother." He bowed, taking off his matching green bowler hat. "If it's not too much of a bother."

This time he met her gaze, and she realized it wasn't a human neighbor standing on her doorstep. Mr. Alfred Howard had arrived early.

CHAPTER 3

Alfred Howard hadn't been what Mia had expected. The man was cheerful, jolly even. And his green eyes sparkled as he talked. She'd brought him inside to sit in the reception area while she went to get Trent and the Majors.

Of course, the rest of the group followed along, so the reception area was now crowded with people as they watched the proceedings. Mia set a plate of cookies on the table in front of Howard, as well as a tall glass of water. "I can get you something else to drink if you want."

"Oh, no, this is fine. I can't resist a freshly made cookie." Alfred Howard's eyes lit up as he picked up an oatmeal raisin one and sniffed it. "This reminds me of home. Thank you, Miss Malone."

"I'm Trent Majors." Trent reached out his hand as he followed Mia to where Alfred Howard sat, eating a cookie, the copy of *Country Living* now lying forgotten on his lap.

He finished the cookie and brushed the crumbs off his hands, looking up at Trent as he shook his hand. "Aren't you a tall one? Six-two?"

"Six-three," Trent responded as he sat in the chair next to the sofa. "Let's all sit. We weren't expecting you until Tuesday."

"Oh, I took advantage of my assignment to come early so I could visit the great state of Idaho. I've never been here before. It's so different here in the mountains. When I flew into the airport, I thought I was in a desert."

"You were. The Boise area and the freeway you took to get here is high desert country. That's why they set up the Air Force Base in Mountain Home. But you get into the Sawtooth Mountain range north of Twin Falls. Magic Mountain is to the north of us, on the other side of Magic Springs River." Trent reached down and picked up Cerby, who had started jumping at his feet. "But I'm sure you're not here to talk about the scenery. This is Cerby."

"Oh, my. I knew he was a Maltese, but he's small for his breed, isn't he?" Alfred Howard reached out to pet Cerby, but he growled and backed away into the corner of the chair. "Well, he doesn't like me one bit. Which is odd for a Maltese, but for a hellhound, it's par for the course. They react badly to magical creatures."

"'Magical creatures?' Cerby loves everyone we know, even those with magic." Mia frowned as she watched the exchange. Howard had already discovered Cerby's alter ego.

"Oh, dear. I let the cat out of the bag, didn't I? Miss Malone, I'm not only a witch—I'm from Ireland. I'm also half leprechaun. My human witch mother was a bit adventuresome, I'm afraid. My father, well, I've never met the guy." He winked at Mia. "Families, what are you going to do, right? Anyway, back to Cerby and Trent. I need to do more testing."

"'Testing'?" Abigail came around and leaned over Trent's shoulder. "The paperwork was filed correctly, and a certified board member was part of the transfer ceremony. Trent doesn't have magic anymore. It was passed to his brother, Levi."

"Maybe it was, and maybe it wasn't." Howard made a so-so gesture with his hand. A large emerald ring sparkled as he moved. "That's why I'm here. There have been situations in the past where magic wasn't completely transferred. I've been studying the issue for years. Sometimes it's as simple as residual magic showing up due to the proximity of other witches. Since Trent hasn't moved away from home, the magic might dissipate when Levi and Miss Adams complete their move to Oregon."

"How did you know . . ." Christina started, but Levi grabbed her hand before she could finish.

"Miss Adams, I am very good at my job." Howard nodded as he pulled out a notebook and pen from the leather bag he had strapped over his shoulder. "Now, I need to verify some details since I have so many of you here today."

Mia listened as Alfred Howard went through the details of Trent's magical life and the transfer of his powers to Levi. After that, he looked around the room. "Any inconsistencies there?"

Trent, Abigail, and Thomas all shook their heads. Mia figured this must be the information the coven had recorded on Trent when he held the power.

Alfred Howard grinned and clapped his hands. "Good. It seems that your coven is keeping accurate records. You wouldn't believe the state of some coven archives. Especially ones like yours, where you're far from a district-controlling body. Some people don't understand the need for order. Okay, I have a few questions for Trent. When did you realize you could talk with your brother telepathically?"

"Excuse me?" Trent glanced at his mom, who slightly shook her head.

Alfred Howard sighed and put his pen and notebook away. "And this is where we always run into a problem. Mr. Majors, when you joined the coven, a link was created between you and the archivist. Every time you used magic from that time forward, it's noted in the logbooks. Now, most of the non-granted magic is inconsequential, like you boys chatting. But when something big happens, like a hellhound being awarded by the Goddess, we check every instance of magic. Do you think the Society didn't feel the power surge when he arrived?"

"If you already know everything, why are you asking me?" Trent asked, rubbing Cerby's back as the little dog let out tiny growls every time Alfred Howard said a word.

Howard stood and adjusted his vest, or was it a

waistcoat? Mia didn't know the difference, but the more old-fashioned word sounded right. Mr. Howard winked at her, confirming the description. Now he was reading her mind.

"I'm here to find out why the Goddess is so interested in protecting you, Trent Majors. Hellhounds are usually only sent to witches in the national leadership hierarchy. And mostly as protectors from assassins. Now, from your archive records, it appears that you would have been promoted quickly in leadership if you hadn't decided to run the family grocery business instead. The Goddess has never granted a familiar with such power as a parting gift before, so clearly, she has plans for you. I'm here to find out how much power you still have since the transfer. We may have to increase it to give you the levels you need to control Cerby. Especially now that he's started to manifest. The dragon seems docile. Have you had any problems?"

"Buddy is Cerby's friend. We will deal with him and Cerby's training needs." Trent met Mia's gaze. Then he leaned back in his chair. "You might as well know . . ."

"Trent, stop. He's baiting you." Thomas stood as well. "This isn't my house to throw you out of, but I'd like to ask you to leave, with Mia's permission. You're taking advantage of my son without a coven advocate."

Alfred Howard nodded and moved to the door. Then he stopped and handed Trent a business card. "You're right. Your son does need to know the penalties for lying about his power to an assigned investigator. I'll let the coven know you've asked for an advocate, so as soon as that's completed, I'll be in touch. For now, I'll go back to the Lodge and schedule some tourist activities. A friend lives nearby, so I'll be experiencing your lovely area like a local. You can reach me at any time at this number. Even in the wee hours of the morning. I don't sleep much."

Thomas followed Alfred Howard to the door, then stood and watched while he drove away. When the Irishman was gone, he shut and locked the front door. "This is a disaster."

At the Lodge the next morning, Mia wondered if Alfred Howard had picked the hotel to be close to Magic Springs or if he knew she worked there. Ambushing her at work would be a bad idea, since most people she worked with were human and didn't know her other occupation. Mia's Morsels still wasn't making enough profit for her to walk away from the day job. When Blake met her at her office door, she wondered if she'd already run out of time. "Good morning, Blake. Are you here to check on the dinner plans for tonight?"

Blake let Mia unlock the office door before she said anything. Then she followed Mia inside her office, closing the door behind her. "I got a visit from one of our guests this morning, asking about you and your boyfriend."

Mia tucked her tote away in a desk drawer, then sat down at the desk. "That seems personal."

"It was, and you know I don't like the personal interfering with our work. I wouldn't have even talked to this Alfred Howard person, except, as a coven member, I'm required to entertain all members of the National Society."

Mia blinked, letting the information sink in. When she spoke, she tried to frame her words carefully. "You're a witch."

"I am. My coven is in a little town north of Boston, Newburyport. We're a small group, and we keep our membership quiet. Especially after the whole Salem thing. But that has nothing to do with either my role as your boss or my presence in Magic Springs. And I told Mr. Howard that. I said that you were a valuable member of my work team and I had no information about your other activities, besides your ownership of Mia's Morsels. I don't believe he liked my answer." She straightened a pen that was on Mia's desk. "I find that when the national office gets involved in your life, things break. So be careful and don't let anything drop. I'll let you get back to your work. I'm sure the event tonight is going to run smoothly, correct?"

"I've got it under control," Mia responded. She didn't like the fact she'd been right about her suspicions about Howard. So, if he'd interviewed her boss regarding her personal life, who else would he talk to if he thought they might have information on Trent's magic?

She texted Trent and Abigail, then wondered which one would call first. Abigail's number beeped on her cell. "Hey, I take it you saw my text. Can you believe he came here to ask questions?"

"Are you okay?" Trent's voice boomed over the connection. He must be with Abigail. "What did your boss tell him?"

"According to her, nothing. Although I'm not sure I trust her. How did I not know she was a witch? She's been here for months." Mia stared at her closed office door, shaken by the visit from Blake.

"Honestly, I didn't know either, and I've talked to Blake several times. She's excellent at masking. Anyway, you need to come home as soon as possible. He's trying to divide and conquer. Trent's here, as well as Christina and Levi. Your grandmother already knew to come over yesterday." Abigail listed off the family members and their current whereabouts.

"Funny how she seems to know things. Anyway, I have a routine catered dinner at six. As soon as I know everything's running fine, I'll head home. The bank's been having this monthly dinner for years. They won't need much hand-holding." Mia hoped she hadn't just jinxed her evening.

"Mia, be careful," Abigail warned her. "There have been times when investigators have gone to extreme measures to get information. It hasn't been reported for years, but Howard has a reputation for underhanded methods."

"I can come over and wait for you," Trent offered.

"No, I'll be fine. I'll lock my office door and ask James to walk me to my car when I leave. No one is getting past Blake's new security doors and guards in the staff office hallway. I still don't understand why she set this up as an employee-only zone, but now I'm happy she did."

No one said anything from the other end of the line.

"Okay, did we get cut off?" Mia glanced at her cell, but the call was still connected.

"No, we're here," Abigail said. "Trent and I were wondering the same thing. Maybe there's a reason we didn't recognize Blake as a witch. Did she give you any information on her coven?"

Mia told Abigail what Blake had told her, but then her business line rang. "I've got to run. James needs to finalize the menu for tonight. I'll be home as soon as I can."

"Be careful," Trent echoed his mother's warning and disconnected the call.

Mia switched to the business line and told James she'd be in his office in a jiffy. Then she pulled the file for that tonight. Why had Blake fortified the Lodge's employee section? Maybe she'd ask after meeting with James. Her boss seemed to be more open to discussing policies today. Especially after telling her she and Mia had something in common. It couldn't hurt to ask.

After working with James—and eating the lunch he'd provided by calling it a "tasting" for tonight's dinner—Mia asked him to walk her to her car when she left.

"Sure, but what's going on? Do you have a stalker I don't know about?" James joked.

"Maybe I do," Mia threw back as she left the office. "But thanks for humoring me."

"Anything you need, I'm here." James rolled his eyes as his phone rang. "Duty calls."

As she walked to Blake's office, she paused at the desk of the administrative assistant whom Blake had hired on her first day. "Is the boss free?"

"As free as a bird," Rena chirped, then laughed as Mia started toward the door. "Sorry, I meant she just left the hotel. She said she'd be back tomorrow and to route all her calls to the appropriate department head or take a message. I think she's dating someone. I haven't seen her go off-grid like this since she hired me."

"Okay, then, thanks." Mia left the office and headed to her own. She needed to follow Blake's example. She decided to grab her tote and handle any issues from the house. If she had to come back, she'd bring Levi or maybe Thomas as backup.

When she got back to James's office, he was heading to the kitchen. He frowned at her tote. "I thought you were staying around for a while?"

"I'm not feeling my best. I can handle any issues from home." She nodded to the door to the employee parking area. "Do you mind walking me to my car now?"

"Of course not," he said as he poked his head into the kitchen area to tell them he'd be right there. Then he opened the door to the outside. "Are you sure you're okay to drive? You look a little pale."

Mia felt a little shaky, but after glancing around the parking lot, she didn't see Alfred Howard waiting for her, so she faked a smile. "I'm fine. Just a lot going on. I'm trying to keep Mia's Morsels handling the Halloween party off my mind, but it's going to be huge."

"Blake would freak if she thought you were even thinking about it on Lodge time. I swear that woman counts the times I go to the restroom in a day." When they got to her car, he opened her door for her, and Mia glanced around the inside before climbing in. "Seriously?" he said. "You're starting to make me paranoid too."

"I'm reading a serial killer book. I guess it's got me jumpy," Mia lied to him. But she was glad she took the time to check the backseat and saw it was clear. Abigail and Trent had her worried.

"I'll see you Monday for the staff meeting, then. Unless you get called in tonight. I'll try to handle everything, so head to bed. You need to be at your best for the weekly grilling from our fearless leader. And maybe I'll be King of the Paperwork this week since you'll be too sick to finish yours." He shut her door and tapped his hand on the top of her car.

She drove away, avoiding the lot by the front entrance, which meant she had to drive another three blocks home, but she didn't run into Howard as she left.

When she unlocked the front door, Muffy and Cerby came running, barking at the door opening, then they jumped on her legs until she acknowledged their presence. Trent came out of the kitchen. "You're home early. Did you lock the door?"

"Yes, I locked the door. You and your mom freaked me out, so I came home. I might need to go back, but so far, so good. Is your dad still here?" Mia set her tote on a table near the stairs.

"He's in the kitchen with the rest of the gang. Did you eat lunch?" He put his arm around her as they made their way to the industrial kitchen, where they cooked for the catering gigs and the weekly delivery service.

"James fed me." Mia took a breath. It felt better being home. Whatever was going on, she was feeling the angst outside the school building.

Grans looked up at her from her spot at the table

where everyone was sitting. "You'll feel much better in a few minutes. The spelling is working well."

"What spelling?" Mia got a bottle of water from the fridge, then sat down with the group next to Trent.

Abigail dropped her gaze as her grandmother met Mia's glance. "Uh-oh."

"I've told you before, or at least I thought I did, the school is warded." Grans looked at Mia like she'd failed math or something. "The wards boost your immune system from the negative magic you encounter when you're outside the school. Your necklace protects you, but the school gives you power and strength. Either Howard or Blake or someone from the coven is sending out a lot of negative energy around you and the rest of us. That's why I decided to stay here. I need to ward Robert's house, too, but there's so much upkeep to the process. I don't think I can keep three places safe."

Mia let that thought roll over her as the rest discussed Cerby and Buddy. By the time they'd finished an early dinner and left to retire for the night, Mia was glad to have everyone gone. Trent and Levi had left around five with Cerby and Buddy. They wanted to get the dragon settled before nightfall. Abigail and Thomas had left, and Grans had retired to her room. She was probably talking to Robert. Christina brought Mia a glass of wine, and they sat in the living room.

"Even with you leaving town, my life is fuller than I'd ever expected." Mia smiled at her young protégé. Her almost-sister-in-law.

"That's a good thing. You need people. When you lived with Isaac, he kept you working too hard to even think about having friends or a life. Now you have a whole house full of people most days. People you like." Christina sipped her wine. "I almost feel jealous for leaving. If it wasn't for the crazy amount of money they offered, I'd stay here."

"Rub it in." Mia laughed as her phone rang. Trent was calling, probably to check in. She took the call. "Hey, so have you got them settled? I bet Buddy loves the backyard."

Trent's house was on the river, and he owned the wooded acres behind the house. It was a perfect place to raise a dragon, although Mia had never thought of it that way before. "Mia, Levi and I were out sitting on the back deck talking when Cerby came running back from the woods barking. I followed him into the woods and found him. Alfred Howard's dead."

Mia set the wineglass down, glad she hadn't taken a drink yet. "I'll be right there. Did you call Mark?"

CHAPTER 4

When Mia arrived at Trent's house, the driveway was filled with police cars and one lone ambulance without its lights on. A black BMW was parked on the street. Mia made her way to the front door, then as she stood there, she watched as four men pushed a gurney with a body bag on top of it into the ambulance. The body inside appeared to be much shorter than the bag or the gurney. Alfred Howard. An evidence bag held a box of Lodge cookies. It looked empty.

"What exactly do you think you're doing here?" Mark Baldwin asked from the doorway. Mia hadn't heard the door open while she was watching the scene.

"Trent called. I wanted to make sure he was all right." Mia stared into the foyer. A flurry of white flew at her, and she picked Cerby up as she talked. The dog was shaking. "Hey there, big guy, are you okay?"

"That remains to be seen." Mark glanced around,

then pulled her inside. "I have a feeling this event is more in your realm than mine. Do you mind helping?"

"Of course. Whatever you need," Mia said as she followed the police chief into Trent's living room. Trent wasn't alone. Abigail, Thomas, Levi, and a man Mia didn't know were gathered around the couch. She could see Buddy watching them from outside the window. Cerby barked at his friend, and Buddy stepped back into the shadows. Rubbing the little dog's head, she glanced at Mark. "What's going on?"

"Chief Baldwin has been asking some very pointed questions," the man dressed in a black suit said, waving Trent down when he tried to stand and greet Mia. "He seems to think that Trent had something to do with that poor man's death. As he's clearly stated, he went out to find his dog and discovered the body. Nothing else to say."

Mark blew out an exasperated breath. "Look, Steve, I'm not saying Trent had anything to do with it. I find it odd that the man who's obviously part of your world from his appearance would wind up dead by the river. Mia, tell them I'm not trying to jump to conclusions here. I need a rational explanation. Even though I know it might not be possible."

"I'm not sure what you mean by 'our world.' You live in Magic Springs as well. I haven't been home except for holidays for years." The man, Steve, glanced at Abigail.

"Steve, Mark is aware of the coven and our special circumstances," Abigail explained.

"Mother, I'm the attorney here. You paid a lot of

money for my law degree. Maybe you should stay quiet like I asked." Steve softened the words with his tone, but Mia could see Abigail bristling just the same.

"You're a Majors?" Mia glanced at Trent, who nodded.

"Mia, meet my oldest brother, Steve Majors. He's my attorney and almost the five-million-dollar man since he charges so much for his services." Trent smiled as Cerby wiggled in her arms. "Let him down. He wants to be with me."

"And as your attorney, I told you to stop speaking." Steve frowned as he watched Mia let Cerby down. "I think it would be better for you to leave, Miss Malone."

"Trent asked me to come, and he'll tell me to leave." Mia stood straighter. Steve might be part of Trent's family, but he wasn't in charge of her. "What happened to Alfred Howard? That was him in the body bag, correct?"

"Yes, the victim is Alfred Howard, according to his passport. As far as what happened, that's what I'm trying to find out." Mark Baldwin groaned as his phone rang. He stepped away and answered the call.

Mia took the interruption as the time to rush over to Trent. She hugged him. "Are you all right?"

"I'm fine. I went out to get Cerby. Levi had let him out without a leash." Trent glared at his brother.

"I thought you'd already set up a perimeter for him, dude. Don't blame me." Levi smiled at Mia. "I'm glad to see you. Is Christina still at the apartment?"

"Yes, she went to bed. I didn't want her involved since Baldwin freaks her out." Mia turned back to Trent. "You found Cerby near the body? Buddy didn't . . ."

Trent shook his head. "There were no marks. Besides, dragons don't tend to leave bodies around. They eat the evidence."

"Gross." Mia blew out a breath. That was one good thing, anyway.

"No one listens in this family," Steve grumbled. "Just because Baldwin's in the other room doesn't mean he can't hear you talking."

"Mark's a good guy. He's not looking for an easy solution. He'll find out who actually killed Howard." Mia was beginning to not like Steve Majors at all. "We work together to solve these situations."

"Except when my son is going to be charged." Thomas shook his head. "Mia, I know you mean well, but let Steve do his job."

"Thomas, stop being so pushy. We know what we're doing," Abigail came to Mia's defense, and suddenly they were all talking over each other.

Trent took Mia's hand. "I'm glad you're here. You, Levi, and I are the only sane ones in the room right now. And I'm not totally sure about Levi."

"I heard that," Levi grumbled as he texted on his phone.

Mia smiled as she sat next to Trent. As Abigail and Thomas continued to argue, she focused instead on trying to hear Baldwin's part of the conversation. "What do you mean, the coroner called in a specialist to do the autopsy?" he was saying. "I don't understand why Frank can't . . ."

Mia immediately knew what had happened. The coven had already heard the news and was pulling strings. There was no way they'd let a mortal cut open a man who claimed to be half-leprechaun.

"Fine, have them send me the results when they get . . ." Baldwin paused as he stared at his phone. "Sorry, I've got to take another call."

Mia watched as he hung up and answered the incoming call.

"Sarah, this isn't a good time." Baldwin paused, then met Mia's gaze across the room. "You know I can't step away from an open investigation. No matter who called you."

He listened for a little while longer, not breaking eye contact with Mia. "Fine, I'll come home. But you tell the coven board that either I have a suspect in my office in seventy-two hours or I'm taking the case back."

As he walked over to the group, he stared at Mia. "Did you call them in?"

She shook her head. "Check my phone. I didn't call anyone after Trent called me. And I told him to call you. I take it the coven has pulled rank?"

"The mayor called Sarah to explain why I shouldn't be interrogating Trent Majors or any of his family members until after the coroner determines if the death was natural or accidental. My boss called my wife. And my coroner has called in a specialist. Your magic group is interfering in my investigation and my family, but they have effectively tied my hands."

"Mark, there are things you don't want to know about—" Abigail started, but Steve reached out to interrupt her. She turned on her oldest son, anger flashing in her eyes. "Do not shush me. I am your mother."

"And with that, I'm leaving," Baldwin said. "Trent, please don't leave town. We will eventually talk about the time when you found a short man wearing all green dead in your woods. Or when your dog found him. But at this point, I've been benched." He wiggled his finger at Mia. "Come outside with me and let's talk. I have some things I'd like you to check into."

"Mia, you don't have to do anything this officer asks," Steve started, but Mia stood and whirled to face him.

"Look, I know you know this isn't a normal investigation, nor is it probably a normal murder. I know you mean well, but we have a system here in Magic Springs that works. Mark handles the human crime investigations, and our team deals with those things that are magical. I'm betting there's a human reason for Mr. Howard's death, but if it is part of the 'magic' side of Magic Springs, there are different rules and, ultimately, coven laws to follow. Besides, you're not even my attorney, so stop telling me what to do." The shocked look on Steve Majors's face told Mia all she needed to know. The man was not used to being told no.

She turned and followed Mark out to the front porch. The night was starting to darken around them, but an almost-full moon was peeking out from over the mountain. Fall nights were the best. You could wear your bulky sweaters and jeans and be okay outside until late without adding a coat, especially when you were hanging around the firepit.

Mark nodded toward where they'd left and where they could still hear Abigail and Thomas arguing. "Thanks for the support back there, but you might have made yourself an enemy. Steve Majors is considered a shark in the criminal defense pool in Denver. He didn't like your defection to the dark side."

"That's the thing. I don't think there should be sides. You know that Trent couldn't have killed anyone. Neither did anyone in his family." Mia leaned on the porch column.

"Mia, sometimes what you want to be true, isn't." Mark glanced at his truck. It was the only official vehicle left in the driveway. The BMW and Mia's decrepit Honda were parked on the street. The BMW must be Steve's rental. "Anyway, can you find out why this guy was even here? And what he has to do with Trent's family?"

Mia knew at least part of the answers to Mark's questions, but after cheerleading the no-sides, cooperative mission, instead of telling him, she nodded. "Call me as soon as you know something."

Mark put his ball cap back on. "Same with you. We'll figure this out, I promise. At least Miss Adams isn't in town this time."

Mia took a breath. "About that . . ."

"Don't tell me." Mark shook his head. "I should have known that if Levi was here, our goth princess wouldn't be far behind. She's always around if there's a murder in town. Have you noticed that?"

"Christina didn't kill anyone. You've never liked her," Mia said as Mark strolled to his truck.

"Not true. I like her. Especially when she thinks I'm watching her because she did something wrong. She gets so flustered." He climbed into the truck cab and started the engine. As he rolled down his window, the look on his face turned serious. "What I don't like is having politics interfere with my investigation. Can you tell your friends at the coven to back off and let me do my job?"

"One, not my friends, and two, what makes you think they'll listen to me?" Mia pointed at him. "You might want to chat with your wife."

He rolled his eyes and turned his wedding ring back and forth. "Like that's going to do any good. Sarah's either all about the baby right now or touting the advantages of coven life for our family. She wants us to join, so naturally, whatever happens, Sarah agrees with the coven. I haven't won many arguments in the last six months. Now that I know about magic, she thinks I should fall in line with whatever that group wants. It's not going to happen."

Mia watched as Mark pulled out of Trent's driveway. She knew the pressure the coven could put on someone. In fact, she was pretty sure the only reason Mia's Morsels got the contract for the Halloween party was because they wanted to show her what they could do to help her. Instead, the gesture made her feel icky, like they were trying to buy her allegiance.

It was exactly how she'd felt about the offer from Isaac to cater to Christina's upcoming engagement party. Of course, it was only the party in Magic Springs Isaac was giving Mia's Morsels. The Boise event would be held at the family mansion on Warm Springs Avenue and be attended by Boise's upper-crust society members, as well as any clients or potential clients Mr. Adams thought would enjoy it.

Levi would find his engagement party to be a work

event for his new in-laws. Hopefully, Abigail and Thomas would keep it together during the party. She and Trent would be there and try to keep the peace. And if this Steve was still in town, she guessed he would attend as well.

She turned back to the house, wondering if Steve had a girlfriend. From his manners, she assumed not, but sometimes women liked pushy, overbearing men, especially when they had a big bank account.

Trent met her at the door. "So that was fun."

"You and your family have an odd idea of fun." Mia glanced inside. "Are your parents still fighting?"

"Yep. But now it's transitioned into the silent treatment. Mom wants to gather around the firepit here with her boys, so I guess I'm stuck here for the night." He pushed a strand of hair out of her face. "How's Mark?"

"Frustrated with the coven. I don't blame him. It's like he's trying to investigate Kennedy's assassination. He's getting stonewalled."

"Mia, Howard was a magical creature. They die for all kinds of reasons." Trent glanced toward the side yard, where Buddy was now jumping from tree to tree, making the branches bend and almost hit the ground from his weight. "I thought having squirrels was interesting. Buddy's going to break all my tree cover."

"Maybe not now, but we probably need to talk about the long term. What do dragons eat? Is he magical and doesn't need to eat? Why is he invisible to most mortals? Is Christina the only human who can see him?" Mia rolled her eyes. "And that's only the beginning of my questions. I'm not sure I'm ready to take on the kitchen witch role. I'm pretty sure I won't pass any test."

"You'll be surprised at how much you've learned. Relax and let your intuition help you if you get stumped. Guessing is usually your subconscious telling you the right answer." He handed her a tote. "I'd better get back inside. Steve wants a complete blow-by-blow of the Cerby delivery."

"Do you want me to take him home with me? Will having family around upset him? He didn't like Mark even suggesting that Buddy could have hurt Howard." Mia dug her keys out of her bag. You would think that the bag had a magical extension charm on it, as hard as it was to find things inside. But that was the nature of a large tote.

"No, I think Buddy's having fun in the forest. And there's a lot of acres of federal land behind me. He can run and fly for miles." Trent pulled her into a hug. "One more reason for us living here when we move in together. Buddy needs a lot of room."

She touched his face in the gathering darkness. "I'm going to have to learn Grans's wellness spell, then, and ward your house."

"Who says it's not already warded?" he asked as he kissed her goodnight. "Thanks for coming tonight. Mom, Levi, and I will all be over in the morning. But if you need us before that, call."

"And Steve and your dad?" Mia stepped off the deck. She hoped they would be otherwise occupied.

"Fishing in Hells Canyon for the weekend. Dad convinced him that until the coven is done with their investigation, there's no need for him here."

Mia walked over to her car after saying goodnight. At least she had the weekend to figure out who killed Alfred Howard. At the car, she felt the wind from Buddy flying over her to say goodnight. She called up to the dragon, "Be safe, Buddy."

A chortle answered her. Dragons didn't worry about safety. She wished she had that luxury.

CHAPTER 5

Saturday morning, Mr. Darcy patted Mia's face until her eyes opened. He was trying to let her know she was late for the party. The noise from the kitchen told her that the apartment was filled with people and she was still in bed. She rubbed his head, then reached over for her phone. It was seven thirty. "I guess weekends don't mean anything when you're self-employed."

Mr. Darcy meowed his answer, then left through the partially opened door. She shut it all the way and got ready for her day. Her suspicions were confirmed when she was handed a cup of coffee as she walked into her sunny kitchen.

Abigail stood at the stove. "Omelet or fried eggs? We have bacon, cheddar cheese, and some veggies we can add."

"Omelet. With everything." Mia sipped her coffee. "Do we really need to be up this early?"

"Stop complaining, you got to sleep in." Trent leaned over and kissed her cheek. "Mom texted me a shopping list at five. Then Levi had to go over and gather her and her overnight case. She's staying here for the weekend. Dad insisted."

Abigail rolled her eyes as she set a cinnamon roll in front of Mia. "That man drives me crazy at times. It's his way or the highway. But he keeps changing the highway's location so I can't find it. I guess I'm stuck with him. I hope you don't mind me crashing here, Mia."

"Of course not. Besides, we've got a lot of planning to do for Christina's party." Mia dug into the cinnamon roll and enjoyed the smell of freshly baked bread. Abigail must have been up long before she texted Trent. A purple face filled the window, and she heard a deep chortle. "Good morning, Buddy. Glad to see you too."

"Sorry, we couldn't leave them home alone." Trent rubbed Cerby's head as the Maltese tried not to fall asleep on his lap. Mr. Darcy stood at the window, batting at Buddy's face through the glass. Muffy was the only animal ignoring the beast.

Grans looked up from the book she was reading. Her plate was half empty, but she was more focused on the material. "Good morning, dear. Trent, you need to make a collar for Buddy. That way you can walk him. Exercise is crucial for his development. And in a few months, he'll hibernate until spring, so he needs a cave on your property."

Grans must have been reading about the care and development of dragons. Mia washed down the rest of the roll with a long sip of coffee. "I guess you had that book in your home library? We probably should have had it months ago."

"Back then"—Grans gave Mia a long look—"Trent was sending Cerby to training camp back then, and we didn't know about Buddy. Remember?"

Had it only been a few days since they'd retrieved Cerby from camp and hanging out with his best friend? Mia covered her mouth and yawned. "My bad. I'm not keeping everything straight lately."

"It's the dragon breath," Abigail informed her as she set a plate in front of Mia. It held an omelet with a hollandaise sauce over the top as well as three slices of bacon. It might not be good for their marriage, but Mia loved it when Abigail came to stay with her. "It can mess with your thoughts and emotions until you're used to it. Most coven kids get shots when they are five for the problem. I guess you didn't?"

Grans shook her head. "Mia's mom, Theresa, refused to let me deal with anything magical around Mia. She didn't want Mia to find out about this life. So no vaccines."

"Who would have expected a dragon to show up?" Mia joked, but the others didn't laugh. Instead they were all staring at her like she'd grown a second head or something.

Abigail finally sat down to eat after turning off the stove. "You're also changing colors. That's not good. Anyway, that's why we give the vaccines. You never know when a dragon will show up, and dragon breath is a real problem. I'll call the coven and have them come over today."

"I thought you said I'd get used to it?" Mia stared at her food. Was her plate empty? Or did she already eat? The room was getting fuzzy. "Grans? I'm not feeling well . . ."

When Mia woke, she was back in her bed. She glanced down at her clothes, but she wasn't in her pajamas. "It wasn't a dream."

Trent sat in a chair next to her. He set the book down he'd been reading. "No, sorry, it wasn't a dream. You went down at breakfast. The coven medical specialist has been here and given you a shot. She says you should be right as rain by the end of the day. I'm sorry Cerby's friend made you sick. I didn't even think."

"How would you know that I hadn't had a vaccine?" Mia scooted up in bed and groaned when a wave of dizziness hit her. "I didn't even know I needed one."

"But I did," Grans said as she came into the room with a tray.

Mia could smell the chicken soup as soon as Grans stepped into the doorway. "I think I'm just overwhelmed with everything. Don't blame yourself. Maybe I'm not ready to take over the kitchen witch role. I'm probably not going to pass my exam Monday anyway."

"Don't say such things, child," Grans scolded as she put the tray on the bed over Mia. "Intentions are half the battle. If you think you're going to fail, you will. You have more natural ability than I had when I started my journey. Besides, I'll be around for a long time to help you out unless I'm traveling. Robert and I want to start seeing the world."

"I love the idea of you traveling." Mia picked up her spoon. "Where are you heading first?"

"Obviously Italy." Grans sat next to Mia on the bed as they talked. Anytime Mia would try to set the spoon down, she'd urge her to eat more. "Just one more bite, dear."

Mia felt the spell's effects before she realized what her grandmother had done. She'd dosed the soup. "I have too much to do . . ."

Then she dropped the spoon in the bowl, and she felt the tray being taken away. She could still hear Grans and Trent talking, even though she couldn't open her eyes.

"Did you have to knock her out?" Trent asked. Mia could hear the concern in his voice.

"When those shots are given to children, they sleep for a week. She'll be fine by dinner, and then her head will be clear. Right now, there's nothing anyone can do anyway until the coven calls about Howard. Since you're here, I could use some help in the library. The archive spell's being . . ."

And then sleep overtook her, and she didn't hear the rest.

When she woke, the sun had set, and she felt back to normal. She slowly sat up in bed. No dizziness. No fuzziness. The shot had cured her reaction to dragon breath. Thank goodness this hadn't happened when she had been at the Lodge. She would have found herself in the hospital getting tested for any number of things. She swung her feet over the edge of the bed. She thought about what she'd say calling in. "Sorry, I can't come to work as a dragon has poisoned me and I'm fighting off the vaccine."

At least her current boss would understand. One positive for working for Blake. She wondered if the newest witch was linked into the coven gossip train enough to have heard about what had happened.

Mia looked around for her phone, but it wasn't in her room.

She slipped on shoes, and then headed out to the living area. No one was there. She grabbed a soda out of the fridge and glanced out the window. A firepit glowed in the backyard, and she could see people gathered around it. "Everyone must be outside," she said, taking a second drink. The sweetness of the soda was helping.

"Duh," Gloria said from behind her.

Mia spun around. "You've never talked before."

This time the doll only giggled.

The apartment felt empty except for the doll and her connection to the Goddess. For a minute, Mia wondered if she was even awake. Maybe this was a dream. Then she banged her knee into a trunk someone had left in the hallway. Probably Grans or Abigail, since she'd come to stay the weekend.

Mia wondered if her staying here was for Abigail's sake or her own. This family, or mini coven, seemed to close ranks here at the academy whenever trouble brewed in Magic Springs.

When she reached the first floor, a knock sounded at the door. She hadn't heard the security system go off when she was upstairs, and she didn't want to take the time to check the screens in her office. It was probably

Mark Baldwin, coming to see if she'd found out anything. He wouldn't understand that she'd been asleep all day, but Sarah could explain it to him.

She swung open the door to find Finley Shiley, Abigail's new hire, on the doorstep. She had a suitcase in one hand and a backpack over her shoulder. "Finn, what are you doing here so late?"

The girl shuffled her feet and didn't meet Mia's gaze when she talked. "I'm sorry, but Abigail said if I needed a place to crash, I should come here. My van broke down and was towed off the street, but they only let me grab my belongings. I walked from Sun Valley and just got into town."

Another stray. Mia didn't question the timing. The Goddess sent who and when she sent. She reached out and held the door open. "Come on in. Everyone's out in the backyard. I'm afraid all the rooms in the apartment are spoken for this weekend, but we'll find a couch or something for you."

"I can sleep on the floor." Finn stepped into the academy and sighed. "Have you noticed that there's something calming about your place? I don't know if it's the décor or what, but I always feel like everything is going to be okay as soon as I arrive here for work."

"Put your suitcase and bag into this closet." Mia opened the door and took a key off the top shelf. "It locks, and we don't use it, so until we get you settled, your stuff will be safe here. I'm sure Abigail has a plan for your stay. She always has a plan."

Finn followed Mia's instructions and took off the heavy down coat she'd been wearing. The girl looked like she'd lost fifty pounds. Her red hair was shaved on one side where she had a row of earring posts shimmering. A crescent moon hung in the lowest piercing. In her other earlobe, she only had one piercing and a matching moon earring. If Christina had been covered in black when she'd arrived years ago, Finn wore an explosion of colors. Over her red jeans, she wore a royal-blue T-shirt, and she had yellow sneakers with a pair of Hello Kitty socks poking out. She grabbed an orange *Virginia Is for Lovers* hoodie and pulled it over her head.

Then she met Mia's gaze, staring at her with bright green eyes. "Are you sure my staying here is okay? I won't be here long. I need to get my van fixed, and then I'll be out of here."

"You think you can live in your van here in Magic Springs? Do you know how cold it gets in the winter? And that's not far off. I'm surprised we haven't had a snowfall yet." Mia took the girl's arm, and they headed to the back doors that would lead directly out to the yard without going through the gym. "We'll figure something out. Don't worry about it. And there are showers in the bathrooms in the gym."

"I know. Abigail's been letting me use them on days I work," Finn admitted as they walked out to the gathering around the firepit. "Abigail is the best."

"Yes, she is," Mia admitted as they reached the gathering. "Finn, you know Abigail and Trent, but this is Christina, who used to work with us. And her fiancé, Levi. And my grandmother, Mary Alice Carpenter. Finn's going to be staying with us for a while."

Grans spoke first. "Are you sure at this time . . ."

Mia shook her head and interrupted. She didn't want Finn to feel like she was intruding. "You're right, we've got all the bedrooms filled this weekend, but we'll figure out something."

"I've got a rollaway in my garage I was going to donate, but I can bring it over tomorrow and set her up in the extra room on the first floor. I'd say set up one of the classrooms, but we haven't remodeled the bathrooms up there yet." Trent was already in problem-solving mode.

"Sounds like we've got a plan." Mia pointed to an empty chair, and Finn sat down, her hands in her hoodie. "If you don't mind sleeping on the couch tonight."

"A couch would be perfect. You don't have to go to any trouble." Finn glanced around at the group.

"The rollaway is in my way," Trent admitted. "You're actually doing me a favor. Moving it here makes it Mia's problem."

Mia sat down next to him. She leaned into him with a shoulder butt. "You're a brat."

"How are you feeling? Your grandmother thought you'd be better after a long nap." He kissed her on the cheek.

"Much better, thanks," she responded as she looked over at Abigail. "So, what have you been talking about?"

"Nothing really. Just Christina and Levi's plans, and the party, of course. Finn, I told you I needed you to help prep on Friday, right? And now, it looks like we have another party the next weekend for Mary Alice's engagement."

Finn leaned close to the fire. "I'd love the hours. I need to fix my van and find a place to live. And I've got nowhere to go right now."

"You started at a great time," Christina added. "You'll get tons of hours. We're always slammed during the holidays."

Mia wondered if that would be true this year, with the changes at the Lodge still not going in their favor.

Before she could fixate on the issue, Abigail handed her a stick with a marshmallow on the top. "We're making s'mores."

"And drinking a dessert wine," Christina added, laughing. "I know you're probably wanting dinner, but the rest of us have already eaten. You slept a long time."

"S'mores sound wonderful." Mia looked over at Finn, who was already roasting her marshmallow. "Have you eaten, Finn?"

"I had a hamburger for lunch, I'm good." Finn didn't look at anyone.

"Not in this house, you're not." Mia shook her head. "We are all about the food, so once we're done with our pre-dinner dessert, you and I'll go in and see if there are any leftovers."

"Mom cooked," Trent said dryly. "What do you think?"

"I made chicken enchiladas. And Spanish rice." Abigail sipped her wine. "I can't help it if I got used to cooking for four men in my house."

"Sounds like we have a dinner to warm up." Mia rotated her marshmallow and brought it out as the tan was beginning to darken. Trent had the graham cracker and chocolate ready for her. "So, tell me a little about you, Finn. You aren't from Magic Springs, are you?"

"No, I grew up in Nampa, but then my mom remarried, and I thought it would be better to give her some space, so after graduation, I tried Boise, but it felt too big and too close to home." She glanced around at the people gathered around the firepit. "So I headed this way to see Sun Valley, and someone told me about a job here in Magic Springs. So here I am, with a broken-down van."

"We have similar stories." Christina grinned. "I took a plane to Vegas before Mom canceled my credit card. Then my brother Isaac rescued me from there and dumped me on Mia's doorstep when Mom got tired of me not following her rules. I was a bit of a wild child."

"'Was'?" Levi asked and got swatted by Christina. He pulled her closer and kissed her head. "That's your best quality, babe."

"No, that's not true. Christina is bright and caring, and for some reason, she loves my troublemaker son." Abigail smiled at the pair. "When did you realize you loved cooking? Don't look shocked, I see you reading cookbooks on your lunch hour. Only true fanatics like us do that."

"When my dad left, Mom went to work, so I started making my own dinners. Then I made enough so she could eat when she got home. I did a lot of research on how to make a grocery budget last," Finn admitted. "When it was the two of us, I cooked everything. Then, when Dale moved in, he took over the cooking. He's good to my mom, so I'm happy for that. I don't fit into their lives."

Mia and Trent exchanged glances. There was more to Finn's story, but Mia wasn't going to push the girl. Not until she found out more. She hoped Finn was accurate about graduating high school. Mia didn't want to be harboring an underage runaway.

Finn sniffed her marshmallow before taking a bite. She made a face, then looked at the others. "Does anyone else smell sulfur in the fire?"

CHAPTER 6

Sunday morning, Grans and Mia headed into the library to try to access the coven library archives spot. Mia glanced downstairs like she could see Finn's bedroom on the first floor.

Grans saw her and waved the concern away. "Just lock the library door. No one is getting in here unless they have a key. The library ghosts aren't the most welcoming to the living."

Peaches, the ghost cat who spent her time warming herself in the sun that came in the large windows, meowed as she wound herself through Mia's legs. Mia reached down to pet her, but her hand went through the cat's body and Peaches turned into smoke.

"Animal ghosts are unpredictable. It's best if you don't try to interact." Grans nodded to a large table. "The archive connection should be on that table. At least it was when I attended school here."

Mia sat across from her and set her grimoire next to her. "Are you sure I don't have to be official in some way to get into the archives?"

"Of course not. Coven children can access the archives years before they take their vows. You're over-thinking this, which is not a good sign for your testing tomorrow. Maybe you should chat with Trent about his testing. It could put you at ease." Grans placed the palms of her hands on the table and started humming.

Finally, she looked up. "Maybe we have the wrong table."

Mia could hear Gloria's laugh from the other side of the wall where Mia's kitchen was located. "That's enough from the peanut gallery over there."

Grans glanced over her shoulder. "Gloria was laughing?"

"She's been a little vocal lately," Mia admitted. "I think it's all the commotion around Halloween and the coven party."

"Familiars aren't supposed to get anxious. They're supposed to calm you when you're anxious." She looked at Mia. "Where did you get Gloria, again?"

"I thought you gave her to me?" A pit was forming in Mia's stomach. "I was staying with you the summer between my freshman and sophomore years. She was on my bed when I arrived, so I thought she was a gift."

"When did she start talking? Making a connection?" Grans pulled Mia's grimoire over to her side of the table and opened it to the first spell page.

"It was after I went home that fall. I was home alone one Saturday night after a football game. My friends had gone to a party, but I'd wanted to go home. I'd found out that the guy I had a crush on was dating a freshman. I was devastated because he'd talked to me the week before, and I thought maybe . . ." Mia felt her face turning red as she remembered the embarrassment. She'd told all her friends, then found out he was already dating Sharon. "Anyway, Gloria said he wasn't worth my tears, and I'd have a great boyfriend soon."

"And you started dating Bodie by Thanksgiving if I remember the timeline. Your mom was furious that you blew off the PSAT training session and went to the movies." Grans looked at the wall of books again that separated the two rooms.

"What's wrong?" Now Mia was concerned. It wasn't like her grandmother to blow anything out of proportion.

Grans met her eyes. "Your familiar isn't supposed to bond with you until after you start your journey to your acceptance. Your mother hadn't abdicated yet back when you were in high school. She waited until after you were out of high school to give me her grimoire. I had started your training as a lark, but you shouldn't have had a familiar yet. And there's one more thing wrong with your story."

Mia watched as Grans returned her grimoire, then said, "I don't think so. I know it was a while ago, but I think I have the timeline right."

Grans refocused on the table. "I'm not sure it matters, but I didn't give you Gloria."

"Then how did she wind up on my bed that summer?" Mia was starting not to like this week at all.

"Now, that is a good question." Grans's face lit up as

the table started to glow. "I knew I had the right table. Mia, open your grimoire to an empty page and repeat after me."

That evening, as the group gathered for dinner, Mia noticed that Finn wasn't in the apartment with them. She glanced at Abigail. "Where's your apprentice?"

Abigail chuckled. "A friend came to get her for dinner. Finn's a nice kid. Thanks for putting her up for a few weeks."

"I didn't have much choice, but I have a feeling it might be longer than a few weeks." Mia sipped her wine as Abigail put the lasagna and garlic bread on the table. "We can't have her living in her van in winter up here. She'll freeze."

"I still think it was very kind of you." Abigail glanced over at Christina, who was texting on her phone. "How's Levi?"

"Bored." Christina grinned as she put away her phone. "I told him he didn't have to work shifts when we got back. It's not like we'll be here long, but someone called in, so he jumped."

"He was afraid we'd rope him into party prep," his mother interpreted. "Levi can smell hard work a mile away."

"Abigail, that's not nice to say about your kid." Mia didn't think Abigail was wrong, but she didn't want Christina to start having cold feet.

"What can I say? He's the baby." Abigail fluffed out her napkin. "And this one here wouldn't let me do anything for him. Trent was an independent soul from the day he went to kindergarten and found out there was a world out there away from the family."

"She says of the one son who actually works in the family business," Trent commented as he picked up a slice of garlic bread. "Maybe you should insist she get her head examined, Mia. She may be running your business into the ground."

"I keep my finger in the pie so I know what's going on." Mia was used to the teasing that went on in the Majors family. "Now I'm glad Finn's not here. She might think you all are actually fighting."

Everyone chuckled at that. Then Abigail set her fork down. "That being said, I am worried about our newest employee and roommate. She seems so disconnected from any family or friends. When this guy showed up to take her to dinner, I was shocked. She hadn't said one word about dating anyone."

"Maybe they're not dating, Mom," Trent said between bites. "Maybe they are just friends, like she said. Sometimes you need to take people at their word."

A dragon call echoed through the room, and Cerby, who had been sleeping on the window seat, jumped up to look out the window. He barked three times, apparently answering the question, then curled up again.

"Then there's Buddy." Trent sighed as he looked out the window and watched the dragon go back and hop onto a tree branch. "It's going to be hard enough to figure out how to train a hellhound. What am I going to do with a dragon? Having another human here, besides Christina, is asking for trouble."

Grans waved her fork at Trent. "Don't worry at all about Buddy. Humans don't notice magical creatures.

They don't have the mental capacity to know they're real. Sorry, Christina, I'm not trying to be mean."

"Well, since I can see Buddy, maybe I'm extraordinary for a mere human?" Christina rolled her eyes as her phone buzzed with another text. "Levi's going to have to wait until I'm done eating. He's so needy."

Gloria giggled, and Christina burst into a wide smile. "Right?"

Grans and Mia shared a look. Christina could see Buddy and hear Gloria. Two things that a human shouldn't be able to do. Trent shouldn't even be able to tap into Mia's familiar, but he also heard Gloria at times. The coven had been right to send out Howard to investigate Trent and Cerby since Trent should have been as human as Christina now that Levi had the generational magic that Abigail would pass when she left the world.

But things weren't always predictable as far as the rules of magic went. Not here in Magic Springs. Mia shouldn't be focusing on the outlying issues surrounding the magical community tonight. She should be studying for her final exam tomorrow at coven headquarters. She'd already taken the day off from work, promising Blake she'd have her report on Friday's dinner no later than noon on Tuesday. Now that she knew Blake was a witch, she didn't even have to make excuses for the kitchen witch duties that took her away from work.

After dinner, Grans pulled Mia aside. "I'm going into the library to use the archives. I'd like to explore Finn and Christina's family trees a little more."

"Do you have what you need?" Mia assumed she'd

need birth certificates even to start a genealogical search. And besides the fact that she'd grown up in Nampa, which was four hours away, they didn't know much about Finn's history.

"Don't be silly. The archives have back doors in all the official vital records departments all over the world. It was one of the first projects they completed to build the archives. We need to do a deep dive into what's available to you now. I'll order a study guide that you can pick up tomorrow at the coven. Cleo can have it available for you once you finish your exam." Grans picked up her phone and texted someone. "There, now, make sure I'm back in the apartment by ten. You know I can get lost in research, and I need my beauty sleep."

Not to mention that the library had at least two ghosts—one with a lot of power who didn't like the living being in their domain.

"I'll set my alarm on my phone," Mia assured her. She watched as her grandmother moved toward the door. "Maybe I should go with you?"

"Don't be silly. You have a houseful of guests. Nothing's going to happen to me," Grans reminded her as she opened the door. "Besides, Christina's here, and you two probably need to catch up."

Mia nodded. She knew Christina wanted to talk about the engagement party that was being held here in Magic Springs. And with Abigail here for the weekend, it was the perfect time to sketch out the details. Mia wasn't looking forward to hosting a party for the Adams family. Especially since Christina was the only one on that side who was happy about the upcoming nuptials.

Even so, Mia had served as a wedding planner for families before that were more reminiscent of the Hatfields and the McCoys. She could do it again. And she wanted to mix up a few potions tonight in the lab, to remind herself of the process. Grans had been a little vague on what her examination might entail, and talking to Trent hadn't eased Mia's mind.

She wanted to be ready for anything. She might even try a transformation spell tonight. Her phone buzzed with a text message from Baldwin.

Have you heard anything?

Mia sighed and added Howard's death to her list of worries. She answered back. *Sorry, it's been crazy here this weekend. Should have something mid-next week.*

That should give her enough time to do some archive research. And she could ask after the exam tomorrow. Maybe if they thought she'd passed, they'd provide her with insider information.

But then again, she had to get ready for her ceremony. The good thing was that traditionally, the ceremony was only for friends and family. She'd planned on having it in the backyard under the full moon. But now they had Finn to deal with. Maybe Mia would set her up at the Lodge for a night so they could get this done. It might actually be good to have her there the full weekend, since the coven's Halloween party would also be held here Friday night. The coven had hired their own servers for the event. Yes, getting Finn out of the school next weekend would be better for all of them.

She went back to the kitchen to see if Abigail and Christina were ready to talk party planning.

* * *

After three failed potions, the last one blowing up in her face, Mia decided to call it a night. She was cleaning up the potions lab, muttering to herself about not being ready for the stupid test after all, when she noticed a woman sitting on one of the old desks they'd left in the room, watching her.

"There's no reason to be concerned. The elders want to know you're serious about taking on this mantle. Besides, no one there has tested a kitchen witch since your grandmother went through the process sixty years ago. I hear they're bringing in someone from Salem to do your testing." The woman floated a few inches above the seat as she talked.

"You heard this, how? Is there a ghost network? Maybe a television station?" Mia had learned not to be afraid of the ghosts who showed up at the academy from time to time. Especially ones who felt friendly, like this woman did. She'd felt someone watching while she screwed up her potion experiments, but she'd thought it had been Gloria or even Grans.

The woman laughed, a clear, happy noise. "Oh, you will be fun to have in our circle."

"Wait, what circle?" Mia asked, confusion making questions flow through her brain.

The ghost was starting to flicker. "The circle of kitchen witches. We don't ever leave the circle once we've been initiated. I'm sure Mary Alice mentioned this before. It's a . . ."

Without finishing the sentence, the ghost disappeared.

Mia glanced around the potions lab. It was back in order, and she was the only one there. At least that she could hear, see, or feel. She had more questions for Grans. As she turned out the lights and locked the lab door, she glanced at the clock on the wall. Ten thirty.

That can't be right. She pulled her phone out of her pants pocket and saw the alarm still going off. When she stepped away from the lab door, she could suddenly hear the alarm. She turned it off and hurried up the stairs. Hopefully, her grandmother was back in the apartment already.

She debated going directly to the library but decided to check the apartment first. Christina was sitting alone in the living room. "Where is everyone?"

"Trent went to get Levi from work, and Abigail went to her room." Christina yawned and set the book down. "I'm on Oregon time and not tired yet, but I'm getting there."

"What about Grans?" Mia headed toward her room and ran into Muffy and Cerby, sleeping in the kitchen with Mr. Darcy. She woke them, and they started barking at her.

"She's not here. I thought she was with you," Christina said as she followed Mia into the hallway, where she opened Grans's bedroom door.

Her bed was neatly made, and she wasn't there.

"Crap, she's still in the library," Mia said as she headed that way.

Christina was still following her. "Is that a problem?"

"Maybe not, but I was supposed to go get her at ten. Can you take the dogs out for me? Now that they're awake, they probably need to go." Mia asked for the favor mostly to keep Christina out of the library. The ghost tolerated Grans and Mia coming inside to research, but it hated humans entering the library. "I'll go get her, and then I'll be back."

Christina agreed, calling the dogs to follow her down the stairs to the front door.

Mia headed to the library. She stood in front of the door, catching her breath and clearing her mind. Going into haunted spots while upset only gave the spiritual entities more to feed on. She wanted to get her grandmother out and back into the apartment. Then Mia was going to crash.

She opened the door and saw Grans sitting at one of the tables. The archives were open and floating on top of the table. Grans was frozen, but Mia knew her mind was in the archives, working. The only part of her that moved was her hand, writing something on a sheet of paper in front of her.

She stepped closer, and the same ghost woman from the potions lab appeared.

"Call her name. Don't touch her, it will rip her out and damage her mind as it returns to her body," the woman advised.

"Okay, now you're scaring me," Mia admitted as she took a breath and called her grandmother's name.

The light in the archives flashed, then the doorway closed. Grans's eyelids flickered, and she leaned back to take a breath. "It's ten?"

"Ten thirty, actually," Mia corrected her. "I was in the potions lab, and my alarm didn't work. Are you okay? That looked a little freaky."

Grans glanced down at her notes. "I'm fine. It's the way the archives work. Well, it's a start, but did you know both Christina and Finn were adopted?"

CHAPTER 7

Christina had already gone to bed by the time Mia returned from the library, so she didn't have to face her to ask about her adoption. Trent stayed over, sleeping in her room. She lay there in the dark, tossing and turning until he sat up, turned on the light, and said, "Spill it. This can't be about tomorrow's test."

Mia propped herself up on the pillows, and Mr. Darcy jumped on her lap. Cerby was sleeping between her and Trent. He opened one eye, watching while Mr. Darcy settled on Mia's lap, then went back to sleep.

"It's not about the exam," Mia admitted. "I am concerned about it, but it's normal test anxiety. I have had it before big tests for as long as I can remember. This is a can of worms I'm not sure I want to open."

"And if you tell me, the can is open?"

Mia rubbed Mr. Darcy's head. She was thinking about Trent's link to Levi. "Maybe. Can you block your thoughts from Levi, or do you two share everything?"

"We don't share everything. The link is more like a conversation. One of us has to initiate the discussion. Why are you worried about me telling Levi something?" he asked, looking at her. He was on his side, his head propped up with his hand.

Now she wished she hadn't said anything. "You know, it's probably the test. I'll go out and sleep on the couch so I don't bother you."

"No way. Your bed. If I'm bothered, I'll go out and sleep on the couch." He reached out and pushed a lock of hair out of her face. "It can't be an issue with work, or you'd tell me. And if it was Mom, you wouldn't tell me or Levi, which leaves Christina. You wouldn't care if Levi knew something about your grandmother, but Christina? That's different. There's something you know about Christina that you don't know if she should know."

"I hate it when you logic out an answer." Mia lifted her chin and stared at the ceiling. "It might be nothing."

"Nothing doesn't make you toss and turn. Is she safe?"

Now Mia turned toward him. "Of course she is. I wouldn't keep something potentially dangerous a secret. She's not sick either. And she's going to rock this new life in Oregon."

"Yet there's something that's keeping you from sleeping," Trent observed. "You might as well tell me. You know you want to talk it out."

"That's the problem. I do want to talk about it. Grans is lost in the research side of the question. I'm more worried about what my friend is going to feel and do when she finds out." She met his eyes and stared for a few minutes. Finally, she sighed. "You're certain you're locked up from Levi knowing anything?"

"I won't be if we keep mentioning him, but yes, he's locked out of my head right now." Trent rested his hand on Mia's arm. "Tell me what's got you tossing and turning at one in the morning."

She needed sleep. But until she talked this out, she'd never relax enough to let that happen. "Fine. Grans found documents that seem to indicate Christina was adopted."

Trent stared at her, then turned over to reach for the light. "Sounds about right. Goodnight, Mia."

"Hold on, don't turn off the light. What, did you already know?" Mia turned toward him, and Mr. Darcy jumped off her lap, annoyed at her movements.

"No, but Christina's normal. Her parents—heck, even Isaac—aren't normal. Sorry, but it's true. Your ex has an inflated ego, along with his parents. They are self-centered and cruel, all about the money and less about anyone's feelings. Christina's too nice to have come from that gene pool." He had lain back down and was now rubbing Cerby's ears. "Although I am worried about her finding this out before the wedding. The girl has expensive taste, and if the Adams money is taken out of the equation, their wedding is going to be at the courthouse with a reception here at the school. She'd hate it."

"She wouldn't hate it," Mia countered, but even as she said it aloud, she knew Trent was right. Christina *would* hate it. She wanted the fairy-tale wedding. And she'd probably go into debt to make it happen. "So you think I should leave it alone?"

"I think you should let the decision marinate. Maybe you'll see clearer in the morning. Or after you ace this test. You'll have more brain cells to deal with Christina's issues then." He yawned.

"Why are you always so calm about everything?" Mia asked as she leaned over to kiss him. "Turn out the light, and I'll put this on my list of things to worry about next week. After the exam and this Halloween party is done."

"Smart girl." Trent turned off the light.

But Mia stayed awake thinking for a while, even after forcing the information into a box marked *Later* in her head. She hoped her friend wouldn't be destroyed by the discovery.

Christina and Levi were still in their bedroom the next morning when Mia left for her test. Trent needed to check in at the grocery store, so he drove her to the Magic Springs Center for Mental Wellness, the coven's hidden-in-plain-sight headquarters. They also had a counseling service available on site for any humans who happened to walk in looking for mental health treatment. But almost nobody did. Trent pulled up and parked in front of the new brick building, then squeezed her hand. "Do you want me to walk you in? They won't let me past the receptionist. Especially now in my mere mortal capacity."

"If only they knew." Mia smiled as she took a breath. "I can do this. I felt the same nerves when I took the SAT my junior year. No hints or crib sheets I can tuck in my bra?"

"Sorry, no. But you'll do fine. As long as you trust your intuition." Trent nodded to the building. "Your future awaits."

"Great, that makes me feel so much better," Mia responded as she got out of the truck. She climbed the marble steps and pulled open the tall, wooden door. It felt like she was entering a castle, and as she walked up to the reception desk, she noticed the large sculptures of what appeared to be Greek gods surrounding the circular entrance. The outside of the building had been flat, not rounded, but the room inside had a circle of columns and bright windows. She'd bet that on rainy days, sunshine still filled the room. They'd added magic to the décor.

"Hi, I'm Mia Malone. I'm here for a test." Now Mia hesitated. Maybe there was more than one type of examination. She hadn't ever asked Grans what the name of the test was.

"Mia, no worries, you're in the right place." The receptionist laughed when Mia gasped at the response. "No, I'm not reading your mind. But your face? That I can read. You should never play poker. The lobby only looks like this for people who have magic. Humans get a boring waiting room at a medical center that looks like it hasn't been remodeled since nineteen sixty. Orange plastic chairs, if you can believe it."

"Okay, I'm definitely in the right place then." Mia grinned. "I don't think we've met before."

"I'm Cleo. Head of the library, the archives, and receptionist, if the door opens. The book your grandmother ordered is right here. I'll give it to you when you get done. And there's your test examiner now. Hugh Charlton, this is Mia Malone. I'll leave you two to get acquainted."

When Mia turned back to thank Cleo, she and the reception desk were gone. In fact, the lobby was gone. They now stood in a large den or library. Two desks were placed in the middle of the room. Hugh motioned to one, and Mia sat down.

"Good morning. As Cleo mentioned, I'm Hugh. I've been doing these examinations for years now, and I've never lost a testee." Hugh Charlton was tall, lanky, and dressed in a light-green tunic and matching pants. He wore open sandals on his feet and a band of silver around his head, pulling his almost silver-hair away from his face. And if that hadn't told Mia he was fae, the point on his ears would have. The man was too beautiful to be human. He chuckled at his joke, so Mia laughed too. "We'll be starting with an oral examination so I can get to know you and your goals and wishes. Then, with the hard stuff out of the way, we'll start the written part. Are you ready?"

"As ready as I'm going to be." Mia nodded.

"Excellent." Hugh smiled and asked the first question.

By the time the exam was finished, it was past five o'clock, and Mia left the building feeling a little dizzy and starving. She hadn't been able to eat much before she arrived, so now that she was back in the truck with Trent, all she could think of was food. He handed her a turkey sandwich.

"Here, I bet you're famished."

"Starving. How did you know I was done?" She put her seat belt on, then moved the book Cleo had handed to her as she'd walked out of the building to the seat next to her.

"Cleo called me about ten minutes ago. She let me know to come and get you and told me to bring food. She can sense hunger." Trent pulled out onto the street. "How do you think you did?"

"Surprisingly, I think I did well. Hugh stumped me on a couple of questions, but then I realized they were trick questions, so I answered based on my gut feeling. I either aced it or failed miserably, not knowing I was that much of an idiot." She wolfed down the sandwich. "How was your day? Anything I should know?"

"I was at the store most of the day. Levi and Christina hung out at the academy, and he got roped into helping cook for tomorrow's deliveries. Finn is amazing in the kitchen and is making Christina jealous and anxious about leaving," Trent slowed down for a rabbit that was trying to decide whether it was crossing the street or not. Finally, the rabbit dove back into the brush by the side of the road. Trent sped back up to the speed limit. "So that's all I heard. Your grandmother has been in the library all day. Don't worry, Mom's been checking on her every hour and even took her lunch to her. Are you glad the exam's over?"

Mia was jolted by the change of subject, but he was probably trying to keep her from freaking out over Grans's day. "I am. Frankly, the whole thing wasn't what I expected."

"It never is. How did you like the lobby remake? Cleo did that a couple of years ago. It gives new meaning to hiding in plain sight." He paused as they got closer to the school. "Did Baldwin reach you?"

"No." Mia pulled out her phone. Twelve missed calls. "What's going on? Anything important?"

"He's anxious about getting back to investigating Howard's death. I don't think the coven has ever pulled him out of an investigation like this. At least not for as long as I can remember. Steve and Dad are back from their fishing trip. Steve stopped at the police station to see what was happening. Baldwin threw him out and told him to ask his friends." Trent kept his gaze on the road. "I'm afraid that with all this meddling, Baldwin's going to think I killed the guy."

"I don't think that's true. Mark is as vested in getting to the truth as we are. He's not a bad cop." Mia started listening to the voice mails. Marks' messages went from checking in to worried, to finally, in the last one, he sounded resigned. "Sarah told him I was doing a test for the coven today and wouldn't be available. Of course, this was after he'd tried to reach me all day. Those two need to learn how to communicate better."

"So he's antsy?" Trent parked the truck at the school.

"That's an understatement. I know you didn't kill Howard. And, hopefully, neither did Cerby or Buddy." Mia slipped out of the truck. She hadn't realized how tired she was. She reached for her half-eaten sandwich, but somewhere between downtown and the academy, she'd finished it.

Trent met her on the sidewalk and put his arm around her. She leaned into his chest, hoping she'd make it up to the apartment before falling asleep. He squeezed her as they walked. "Cerby and Buddy didn't do this. I told you, dragons don't leave evidence, like bodies, behind. And Cerby, he would rather play with someone than end their life. That was one of the problems Cerby had at training. The camp directors had a pen full of bunnies. Cerby opened their cage and let them go. He didn't like the idea that they were being used as food or as training snacks."

"He has a kind heart," Mia said. She glanced at the stairs as soon as she walked in. "I'm not sure I can do it."

"There you two are." Grans came out of the kitchen. "No going upstairs to sleep. You need to stay awake until midnight, when your results download onto the website. We've made margaritas and Mexican food to fortify us while we wait."

Mia stared at her grandmother. "I don't think I can make it that long."

"Don't be silly. Drink this, and you'll be as good as new." Grans handed Mia a drink that smelled like almonds and apples. And maybe a bit of copper.

"I'm not sure," Mia started but then saw the look Grans had given her. She drank the potion. And felt more awake. She handed the glass back to her grandmother. "What I was going to say was I'm not sure we should be celebrating my other side. Not with Finn in the house."

"Don't be silly. We told Finn you were taking a real

estate test. She'll never know the difference." Grans pointed to a table. "Sit there, and I'll let the others know you're back. Abigail was finishing preparing for tomorrow's deliveries."

Her grandmother disappeared into the kitchen as she and Trent sat down. "I don't think I've ever won an argument with my grandmother. She's always covered whatever opposition I've had before I even tell her."

Trent considered this information. "It could be one of two things. She can read your mind, or she can see into the future. Maybe not too far, a day or so. She watches the interaction between the two of you and modifies her reaction in real time. It's a handy talent to have, but it's usually only present in families, and you have to be pretty close to the person you're reading."

"Maybe that's why we're celebrating. She already knows?"

"I don't think it works that way." Trent started to tell her more, but Finn came into the room with a pitcher of margaritas and a tray of glasses.

"I hear it might be celebration time." Finn set the tray on the table and poured the frozen treat into the glasses. "I didn't know you were into real estate. My new stepdad is an agent. He helped Mom find the new house. That's how they met."

"I hate counting chickens, you know." Mia also hated lying to the girl, but telling her she was taking the entrance examination to be a kitchen witch was a little complicated.

"Oh, I get it. I told my cousin last night about you guys setting me up with a room here, and he was so happy for me. I haven't had the best news to share with anyone for a while. Now I have a job, and a place to live, and hopefully, my van will be fixed in no time. Next step, a real apartment." She held up her glass. "Here's to new beginnings. Yours and mine."

Mia clinked glasses with her newest employee. "I can drink to that."

CHAPTER 8

When the results showed up on the coven's website, Mia was ready to head to bed. Finn had already retired to her room. Mia knew the rest of the group was ready to crash too. Abigail had left at ten, when Thomas showed up to drive her home. Grans was nursing a cup of coffee she'd poured thirty minutes ago.

"Refresh the screen." Trent nodded to the laptop in the middle of the almost-empty table. Christina and Levi had cleaned up a few minutes before, and now everyone was gathered and watching the laptop screen.

Mia met her grandmother's gaze. "If I failed, this is no reflection on you. You did your best. I came into the training way late."

"Just push the button." Grans patted her hand. "We'll deal with the consequences tomorrow. Well, actually, later today."

"Okay, here goes," Mia said as she refreshed the screen . . . and it went completely black.

"Did the battery die?" Christina leaned in. As soon as she did, fireworks exploded on the screen and came out into the room. A man dressed in a tuxedo stood in their reception area.

"Mia Malone, you are now officially a Level Three Witch with all the rights and responsibilities that come with the title. Your coven representative will be arriving soon with a handbook and your entrance paperwork. If you choose to continue your studies, the examination board feels that based on your answers during your entrance exam, you should be ready to take the test for Level Four next year. Good luck in your endeavors, and welcome to our society. We are certain that a witch of your talents will do great things."

The man disappeared, and the laptop closed with a *bang*.

"Huh," Grans said, staring at the spot where the man had made his announcement.

Christina hugged Mia, but the other three, Grans, Trent, and Levi, looked at each other. No one said anything.

Mia stepped out of Christina's hug. Something was wrong. "What? Didn't I test high enough? I told you I was worried about taking the test this soon. We should have waited. How bad is it to be a Level Three? I bet you all are Level Five or more."

Trent shook his head. "That's not the problem, Mia. Everyone I know tested Level One. I only know one guy who tested out as a Level Two, and he was the smartest in our high school and coven class. He's working for a coven in Europe now. I've never heard of anyone on their first test hitting Level Three, nor getting an invitation to test for Level Four in a year."

"I tested too high?" Mia shook her head. "The test must be wrong. There's so much I don't know."

"The test doesn't only test your knowledge, Mia." Grans finished her coffee. "It tests your potential. There's never been a kitchen witch over a Level Three, not since we started taking the exam. We might need to re-think your career plan."

"My career plan is to build a catering business here in Magic Springs. Without having to moonlight at the Lodge to keep the lights on." Mia picked up her laptop. "I'm going to bed. I'll probably get a correction notice tomorrow morning."

"You mean today." Grans kissed her cheek. "I'm taking the elevator, if anyone wants to ride with me."

Christina and Levi followed Grans, but Trent grabbed Muffy and Cerby. "I'll take these two out one last time."

Mia put the laptop away in her office and started turning off the lights. Trent was still at the door, watching the dogs, so she went to stand with him. "At least I passed."

"Mia, you don't understand. If you truly are a Level Three, you will be expected to work with the coven hierarchy. Maybe that's why you can read my mind." Trent watched as the pups jumped on Buddy's belly, waking the dragon. "And maybe the Goddess sent Cerby to me because of your power."

"What, you need protection from me?" She leaned closer. The cold was making her shiver. At least she thought it was the cold air.

He pulled her closer and into the curve of his body, with one arm around her. He was still watching Buddy and the dogs wrestle in the small yard. "I'm beginning to think that maybe I'm supposed to be your protector, not just your boyfriend. This sheds a whole new light on what happens next in our lives."

"Let's not go crazy." Mia snapped her fingers, and the dogs came running. "I'm betting I'll get a correction tomorrow morning. Good night, Buddy." The dragon snorted and jumped back into a tree.

Trent followed her and the dogs inside the house and locked the door, making sure the outside light was still on. "I'm sure you're going to get a message tomorrow, but I don't think it will be a retraction. Let's go to bed. Morning is going to come early. I have a truck coming at six."

Mia wandered up the stairs, her thoughts on the exam results. She'd been so afraid of failing that she hadn't thought about what it meant if she aced it. All she wanted was to continue her grandmother's work as a kitchen witch.

Gloria's giggle could be heard through the apartment's front door.

When Mia walked into the Lodge the next morning, Carol, the front desk manager, waved her over to the desk, where she was stacking boxes of Lodge cookies to give to guests when they arrived. "Congrats on passing your test. I can't believe you tested so high. What's it like to be a genius?"

"I'm not a genius, and I didn't realize you were part

of the coven," Mia admitted. She'd talked to Carol Hathaway a lot and had missed that.

"Flying under the radar is what we do best, right?" Carol grinned. "Anyway, we're not supposed to talk about witch business until after someone passes their initial test. It might skew the results somehow. I don't know, I'm a Level One and just lucky to have passed. Anyway, Mark Baldwin is sitting over there in the lobby. He's been here for about ten minutes. I was about to call you. And Brandon Marshall has called three times, trying to get ahold of you. You're a popular girl today."

Carol handed Mia a phone sheet with Brandon's name and number. The only message was *Please Call ASAP*. "Thanks, I'll call him as soon as I finish with Mark."

"I wouldn't wait too long. He is the coven board president," Carol reminded her.

"Physical presence tops call returning. It's a basic rule of customer service." She smiled as she walked over to where Mark sat. He'd been watching her chat with Carol since she'd walked in, but only now did he stand up. "Hi, Mark, what can I help you with?"

"You haven't heard anything, I take it?" Mark asked as he started toward Mia's office. This wasn't going to be a quick chat, then.

"No, I'm sorry. I was tied up yesterday. I got your messages." She didn't say "fifteen messages," but by the blush on his face, he knew what she meant. She held up the pink slip in her hand. "But I'm supposed to call the coven president. Maybe he has news for me."

"Or he's congratulating you on this test thing. Sarah

tried to explain it to me, but what I got was you did better than anyone expected." Mark followed her down the hall.

"Including me. Of course, I didn't know what to expect, so there's that." Mia unlocked her office door and saw Blake heading her way. "Come on in, and we'll call him now."

Blake met her gaze, then nodded and walked by them. What she had to say must not have been important, or she didn't want to talk in front of the Magic Springs police chief. Maybe Mark could hang out in Mia's office more often.

Mia booted up her computer and stashed her tote. "Can I get you some coffee?"

Mark nodded. "I left a little early from the house today. Sarah says I'm obsessing about this death."

To his credit, Mark didn't point out to Mia, and probably not to his wife, either, that he was paid to obsess over deaths in the small town. Mia pushed the intercom, and someone from the kitchen answered. "Hi, would you send a carafe of coffee with service for two and a basket of breakfast rolls to my office? The local police chief is here."

He chuckled as she ended the call. "Is telling them that supposed to make the coffee come faster? Or not be brought by someone on my wanted list?"

"I don't think we have anyone working here who's on your wanted list. Besides, you actually have a wanted list? I would think it would be on your computer. Or do you have a board with wanted posters in the back of the building?" When Mark smiled, she continued, "I wanted to make sure that James didn't burst in here talking a mile a minute with the tray. Sometimes he can be less than professional unless there's a client in the room. He's a great source of local gossip, though."

"That makes sense. Before I forget, Sarah said to congratulate you on the exam results. What does this make you, head witch or something?" Mark grinned like he was kidding, but Mia could see the questions in his eyes. Did this mean she was one of them? Or could he still trust her?

They paused the conversation as a knock came on the door and a server from the dining room came in with a tray. She set it on the table and poured the coffee into cups. Then she stepped back, staring at Mark Baldwin. "Anything else I can do for you?"

Mia smiled and shook her head. She could hear the stories that would be going around the kitchen staff regarding why the police chief was sitting in her office first thing this morning. She checked the woman's name tag before saying, "We're good. Thank you, Dana."

After the woman left, closing the door behind her, Mia set down her coffee. "I don't know what the test results mean. I know too many people already know about my test. I liked being on the edge of both worlds. Now I feel like they are going to force me to choose one or the other."

Mark held his cup with both hands and stared down into the dark coffee. "I feel the same way. Now that Sarah told me about our heritage after Elisa Marie was born, I question everything. Even the people I work with."

"I guess you knowing about Magic Spring's secret made it easier for the coven to put a hold on the investigation around Alfred Howard's death." Mia decided to get right to the point. "That's why you're here, right? To find out if this new status of mine has given me insight into the man's death?"

In Mark's defense, he blushed before nodding. "Sorry, I don't know how these things work. Do you have any more information?"

Mia shook her head. "I found out about my test results less than ten hours ago. They haven't handed me the keys to the vault where they hide all the top-secret information. But maybe soon. Or maybe they just download everything into my brain."

"You're pulling my leg." Mark leaned back and set his coffee on the desk. "Mind if I have a muffin while you make fun of my ignorance?"

"I'm not making fun of you. I'm telling you the cold, hard facts. I'm as ignorant on this subject as you are. I don't know anything about Howard's death, except that Trent and Cerby didn't have anything to do with it."

"What, you think I actually thought a five-pound Maltese killed a guy?" Mark laughed as he broke the carrot cake muffin in two. "Besides, Trent doesn't have a mean bone in his body. His brother Steve? Now that's another story. He was a senior when I entered high school. He was dangerous on and off the football field. You didn't mess with him. If he was in the weight room when I went to work out, I ran cardio instead."

"So you aren't looking at Trent as a suspect?"

Mark ate half the muffin in two bites, then went back for the second half. He paused and looked at Mia.

"Just because the body was found on Trent's property doesn't mean he killed him. Why would he call the police when he could have buried the body somewhere in those woods and no one would have known the difference? Hikers get lost in the mountains all the time, but somehow Magic Mountain is notorious for attracting wandering hikers. You should see the reports I get for missing kids. It's like they're drawn here by some ancient calling signal."

Mia wondered if Mark hadn't hit closer to home than he realized.

Mark left her office soon after asking one more time for her to call as soon as she knew anything. As she moved the coffee service over to the table in her office, she thought about Mark's words. Christina had been drawn to Magic Springs. Mia had assumed it was because she had moved here, but what if there was something that called to a certain type of person? Now Finn was here. Mia grabbed her phone and called her grandmother. When she got Grans's voice mail, she quickly broke down her theory. What if Magic Springs did have some sort of homing beacon for people with special powers? Even if they didn't know they had any. And if that was true, did both Christina and Finn come from families with magic in their veins?

She opened her computer and scanned her emails. One was from Blake. She opened it and read the subject line: *Call me when Mark Baldwin leaves.*

Nothing else was in the email.

She glanced at the message from Brandon. She'd get this over with first. She dialed the number and was surprised when he picked up on the first ring. "Hi, Brandon. This is Mia Malone. We met at the Harvest Queen Pageant?"

"Mia, I called you." He chuckled. "I definitely know who you are. Congratulations, young lady. Your test scores are amazing. The society is expecting big things from you. Now, I know that your power acceptance ceremony is being held at the school on Thursday, and naturally, it's only open for friends and family, but I wanted to follow up and make sure you knew that you are welcome to participate in a coven initiation during the Halloween party on Friday. It would be precisely at midnight, and we'll be out of your hair no later than two that morning. No one likes a party guest who won't go home, right?"

Mia took a breath. "I'm sorry, Brandon. I haven't decided about the coven membership yet. I'll let you know as soon as I do. Sabrina told me I could tell her on Friday at the party."

"Well, of course, you can wait, but if you accept our invitation, I'm sure a lot of members will make sure to be at the ceremony to welcome you. Most of our older members don't attend the Halloween party unless they have family being initiated. You'd meet all the board and the founding members of our coven." He paused, then kept going. "But I hear the hesitation. Sabrina will be in contact before Friday. I hope you take our invitation seriously. We need you in the coven. Especially now that things are changing."

Mia thanked him again for the opportunity, but it wasn't until she hung up that his words hit her. What was changing in the coven world? She didn't have time to think about what Brandon said before Blake burst into her office.

"Seriously, don't you read your emails?" Blake put her hands on her hips, staring at Mia. "I know Mark Baldwin left over twenty minutes ago. I thought you would have called me by now."

"Sorry, I was taking care of a phone call." Mia crumpled the pink slip and threw it away. Blake was already paranoid about the local coven, and there wasn't any reason to let her know that she'd just talked to Brandon Marshall. "What can I help you with? I'm almost finished with the report on Friday night's event."

It wasn't true. She'd filled in as much as she could before the event, but she needed to review the kitchen report to finish it off.

Blake rolled her eyes. "You think I'm worried about a report? I saw the coven announcement. What are you going to do? You know if you join, they're going to force you into a leadership role. Then you'll have to tell them about me."

"I don't know anything about you except you were in a coven back East." Mia paused, looking at her boss. "Wait, if you're not part of the Magic Springs coven, how did you find out about my test results?"

"I keep an active email address with my original coven. I hate to tell you this, Mia Malone, but every coven-attached witch in the world knows about your test results. You're the first in several generations to even come close to testing out to Level Three during the first examination." She narrowed her eyes. "This was your first examination, right?"

Mia nodded and leaned back in her chair. The pressure from this was going to be extreme. The good news was, if the coven offered her a position, she probably would be making enough to quit the Lodge and just run Mia's Morsels.

The bad news was, she probably wouldn't have the time to run her own business.

Every gift also came with a problem. She knew the story of Helen and the Trojan horse. She didn't know if this gift was going to be worth the problem it caused.

She heard Gloria giggling from her perch on the kitchen baker's rack.

CHAPTER 9

Trent was parked in front of the door Tuesday afternoon when Mia left work. She climbed into the truck and leaned over Cerby to kiss him. "This is a nice surprise. I could have walked."

"Mom says that you shouldn't be alone or walking by yourself until after Thursday's ceremony," Trent said as he pulled the truck out to the street. Cerby cuddled on her lap, his head on the door, looking out the window.

"Why, is she afraid someone will kidnap me?" Mia joked, but when Trent didn't respond, she turned to stare at him. "Seriously? Has it happened before?"

"Unfortunately, it has happened with several witches who weren't even as powerful as you are. There is a process, a dark spell, that if used before you have the power transfer ceremony, it can siphon off your essence. It also kills you, but first, the one performing the spell gets a portion of your power. People will do weird things for power."

"Then why did the coven announce to everyone and his dog my test results?" Mia asked as Cerby licked her arm. "It's a good thing that I took the rest of the week off. Blake's being weird, and there's nothing on the schedule. I can do reports and field calls from home. I don't think I'll be leaving the house until after Thursday."

"Now, that's the smartest thing I've heard you say lately. Did Baldwin call?" Trent turned the truck down the road to the house. He was watching something in his rearview mirror.

"He was parked on a couch inside the Lodge when I showed up." Mia turned and looked behind them. A black van with no side windows was turning off the road toward the ski resort. "Are you expecting trouble?"

He grabbed her hand and squeezed. "It wouldn't be trouble if you knew when to expect it. I'm being cautious. I'm ecstatic you're taking the rest of the week off. I was going to try to talk to you about that."

"Life was a lot easier when all I had to deal with was a job that needed me fifty or sixty hours a week and a cheating fiancé. Oh, and a grumbling Christina. The girl was never happy growing up. So much different than she is today." Mia smiled at the memory.

"As long as you get her after ten in the morning. Levi had to wake her up to go do deliveries with Mom and Finn today. She almost bit his head off."

Mia chuckled. "Christina needs a very loud alarm or Levi to make sure she's awake before he leaves for work. Has he found anything in Portland yet?"

"He's on a hiring list as a temp for an EMT service. He wants to get in with a fire station, but he has to test for those positions. He's got tests and interviews set up for the next month. He might be going back sooner than Christina." Trent pulled the truck into the parking lot. "I'll be the last kid in the family standing here in Magic Springs. I didn't plan on staying here."

"I thought you wanted to live here." Mia unbuckled her seat belt but didn't move. "Do we need to talk about future planning? Like, where we see ourselves in the next five or ten years? I could do the business anywhere."

"I'm sure Seattle or Los Angeles would be a perfect place to raise a dragon." Trent pointed out as he nodded to Buddy, who had dropped out of the tree where he'd been sleeping and waiting for Cerby to come home.

"I think he might fit into those towns. In Los Angeles, people would think it was a promotional event if they saw him. Now, if we're looking at Houston or Boston, we might have a problem." Mia rubbed Trent's arm. "Seriously, if you want to live somewhere else, we can make it happen."

"Then who watches out for your grandmother or my parents when the time comes?" he asked. He picked up Cerby and opened the door. "Don't mind me. I'm just feeling a little trapped here with my circumstances.

Being around Steve always brings out my grumpy side. He makes me feel like I chose a smaller life. It has nothing to do with us. Come on, Mom probably has dinner ready for us. Everyone's here again."

That must have included Trent's older brother Steve because his BMW was parked on the other side of the lot. Under the tree where Buddy liked to hang out. She wondered what dragon poop would do to a car's paint.

Trent put his arm around her, then looked her in the eye. "For someone who was in such a serious conversation, you've got a huge smile on your face. Want to share the joke?"

"Nope." She leaned on his chest as they walked. "So, did you talk to Mark?"

Trent unlocked the door and called Cerby to come inside. The little Maltese was talking to Buddy at the side of the yard. "Not yet. I called, but he said he'd told the coven he'd wait for their investigation, so he's waiting. Badly waiting, but waiting."

Steve Majors was coming downstairs. "There you are. Mom sent me down to tell you that dinner's ready. You're not talking about Chief Baldwin, are you?"

"No. Just pillow talk." Mia took Trent's arm, then kissed him.

The public display of affection made Steve squirm. "Well, anyway, food's ready."

He turned and almost ran up the stairs.

"Huh," Trent said, smiling at Mia. "You figured out how to get my older brother out of my business. And it's a fun way too."

"It won't always work, but he is a little squeamish around PDA, so I thought I'd use it." She smiled at Trent. "I know he's your brother, but he bugs me. Too much like the guys Mom was always trying to hook me up with during college."

"Tall and ruggedly handsome?" Trent asked.

She laughed. "No, arrogant and unable or unwilling to listen."

"Okay, I'll give you both points." He opened the apartment door, and Cerby went tearing inside. "Time for the madhouse. Welcome home."

Christina and Levi sat in the living room, looking at something on her laptop. From the glaze across Levi's eyes, it was either wedding venues or dresses. Cakes would have at least gotten a bit of a spark from him. Cerby jumped on the couch and cuddled into Christina's lap.

As Mia walked farther into the apartment, she heard Thomas and Steve talking to Abigail. The only person she didn't hear was her grandmother. And Finn. Was she still in the building?

"Mia, I'm so glad you're home safe. I started worrying as we finished off our deliveries. I can't believe I didn't think of the problem sooner." Abigail was stirring something on the stove. "Sit down, we're going to have to eat in shifts. Maybe when it's all of us, I should cook in the downstairs kitchen."

"Whatever you want." Mia nodded toward the hallway with the bedrooms. "Grans in her room?"

"No, she's in the library. I was going to go get her as soon as you arrived."

"I'll do it. What about Finn?"

Abigail sighed. "She went to eat with her cousin again. I think she's afraid she's interfering with our lives. I tried to tell her she was invited for dinner. I hate to think she's wasting her money on food when she should be saving for an apartment."

"I think it's a bad week to look welcoming around here." Mia looked around the room. "Why do we have so many bouquets? Are these for Friday's party?"

Abigail looked at Trent, who shrugged as he answered his mother's unasked question. "I didn't tell her. We had other things to talk about on the way home. Like why I was there in the first place."

Abigail turned back to Mia. "These are for you. There are more downstairs. I'm surprised you didn't see them coming in. And there's a lot of food. I put everything in the main kitchen and did a decontamination spell on the batch. We don't need any problems because we let some roses get the best of us."

"People are sending flowers and food because of the test results? This is crazy town." Mia reached out to touch a daisy in one of the arrangements. "They're pretty, though. I suppose I'll need to send thank-you notes?"

"Don't you dare!" Abigail's eyes widened. "Our tradition is to only thank the people you plan on letting into your new witch life. If you send notes to all of them, well, you'll be bombarded with people in your circle. Remind Mary Alice that you need to finish your initial circle invites before the ceremony on Thursday. She'll talk you through the process. I hope I'll be one of your invitations."

"Of course." Mia felt confused. Now she understood why her grandmother insisted that she take this week off from the Lodge. Her phone rang. Glancing at the display, she answered, "Hi, Mark, what's going on?"

"Why is he calling you?" Steve stood and reached for her phone. "Give me that."

"Hold on a second." Mia held out her hand, and Trent blocked his brother's advance. She threw Steve a *What do you think you're doing?* look as she stepped out of the apartment. She moved away from the door and stood between the apartment and the library. "Sorry about that. The house is filled with people and a little crazy right now."

"Steve Majors doesn't want you to talk to me. I get it." Mark didn't even beat around the bush. Somehow he knew what Mia was dealing with.

"Don't tell me you planted a bug in a bouquet of flowers today so you could keep an eye on me." Mia was half-joking.

"No, but from what Sarah told me when I took her to lunch, I wouldn't be surprised if a few were sitting in your house. Beware of friendly gifts." He sighed. "I can't believe we're even talking about these things. In small-town Idaho. I took this job because I didn't want the peculiarities of a big city. Anyway, the dead guy found in Trent's yard, according to your friends, had a heart attack. He was older than he looked, from the reports."

"Probably older than what was on the report too." Mia imagined a half leprechaun had a completely different life cycle.

"I was afraid you'd say that. I thought the same thing. But the question is, should I have Frank, the actual coroner, do an autopsy? Your group left it to my discretion." Mark sighed. "I called to see what you think. Besides that, I don't think your boyfriend killed the guy."

Mia knew Mark was giving her a way out. She could tell him to accept the coven's story about how Alfred Howard died and close the case. Heart attacks happened, especially with older, overweight men in the mountains. They always thought they could do more than they could. But she didn't think Howard came all this way to die on Trent's property. Besides, why was he even there?

Was he spying on Trent to see if his house held potions and spell work? Or maybe he'd been already told about Buddy. The training camp had an NDA, but who knew if they didn't whisper, especially when a hellhound turned the camp pink with fairy lights and had a dragon friend. Then again, weres didn't trust the witches.

That was probably something that didn't happen every day.

"Mark, he was here to see if Trent still has powers. He's not supposed to since he turned over his inheritance to Levi years ago. But when the Goddess gave him Cerby, well, the coven got curious." Mia knew Steve and Thomas were going to hate her for sharing, but Mark needed to know what was going on. She'd never forgive herself if she found out Howard had been murdered but they'd helped to cover it up to keep Trent's secret.

"That sounds like a big deal. Sarah told me she still has powers, and she wasn't supposed to either. That's why she was worried about the baby." Mark was quiet for a long time. "Mia, I think this is a bigger problem than we know. I'm going to continue the investigation, but please tell Trent my investigation is not aimed at him. I'm wondering if the people who *are* directing this want it to be aimed that way, though."

"And if they think you are clueless about the magic world, the evidence points right at him." Mia felt like she was in a spy movie. "Don't get yourself in a bad situation."

"I could say the same thing to you, missy." He chuckled. "So I guess we're covert partners in this investigation?"

"I won't tell your secret, and you don't tell mine. Or really, Trent's. I kind of love the guy."

"Family is important. Okay, so I'll start the file. I'll label it an unattended death case. Tell Trent I'll call him for an interview tomorrow. I'm sure Steve is going to throw a fit. I'll give the go-ahead on the autopsy. I'll send you the report from the coven's specialist via email. Let me know if something stands out."

"Sounds horrific, but okay. I'll be home until Monday. I took a few days off." Mia said her goodbyes and tucked her phone into her jeans pocket. Then she went into the library.

A book slammed into her chest as soon as she entered. "Hey, stop that."

Grans looked up from the table where the archives were open before her. "What did you say, dear?"

"Someone threw a book at me." Mia held up the book. She set it on a table. "Dinner's ready."

"Is it that late already?" Grans closed the archive link and tucked her notebooks into her tote. "I'm starving."

The book Mia had set down jiggled, then flew back into her chest.

"Okay, fine, I get it. You want me to read this." Mia grabbed the book and glanced at the title. "*The History of Magical Creatures.*"

"I'm sure it has a chapter on leprechauns." Grans took Mia's arm. "And it's not nice to yell at the ghosts. They'll stop talking to you if you're not polite."

"I wasn't yelling. I don't like having things thrown at me," Mia explained, but the look on Grans's face told her she needed to do more. She looked up at the ceiling and called out, "Sorry, I was testy about the book delivery. Thank you for your guidance."

As Mia closed and locked the library door, Grans patted her arm. "Now, was that so hard? It's important to keep your channels clear of negative energy. Especially when they're so close to where you sleep at night. Ghosts have been known to get a little aggressive when they think they are being ignored."

Mia decided to ignore that statement. "Abigail said I need to invite my circle for Thursday. What does that mean?"

"Your circle of advisors. The ones who have helped you so far. Only you know their names before Thursday's event. Except for me. You have to invite me since I've been training you. And Abigail, of course."

"Can I invite Trent? Or will that out him to the

coven?" Mia hated secrecy, but this was one secret she thought was important to keep. Except she'd already told Mark. She needed to get Trent alone so he knew that Mark knew. And this was why she hated secrets. She was horrible at keeping them.

"It's your circle. Humans can be invited, but they rarely are. It wouldn't look odd to the coven. You two are a couple, and Trent knows about magic, even if he isn't supposed to have powers."

Mia nodded. She hadn't told her grandmother about Trent, but she'd known. And when Cerby and then Buddy showed up, that cinched it. She opened the apartment door to chaos.

Trent and Steve were yelling at each other in the living room, with Levi trying to keep the brothers from coming to swings. Mia could hear Abigail and Thomas yelling at each other in the kitchen.

Christina was holding a barking Cerby back from attacking Steve's ankles, and Muffy was hiding behind Christina. He ran to Grans and begged to be picked up as soon as Mia and Grans stepped inside. Mr. Darcy was up on the mantel, his back up, and spitting at the men who were still yelling at each other.

Gloria was laughing.

Mia had one skill she'd learned early on the playground of Roosevelt Elementary. She put it to use now, and with two fingers, she whistled loudly, breaking up both fights.

"What in the world is going on?" Grans held a shaking Muffy. "You all sound like you've gone crazy."

CHAPTER 10

By the time the fighting had stopped, Abigail had sent Thomas and Steve out of the apartment and back home. Levi had gone along with the men, after kissing Christina goodnight and promising to be back tomorrow. Now, without the father and two of the sons, the rest of the group sat at the table.

"What on earth started this?" Mia looked around the table.

Abigail met Trent's eyes, and he nodded. She took Mia's hand and said, "Dear, we found out that Steve put a listening spell on you when he arrived. He's been monitoring everything you've said or done the last few days."

"He what? I thought he passed on his powers to Trent?" Mia was beginning to think that the action of passing your powers was more of a ceremonial act than an actual one.

"Steve showed no signs of having any magic since

he'd completed the transference when he went to law school. But Thomas knew. All along. I'm going to have a long talk with my husband about keeping secrets from me as soon as your initiation is complete. But now we have to be concerned with keeping you safe."

"Two days, and this will be behind us," Trent said as he pulled Mia into a hug. "Let's just get through the next two days."

Mia closed her eyes and leaned into his strength. "Okay, so you know what I said to Mark. And you probably know Mark's secret too. We need to keep that quiet."

"I'll make sure Steve knows not to let that out. He has a vested interest in us keeping his secret as well." Abigail dished up spaghetti as she talked. "He told his dad about the spell this weekend when he was caught monitoring Mia on his phone while they were fishing. He said he'd canceled it, but then he went crazy tonight when you told Mark about Trent's powers. That's when it all came out."

"Dad always treated Steve differently," Trent said as he passed a bowl of spaghetti to Grans. "He was always Dad's favorite."

"I can't deny that. I think it was because he came first. Then, when you two came so close together, you boys bonded, and Steve was the odd guy out. It didn't help that there were seven years between you and him. He didn't have much in common with two babies. There's a lesson here for all of you. If you're having more than one child, and I hope you do, have them all close together. Your life will be chaotic and messy for several years, but then you'll have time for yourselves."

"Levi and I haven't even talked about kids." Christina blanched as Abigail talked. "I'm still busy creating a career, and Levi hasn't even decided on one."

Mia shook her head. "Don't look at me. We're not even engaged. Talking about kids is off the table. Especially since we have Cerby and Buddy. I'm not sure having a toddler around a young dragon or hellhound is a good thing."

Grans patted Abigail's hand. "Don't worry, Abigail. Grandbabies will show up sooner rather than later. Not to change the subject, but tell Mia about your circle and your initiation. It's been so long since my own, I'm not sure I remember all the fine points."

As Abigail talked, Mia started a mental list of those whom she wanted to invite to join Grans and Abigail in her circle. Her mother, Theresa, had already told her not to invite her. The farther away from magic and Magic Springs for her, the better. Christina would be her honorary human member. Mia had almost told Christina about her adoption when they'd started talking about kids, but Grans had changed the subject. By the time the evening was over, she had at least the start of a list.

After Grans and Abigail went to bed, Trent went out in the backyard to let Cerby play with Buddy. Christina went to her room to call Levi and talk about wedding plans. The girl had a binder she kept adding to. This wedding was going to be massive. Mia hoped Levi was up for it.

When the parking lot alarm went off, Mia watched as Finn got out of a large Ram truck. She grabbed the Tupperware dish of spaghetti and a bag of cookies and headed downstairs to meet her.

Finn opened the door and stepped back when she saw Mia. "I'm sorry, did I wake you?"

Mia waved her inside. "Don't be silly. I wanted to bring down some spaghetti in case you get hungry before breakfast or want to have something available for tomorrow's dinner. I cleared off a shelf in the fridge behind the takeout counter for you to use. You can put groceries in there, too, and anytime you want to cook, just tell Abigail to leave the kitchen open for you. Of course, you're also welcome to eat with us."

Finn looked shocked. "Thanks."

Mia handed her the bag. "I put your favorite soda in the fridge too. Just in case."

"You don't have to do this." Finn took the bag. "I'm already indebted to you for letting me sleep here. You don't have to feed me as well."

"I love feeding people." Mia smiled. "It's what I do. I don't want you to not be able to save to get an apartment."

"I was talking to a friend who works at the Lodge. Her roommate is moving out at the end of November, and she said I can rent her room. It's on the highway into town, but it's a converted garage, and the lady who owns the house is cool. According to my friend, that is."

"See? Your luck is changing for the better already." Mia smiled as they walked over to the takeout counter. "Oh, and there's a microwave back here and some dishes. There's a small sink, or you can use the main kitchen to clean up during the day."

"I knew that Magic Springs was going to be the right place." Finn put the spaghetti into the microwave.

"My mom told me how my dad always talked about this town. Before he died, I mean. Since I've been here, I've tried to see if there are any Shileys in the area, but I haven't had any luck."

"I'll ask Grans. She's lived here forever and knows everyone," Mia said as she watched Finn heat the spaghetti. Whatever she'd had for dinner hadn't filled her up. Teenagers were bottomless pits. Mia wished she could still eat like that. "Anyway, I'll let you get settled. Thanks for all the good work you've done with Abigail. She raves about you."

"Abigail's the best boss I've ever had," Finn replied as the microwave announced that her food was ready.

"Trent's outside with Cerby, so don't be scared if you hear them come in." Mia walked away, glad she'd thought about bringing Finn food. Now, if Grans talked to her about her history, at least it wouldn't be out of left field. Sometimes things worked out for the best. Like Finn finding an apartment so she could stay in Magic Springs and work for Mia. Well, work for Abigail.

Mia was beginning to wonder if she'd ever be able to take back running Mia's Morsels without having to sell her soul to the coven for a better-paying day job.

When Trent came upstairs with Cerby, the little dog ran to the water dish, then jumped on the couch and promptly fell asleep. She grinned at Trent, who had gotten a bottle of water and sat in a chair near the fire. "You wore him out."

Trent shook his head. "Not me. He played with Buddy until he fell over on his last circle around the yard. I had to pick him up and tell both of them it was time for bed. He loves his little dragon friend."

"You're such a good dog-and-dragon dad." Mia smiled as she held up the book she'd been reading. As predicted, it had several chapters on the Irish folk, including their history and the results of human and leprechaun mating. "I should make you a T-shirt. Anyway, it says here that a half blood should live for at least five hundred years. They're considered to be in childhood until they're fifty. I wonder how old Howard was."

"Didn't you say that Baldwin sent you the original autopsy report? It would say, right?" He leaned back and closed his eyes. "I'm sorry about Steve. If I'd known, I would have beat him until he took off the spell. He's such a tool."

"I'm getting kind of used to Majors men knowing what I'm thinking and saying." Mia glanced up at him.

"I told you as soon as I realized I was actually in your head. At first, I thought I was just good at understanding your every need." Trent held his hand out as he tried to explain.

"Whatever, you knew. You got caught sooner than you expected," Mia threw back. She wasn't mad about the connection, more curious about why they had it. Was it their relationship? Or did everyone click this way once they accepted their role as a witch? Of course, neither she nor Trent were supposed to be doing much as a trainee and someone who had given up his power. She needed to do more research on this, but who had the time? She realized Trent was staring at her. "What, did I miss something?"

"I asked if you wanted me to look at the coroner's report. I could filter out the bloody parts." He held out her laptop. "Load it up, and I'll read it. I'll let you know what seems important, and you can ask me questions."

"I feel like I'm being a wimp," she admitted as she took the laptop. "But I'm going to take your offer of assistance since no man is an island. Or something like that."

It took a few minutes but then she found the email. Right next to one from Blake. Before she opened Mark's, she opened the one from her boss.

Call Me.

Short, sweet, and totally not helpful, since Mia was taking a vacation day. She opened the link for the autopsy, and as it loaded, she handed the laptop back to Trent. "Here you go. Give me a second, I need to call Blake."

"After nine?" Trent took the laptop.

"She interfered with my vacation time, so I get to choose when I respond. This is my time, not hers. Besides, I'm pretty sure the woman doesn't sleep. If I didn't know she was a witch, I'd think she was a vampire. Blake, Mistress of the Night. Has a good ring, right?" Mia stood and went to find her phone, which was probably in the kitchen on the charger.

"You're a nut." Trent glanced around. "Do you have a notebook so I can write some of this down?"

"Of course, in the drawer in the rolltop desk." Mia had found the desk in one of the second-floor rooms. One of the teachers must have used the smaller room as an office. She located her phone and called Blake. When she answered, Mia said, "What can I help you with?"

"I didn't expect a call until morning, but thanks. I'm wondering if anyone has said anything about seeing a demon around town."

Mia tried to breathe. Surely she'd misheard. "I'm sorry, what?"

"A demon, Mia. Specifically, an incubus. I'm wondering if anyone in the coven has seen one in town." Blake sounded like she was talking to a child.

"Not that I've heard. I take it they're real, like werewolves?" Mia's eyes went to the book she'd been reading, now sitting on the coffee table. She had so much to learn.

Blake sighed at her question. "Duh. Okay, so if you hear of any being spotted, please call me immediately. I don't care what time of day it is. Maybe your connection to the coven won't be a problem for me after all."

Mia started to ask what she meant, but then realized her boss had ended the call. She went back to Trent and set her phone on the table. "That was weird."

"What, is she being nice for once?" Trent didn't like Blake. She'd ignored him once when Mia had tried to introduce them. "Or do you have an emergency catering event she's known about for weeks?"

This made Mia laugh. "That was Frank's MO. She wanted to know if I'd seen or heard of an incubus being in town."

"That's pretty specific," Trent said, concern filling his face as he watched her scan the table of contents of the book. "I don't think I've heard of one being in town for years. We had one when I was in high school that used to show up around prom as a transfer student and see how many girls he could get to fight over him. Prom turned into a madhouse."

"I guess it's magical creatures week. Buddy. A half leprechaun came to examine Cerby. An elf did my testing. And now an incubus. What's next, Santa Claus?" She set the book down. "I need coffee."

"Me too." He followed her into the kitchen. "Besides, it's only Halloween. Everyone knows that Santa Claus doesn't come out from the North Pole until Christmas."

"I hope you're kidding, but if you're not, don't tell me." Mia used the one-cup machine and made coffee for both of them. She opened a bag of cookies that Abigail had brought up from the main kitchen. "Did you find anything in the report?"

"Some things. Not quite done reading, but I think you may be on to something with the magical creatures. It's the week before Halloween, a full moon, and Samhain. The veil is thin during this time of the year." He took a cookie and demolished it. "I'm glad we brought Cerby home last weekend. The woods can get a little dicey this week."

"So everyone's acting on instinct?" Mia asked, replaying Blake's conversation. "Blake sounded freaked out. Maybe this isn't the time to have the coven here in the academy on Friday night."

"Don't worry. They haven't performed sacrifices for years." Trent took another cookie. "But there seems to be a connection I can't see right now. Why was Howard here early? What was he planning on doing over the weekend? Spying on me? Or was he meeting someone here?"

"Didn't he say that he was on vacation, but we'd see him on Tuesday, when he would schedule an interview?" Mia tried to remember their conversation the first and only time she'd met him.

Trent nodded. "I'd forgotten about that. I wonder who he was meeting or if he was here alone. If he was here on vacation, he might have booked a fishing trip with my dad. Let me text him."

As Trent did that, Mia looked at his list in the notebook. *Age: 147. Well-developed male with obvious leprechaun features. Cause of death: heart gave out.* She went back to the book to see if it had any notes about cross-breeding with humans. She found it almost immediately. "Trent, according to this, being a half breed shouldn't have affected his heart or any other body part. I'm thinking that maybe the coven is trying to sweep his death under the rug."

Trent read the page in the book. Then he put her bookmark back inside and closed it. He checked his phone. "Dad might have already crashed for the night."

Mia knew he was thinking about Howard's death, so she changed the subject. "I wonder what Grans has found out about Christina and Finn's heritage. Do you think there's any chance they have some witch blood in their original family histories?"

"I've always wondered about Christina. She and Levi bonded so quickly. Typically, there's a disconnect when you date someone outside your, well, bloodline. I'm surprised you lasted with Isaac so long. Didn't you ever feel like he wasn't your soul mate?"

"Before or after I caught him cheating?" Mia smiled and waved away whatever response Trent was going to make. "I guess I didn't believe in soul mates. Mom was practical. She told me she loved my father because of who he was, not what he was. I always thought that was a weird way to put it, but no, I didn't have stars in my eyes with any of my prior boyfriends before you, up to and including Isaac."

"Does that mean you do have stars in your eyes with me?" Trent had moved over to the couch, where Cerby had been sleeping. He'd put the sleeping pup on the floor. He ran his finger up Mia's arm.

"Dude, we're working." Mia giggled as he scooted closer.

"Not until you answer my question. Am I your soul mate?" He turned her head and stared into her eyes as he waited for an answer.

Mia ran her fingers over his craggy face. "Trent Majors, you are the most exasperating man I've ever met."

He nodded and glanced at his phone when a text message alert sounded. "I'm going to take that as a yes. And stop being all mushy. I'm trying to focus on figuring out who killed Alfred Howard. I guess I'm going to have to move to the other side of the room to make you stop tempting me."

"Oh my Goddess." Mia laughed as she threw a pillow at him. It bounced and hit Cerby instead, waking the dog and sending him into a frenzied barking cycle.

"Now, see what you've done." Trent tossed the pillow on the couch. "You woke up the baby. Dad says he had a no-show Friday afternoon. He was supposed to be on a weekend fishing trip down the River of No Return."

"Maybe Howard showed up at the wrong Majors house and someone followed him." Mia wrote down what they'd found out from Thomas.

Trent leaned over and picked up Cerby, who still looked like he was asleep. "Or maybe someone sent him to the wrong address on purpose."

CHAPTER 11

The next morning, Levi arrived for breakfast with a note from Thomas. He handed it to Trent as he sat down at the table. "Here's the guy's name who booked the adventure. And the credit card. Two nights, two guests. Dad said the charge went through, but the number he was given to contact the client was disconnected when he called Friday at noon to confirm arrival. Then they never showed. Dad got paid upfront since the booking was done within his cancellation period."

"Does that happen often?" Mia looked at the paper when Trent passed it to her.

Levi nodded. "According to Dad, yes. That's why he has a thirty-day no-cancel policy. He provides all the meals and food, so when he got burned by a bunch of bankers a few years ago, he implemented the policy."

"So he didn't even question it." Mia wondered if the

client had known that not showing up wouldn't throw up a red flag. "The killer could have taken Thomas's trip, then killed Howard on the way. Accidents happen."

"Not on Dad's watch. He doesn't let people get out of his sight. He's got a perfect record so far." Trent tapped the paper that Mia had set on the table. "I wonder if he's a local? They would know that Dad's trips are super safe."

"Maybe he didn't know that when he booked it. Or maybe he always planned on having the body found on Trent's property?" Christina set her coffee down. "It's misdirection. Look here at the rafting trip, but really, I'm going to kill him before he even gets on the boat."

"Possibly." Mia ate a bite of her cheese omelet. When Christina made a face at her, she grinned. "Something is missing. I don't think he planned on killing Howard on the rafting trip. Besides, what if he pushed him out of the boat and he survived? Howard could point a finger at the culprit. According to the book, leprechauns are hard to kill."

"There's the Emerald Potion," Grans said as she took a bite of fried apples. "If he gave him that, maybe mixed into an energy drink or baked into a cookie, Howard would have been dead in minutes. Anyone would be affected, since it has foxglove or fairy thimbles in it. But the compounds were first used in Ireland to weed out some of the less-than-kind leprechauns when they were trying to settle the land."

"Mark needs to run a tox screen soon, before the chemicals disperse. If they haven't already." Mia was already texting Baldwin. She also told him about the missed appointment with Thomas Majors for a fishing trip. "This is good stuff, guys. We'll have his murder solved before tomorrow's ceremony."

Grans met her gaze. "I think you have something to say about that, right, Mia?"

"Oh, yeah. I need a circle, and you all are family, so will you be my circle?" Mia smiled at the five sitting around her table. "I mean, you're all here enough, and our lives are already entwined. Why not add one more level of connection?"

"That sounds so sweet—almost." Christina laughed. "But Levi and I will be in Portland. Is that going to be an issue?"

"No," Mia answered, then looked at her grandmother, who nodded her confirmation. "Basically, as I understand the group, you're my mastermind group. You vow to help me when I ask and when I don't."

"Which you never will ask, so we'll have to guess when you need help." Christina shrugged. "I'm in. If you and Trent ever get married, we'll be sisters-in-law, at least. This is like you said, one more level."

As they each listed off what they were doing for the day, Mia started to relax. She had an event to get ready for—two, actually. But she was hoping her initiation would be a small family gathering. Most of the group went downstairs to start cooking and getting the gym ready for the Halloween party on Friday. Grans was in the living room paging through the book Mia had left on the coffee table.

"What are your plans for today? Anything I need to get done before my ceremony tomorrow?" Mia sat down and put a full cup of coffee on the table for her grandmother. She wanted to talk about this level thing.

The parking lot alarm went off, and Mia saw the florist van again. "Seriously, more flowers?"

"Let Abigail or Trent handle that, dear. I don't want you to bark at the poor delivery guy. He's only doing his job." Grans pulled her down onto the couch. "So, who else are you going to invite to your circle?"

"I thought I was done?"

"You need at least seven. Thirteen, counting you, would be nice, so two to seven more is common." Grans closed the book.

Mia leaned back and threw her hands over her face. "I don't even know two more people that I trust."

"I'm sure that's not true. Think on it for a while, and if you don't come up with anyone, I'll reach out to my charms class. Maybe one or two of them could stand in until you get a quorum. But don't dawdle in replacing them. They're all older than dirt."

"Well, okay, I'll let you know." Mia rolled her head on her shoulders, hoping to dispel some of the tension. She needed to run or work out or swim or something besides working, but right now, she had no time.

"That's my girl." Grans patted her arm. "I'm making good progress with Christina's genealogy chart. I think we'll have some answers soon. Finn, on the other hand, she's a mystery. It's like she showed up at Nampa High School for her sophomore year. Almost all fully grown."

"Just don't get lost in there," Mia warned. She hadn't liked the way her grandmother looked the last time when she'd collected her from the library. "I'll come get you for lunch. Maybe the library will have another book on magical creatures for me. Oh, what do you know about an incubus?"

"Is someone bothering you? With this level of power, you know there are some dangers until we get you sealed tomorrow night." Grans watched Mia closely. "You don't look like you're under a spell."

"I was yesterday, and you didn't notice it," Mia reminded Grans of Steve's listening spell.

"My bad. I get distracted when I'm tired. But I have to say, he's a very accomplished weaver. That's not the first time he's used that spell." Grans reached down and rubbed Muffy's head. "Do you mind taking him out so I don't have to go all the way downstairs? Oh, and I have a moving truck coming today with a few items for safekeeping."

"We can put it in your storage room on the second floor," Mia said. She stood to grab Muffy and call Cerby, who was sleeping in the kitchen with Mr. Darcy.

"That room is already full. Okay to use the next one?" Grans asked as she finished her coffee.

"Sure." Mia started to ask what was in the room, but Muffy barked at her. It was time to start her day.

When she got down to the front door, Trent was carrying a bouquet of flowers into the storage room. The reception area was filled with the ones that they'd moved out of the kitchen so they could cook.

The room smelled like a greenhouse garden. Mia didn't wear perfume mostly because it interfered with her sense of smell while she was cooking. As she came down the stairs today, though, she felt like she'd waded into a vat of floral scents.

Trent smiled. "At least we won't have to do any centerpieces for the event on Friday. We have enough, and Fred from the florist shop said you have a couple more deliveries they were still working on when he left."

"Can we have him deliver the rest of the flowers directly to some place that needs them? Like the local nursing home? I'm sure we can get one per room if we move some of these we've already received. Since Abigail said I can't respond to thank anyone, there's no reason for them to come here first." Mia waited for the van to leave the parking lot before opening the door for Muffy and Cerby.

"Great idea! I'll call Fred in a few minutes after Mom picks out what she wants for Friday. Then the rest will go to the nursing home. When that's full, maybe we should think about sending some to the children's hospital in Twin? Or a nursing home in another town?" Trent stood near her, watching the dogs climb all over Buddy.

"Either one. Hopefully we won't be dealing with this long." With the great flower flood finally dealt with, Mia could deal with her day. Or she could have if she wasn't getting a headache from the overwhelming floral scents. She headed to the kitchen.

Everyone was at a station, focused on their tasks. Here, the smells filling the air were from bacon and sugar and something tart. She grabbed an apron and moved to Abigail for her assignment. As soon as she came in the door, though, Abigail shook her head. She'd been watching for her.

"Not today. We've got this handled. You need to go up and play in your lab. Your grandmother put a list of projects there you need to complete." Abigail pointed to the door. She glanced over at Finn to see if she was listening. "You need to do the work or you'll never level up."

"I'm beginning to believe that leveling up isn't in my best interest." Mia glanced around the happy kitchen. This was where she belonged. Cooking food for others. That's why she loved the idea of being a kitchen witch— it played on her strengths. Now she was managing events and doing the forecasting for both the Lodge and Mia's Morsels. Not making cookies. She missed baking freaking cookies. "Trent's taking the flowers to the nursing home. You need to choose what you want for Friday."

"I'll do that." Christina grabbed her tray and put it in the refrigerator. "I was going to start a new batch of cookies. Mia, we've got this handled. Go work."

Finn glanced up, questions in her eyes, but at least she didn't ask. Mia gave her a smile and nodded. "I told Grans I'd grab her for lunch, so don't forget to come get us."

Mia avoided mentioning the library in mixed groups. If Finn was a reader, she'd love to go visit a home library to see what books were there, maybe grab a few to read while she was staying here. The problem was, their library wasn't like that. It was more specialized, and humans weren't welcome.

Mia sighed and left the kitchen, hanging her apron back on the hook. "Okay, then, bake sweet."

As she walked through the reception area, she saw the table was filled with books. She stopped because she was sure they hadn't been there before. A white card in front of the books said, *Finn.* The library must have overheard her thoughts and brought down a selection of books that it thought would be appropriate for Finn's reading pleasure.

Mia looked upward and whispered, "Thank you." As she scanned the pile of books, she saw some romances and some paranormal mysteries. And quite a few of the fairy-tale books Mia had read during her studies to be a kitchen witch. The books served dual purposes, as instructional tales for young witches as well as entertaining stories for humans.

She patted the table. Finn would find them when she left the kitchen. Mia would make sure of that at lunch. Mia loved it when the academy worked with her. That hadn't always been the case. Trent wanted to move to a regular house when they made their relationship permanent. What was he thinking?

Her phone rang. It was Baldwin.

"Got time for coffee this morning?"

"Sure. I'm at the house." Mia hurried upstairs to grab a jacket and her wallet. "Where do you want to meet?"

"I'm parked at the greenbelt opening down the street from your house. I don't want anyone seeing us together, so can you go out to the walkway and head south?"

"Okay." Mia wasn't sure why Baldwin wanted to meet in secret, but it was either this or working in the potions lab. Alone. "Give me ten minutes."

As she walked past the tree where Buddy was perched, he chirped a good morning. Or at least a greeting. Mia guessed she needed to learn dragon language. "I'm heading to meet with our human police chief, so don't go scaring him," she told him.

Buddy sank back into the tree, probably trying to show her that he could hide from any human eyes.

"Good job, stay here. Trent will bring Cerby out to play soon," Mia called back as she went through the gate that led to the greenbelt.

She heard the answering chortle clearly. Buddy loved Cerby.

As much as she loved living in the apartment at the school, she knew it wasn't the best place to try to keep a growing dragon and an untrained hellhound in Maltese clothing. The school was too close to town and prying eyes. She didn't even know what the coven would think about Buddy. This reminded her to tell Trent to take Buddy and Cerby home before the coven's party on Friday. He probably had already thought of that. Or Abigail had. At least she hoped. So many spinning plates, and she had no idea how half of them had started spinning in the first place.

She climbed into the cab of Mark's truck, and he handed her a travel mug. "Coffee, black. Right?"

"Perfect. So, why the secrecy?" She looked around at the forest surrounding them. "I have to admit, this is a great place for coffee."

"The coven said they were turning the investigation over to me, but then I got a call from the mayor yesterday wondering why I was investigating a natural death. I threw the unattended death regulation at him, and he shut up, but he did ask me to make the investigation quick." Mark turned to focus on her. "So, who was this guy?"

"He works for the National Society, I think. I've already told you he was here to see why the Goddess gave Cerby to Trent." Mia sipped her coffee, but it was too hot, so she set it down in the beverage carrier. "I'm beginning to think whoever called in the tip on Cerby and Trent might also be the killer. Howard wasn't supposed to be here until yesterday. But instead, he dropped into the school on Thursday to introduce himself."

"Trying to catch you unaware?" Mark nodded. "Smart idea."

"I thought that was why too, but then he said he was taking some personal time to explore since he'd never been to Idaho before and that he'd see us on Tuesday. Maybe he was being nice?" Mia suggested.

"So all I have to do is find out what this guy was

doing between the time he visited you at the school and when he wound up dead at Trent's," Mark said as he scribbled in his notebook. "He checked into the Lodge on Wednesday night. Did you talk to him there?"

Mia shook her head. Had Blake talked to Howard, or was she freaked out he was there? "No, but I've been off a lot recently, getting ready for my test and now the party on Friday. Blake Sandburg, my boss, said he talked to her on Thursday about me and Trent. She wasn't happy that my 'personal' life was interfering with my time at work."

"That's interesting. I talked to Blake yesterday, and she said she never met the guy." He narrowed his eyes. "How much trouble are you going to get into if I call her on her story?"

"Maybe none. Don't mention that she's a witch, though." Mia sighed. "I was supposed to keep that part a secret. So please don't tell her I told you that. Although she called yesterday all upset and asking if I'd seen an incubus in town?"

"Excuse me?" Baldwin wrote that information down, but Mia could see he was uncomfortable. "I should have taken that job in Boise. At least there the freaks were human."

Mia had an idea. "Ask Sarah about the incubus. I forgot to ask Abigail or Grans, but I'll do that at lunch."

"You realize you're dragging me into your delusions." Mark snapped his book shut. "Anyway, can you talk to the hotel staff quietly and see if there's anyone else Howard talked to between Wednesday, when he checked in, and Friday night? And quickly? I don't know how long they'll let me keep this case open."

As Mark drove away, she glanced at her watch. The Lodge was on the greenbelt a mile past her house. If she hurried, she could get there and back before lunch. All she had to hope was that the people who wanted to kidnap her and steal her magic weren't watching her now.

Great, now she was going to be the girl whom everyone thought was too stupid to live in the horror movies. "Okay, then, let's go down in the spooky basement with a single candle for light and not tell anyone what we're doing."

CHAPTER 12

A *chuff* came from the tree next to the greenbelt. "Buddy? You followed me?"

The dragon hopped down on the greenbelt and walked with her. He rubbed his head against her leg. Apparently, she was one of his people now. And she wasn't alone.

Mia swallowed back tears. The fact that he'd been here, just in case, made her feel a little bit better about her upcoming clandestine visit to the Lodge. "Okay, then. Let's get this over with before they notice we're gone?"

"Gone from talking to Baldwin or from whatever else you're planning?" Trent came around the bend and glared at her. Cerby was on his leash and barked at them. "What? Does a dragon have your tongue?"

"Ha-ha. I was just—" Mia paused. She didn't know what she'd been going to say because she knew she shouldn't be out alone—or even at all—until after her ceremony. "Look, Baldwin called and needed to talk this out. The coven's putting pressure on him to close the case. Don't you want to find Howard's killer?"

"At the risk of losing you? No. But I can see your point. Let's go back, get my truck, and I'll take you wherever you want to go. After we tell my mom where we're going and when we'll be back. In case *we* need rescuing." He put his arm around her. "I was worried when I couldn't find you. I got the flowers packed up, and Finn's taking them over to the nursing home in the catering van."

"I'm sorry I worried you." She glanced down at Cerby, who was now walking with Buddy and chatting. "I take it that Cerby found us?"

"He followed me outside and barked at the gate until I put him on a leash and gave him his head. I think he'll be a strong tracker." He nodded at Buddy, who was walking in front of them, his tail dragging on the asphalt and making a line in the hard surface. "How did you get him to come with you?"

"I didn't. I told him what I was doing, and when I got out of Mark's truck at the parking area, he was hiding in a tree, watching us. He said I was one of his people," Mia felt the overwhelming emotion again. "Anyway, Mark wants me to chat with the hotel staff and see if Howard met anyone there between Wednesday, when he checked in, and . . ."

"Friday, when someone checked him out." Trent grinned at his joke. "Okay, not funny, but a little funny, right?"

"You're a card." She opened the gate, and they stepped into the backyard. "Do you want me to tell your mom?"

"No, I'll text her before we leave. Cerby, you have to go inside while we make a trip to the Lodge. Buddy, thanks for looking out for Mia." Trent patted the dragon on the back, and Buddy chortled and hopped back into his tree. His eyes closed. It was time for a nap.

They let Cerby into the house, and Trent texted his mom. Then they were on the way to the Lodge.

"We probably can't grab lunch out, just the two of us, right?" she asked as he turned the truck into the Lodge parking lot. "Maybe that place in Twin on the canyon?"

"Are you kidding me? We shouldn't even be doing this." Trent turned to look at her and saw her laughing. "Not funny."

She got out of the car. "It was a little funny. Let's get this over with before Blake catches me at work."

The Lodge was decorated with full-on Halloween glory. Jeani Langston had been busy. She was a local event decorator with a magical flare. The theme was "Witches of the Ages," a tongue-in-cheek nod to Magic Spring's hidden history. A loud witch's cackle announced their entrance, but the decorations had been up so long that the front desk staff didn't even look up at the noise. Carol was manning the desk, looking at something on the computer.

"Hey, Carol, I'm glad I caught you. We had a friend come to visit last week, and unfortunately, he had a heart attack while he was out hiking. I was wondering if he had other friends in the area we need to let know about his passing." Mia figured a version of the truth was the way to go. Especially since Carol was part of the coven.

"I heard about the little guy. I was shocked to see a leprechaun here in Idaho. Even one who's not pure-bred. I'm not a snob or anything, but it was rare." Carol looked around. "He was very charming. I was there when he checked in on Wednesday. He already had a message waiting. I accidentally saw the number. It was local, but the name was Nick. No last name, and I can't tell you the number besides the two-oh-eight area code."

"That's interesting, maybe a local friend?" Mia glanced at Trent. "Did he have dinner here with any-one?"

"Oh, hold on. I can check his bill. The National Society credit card he used was a black card. We don't see many of those up here." She hit a few keys but kept looking at Mia and Trent. "Isn't your ceremony tomor-row? I can't believe you're not busy setting everything up. I'm looking forward to Friday's party. I bought a new little black dress weeks ago. I hope it still fits."

"Just trying to tie up some loose ends. Trent wanted a few minutes out of the house," she replied, grabbing Trent's hand and squeezing. "So, about Alfred?"

"Oh, right. Here's his bill. He had dinner for two sent up to the room on Wednesday and Thursday nights. Same meal both nights. That's odd," Carol noted, look-ing up at Mia and grinning. "Even for one of us. Break-fast for two on Thursday and Friday in the dining room. And it looks like he had lunch for two on Friday, and it was moved from his bill to an employee account."

"Can you see whose?" Mia leaned forward, trying to see the list of charges, but the angle was wrong.

"Funny, it was Blake's personal account. Not the marketing account, like she typically charges meals with others to." Carol shrugged. "That was it. Maybe he was friends with our amazing boss."

Carol had put air quotes around the word *amazing*, which made Mia laugh. "Can you ask around and see if anyone saw Alfred with someone specific? I'd hate for someone to find out through the news or something. Anyway, Trent's getting antsy, so we need to go. See you Friday night. I'll probably be running around trying to keep the wheels from falling off."

"Your parties are always beautiful. Are Jeani and Cheryl decorating?" Carol closed up the computer and handed her a printout. "Just in case you need it for some reason."

"Thanks. Abigail Majors is dealing with the details, so I'm not sure who's decorating. It will be beautiful either way." Mia said goodbye and tucked the printout into her jeans. She took Trent's arm, and they hurried out of the lobby area and back to the truck. Buddy was in a tree near the edge of the parking lot, watching them, and he gave a quick chirp when he saw them leaving the building.

Mia didn't speak until after they were on the road headed home. "If Jeani's decorating, we need to tell her that Levi and Christina are home."

"Cheryl's dating a witch from Twin. He's in a rock band. Levi will be safe." Trent glanced out the rear-view mirror. "Buddy's following us. I hope there aren't any drones out taking pictures of the mountains. They're going to get a nice shot of a baby dragon."

"They'll think they're being pranked. I'm happy for Cheryl." Mia peered at him. "You already knew that

Jeani was doing the decorating. Abigail needs to keep me as updated as she does you."

"Then you need to come to the Majors Sunday night dinner. I get all my gossip there unless members of my staff at the store are being chatty." He tapped his fingers on the steering wheel. "Just checking . . . as soon as these dual engagement parties for Levi and Christina are over by the end of November, can I ask you *the* question?"

"You can." Mia's heart fluttered. "Some people think it's tacky to get engaged over the holidays, but it's a great time for professional photo shoots since every place is already decorated."

"Good to know." He pulled into the school lot, and they watched as Buddy did a circle, then landed.

Christina opened the door, and Cerby ran out, barking. Trent caught him up in a swoop. "Hey, little guy, what's wrong?"

"He's been that way since you left." Christina grabbed Mia's arm and hurried her inside. "Abigail's been a worried mess, and Cerby wouldn't shut up. Your grandmother even came down from the library to see what the commotion was all about."

"We were only gone a few minutes." Mia met Trent's gaze.

"I'm taking Cerby out to play with Buddy. I believe he's mad we left him at home and Buddy got to go." Trent smiled. "Don't eat all the ham sandwiches."

Finn stood in the reception area watching. "Man, he's good. How did he know that Abigail sent me out to tell everyone that lunch was ready?"

* * *

Mia was upstairs working in the potions lab later that afternoon when her grandmother came to find her.

"Are you trying to get yourself kidnapped?" Grans came over and glanced at the potions book as well as inside the cauldron. "You need a bit more rosemary for the cleansing oil. I'm so glad you decided to do your own preparation potions for tomorrow night's ceremony. While you're here, you should make some salt and herb bath salts for your bathroom. There's a lovely decanter in the cupboard."

"I wasn't—" Mia stopped. It didn't help to argue with her grandmother. "I've been thinking about my circle. Both Christina and Trent are considered human, at least in the coven's mind. Is this something I have to report to them, about who I asked?"

"Oh, dear, no. The ceremony tomorrow is between you and the Goddess. She is the only one you have to think about pleasing." Grans went ahead and added the rosemary to the cauldron. She couldn't help herself.

"Okay, so I'm not ratting anyone out to the coven about hidden skills." Mia stirred the pot with a wooden spoon. She moved back and started pulling the ingredients for the relaxation oil that would be administered right before she made her vows to keep the light and use it to brighten the dark corners of the world. She wasn't quite sure what that meant, and she hoped she wouldn't have to go out looking for evil to smite it. She was a kitchen witch, not a medieval knight. And she'd gotten yelled at for going to talk to Mark today. "I'd like to ask Sarah to join the circle."

"Oh, she's a lovely choice. I wish your mother would change her mind. Theresa's so narrow-minded about all these things." Grans picked up each of the new bottles and looked at them. "You should put away the ingredients from your last potion before starting a new one."

"I did, well, except the rosemary. I wasn't sure you were done adjusting." She didn't mean to call her grandmother out, but she was supposed to be making these potions on her own. According to Grans, many witches didn't nowadays, using ones bought in the coven store.

Grans handed her the container of dried rosemary. "I'm only trying to help."

"I appreciate you." Mia put the container away on the herb shelf. They were all stored in alphabetical order, and she was trying to keep them that way. "How's the research going?"

"Well, I'm verifying some records, but I should have Christina's genealogy chart finished tomorrow. When are you going to tell her she was adopted?" Grans sat in one of the lounging chairs that they'd found in the second-floor office as well. Whoever had had that office, they'd liked nice furniture.

"After the ceremony, I guess. I'd like to wait until the engagement parties are done so she doesn't blow up on her mom for not telling her, but I'll have to trust that Christina is going to handle the information like an adult. Are either of her birth parents still alive? Maybe in the area?"

"Not in the area, and it doesn't look like she has any

full siblings." Grans paused, then stopped. "Let me finish up, and I'll give you a copy of her chart. That way I can make sure it's valid."

"Sounds good." Mia was only half-listening now. She'd started the next potion. After mixing all the ingredients, she grinned at her grandmother. "Two almost done. So, what about Finn?"

"Her background is a little harder to verify, but I think we can expect great things from our newest Magic Springs resident. The Goddess is pleased that you gave a stranger a place to stay in a storm."

"One, she wasn't a stranger. She'd been working for Abigail for over a month. Two, there was no storm, and three, I couldn't bear the idea of her sleeping in that van. It's not done. Not when we had an extra room we could turn into a bedroom." Mia only had the two cauldrons, so now she had to wait for one to cool so she could clean it and put the potion away. She put away her ingredients and then went to sit next to her grandmother. "I kept thinking about how angry Christina was when she came to live with me. She hid it well, but she was so mad at her mom, at Isaac. I think the only reason she came here was that she didn't hate me because she thought I hated Isaac."

"As you should have. That man was horrible to you. And he wanted to get married? You dodged a bullet there." Grans took her hand and squeezed it.

"We were good, for a while. But even on our best days, Isaac and I weren't close to what I have with Trent. He gets me. Anyway, I need one more at least for my circle. Any ideas?" Mia could feel the minutes ticking past her. She was on a time crunch. "What happens if I only have five? Or six?"

"We'll find someone. Don't you worry about it." Grans hugged her and went to leave.

Mia wouldn't have been worried except for the worried look on her grandmother's face. "Don't tell me not to worry when you look like the world might end."

This kitchen witch ceremony was beginning to feel more like work than a good way to transition from one reality to another.

She opened her phone and scanned for any new text messages. Nothing from Baldwin or Carol, but since she had a few minutes, she updated him on the information she'd received from Carol this morning.

Then Mia texted Sarah and asked if she would be part of her circle. She gave her a way out, explaining that if she was too busy with the baby and life, not to worry about it. When she pressed *send*, she wondered if she should have called instead. Was this like breaking up over text messages, a no-no?

The quick response she got back could only mean one thing. No.

Bracing herself for the letdown, she was pleasantly surprised when not only was it not a no, but Sarah said she'd bring Mark and the baby along to help celebrate. And her famous chocolate cake.

Mia smiled as she responded. Then she texted Abigail to let her know of the increase in the number of people at the ceremony, as well as the cake.

From knowing no one when Mia had first moved here but her grandmother and Adele—her grandmother's best friend who died soon after Mia arrived—Mia had built a small community. She had both witch and human friends. She felt like she was part of Trent's family. And she had kept Christina when she'd broken ties with Isaac and his parents.

Not a bad place to be. Even without joining the coven for support and friendship. She knew Sabrina would be arriving at any time to chat about her possible initiation on Friday at the apex of the party. Abigail had said there were three others who were joining on Friday. She got the coven newsletter, *News from Magic Cove's Witch Central*. The lead reporter had left three messages, trying to get an interview with Mia since her test results had come out.

"I wonder if the tests could have been wrong?" Mia asked as Mr. Darcy jumped on her lap. He must have escaped from the apartment when Grans went back upstairs a few minutes ago and he'd come looking for her.

He didn't get to move around quite as freely as when Dorian had been residing in his body. He'd thanked the cat for housing his spirit by opening doors and getting down treats whenever Mr. Darcy wanted one.

Now Dorian's spirit lived in a golem body somewhere near Boston and was rebuilding his almost-human life.

She wondered if he was having as much trouble with his life transition as she was with hers.

CHAPTER 13

"Thanks for the books," Finn said at dinner. Abigail had convinced her to join them tonight. "I don't know who got them for me, but you hit the nail on the head with what I like."

"We pulled them from the ones we had." Mia glanced around the table, hoping no one would mention the library. "Glad you're enjoying them."

Abigail met Mia's gaze. "Oh, and there's one more thing. Two, actually. Thursday night, we'll be having a private affair in the gym and reception area. I hate to ask but . . ."

Finn held up her hand. "Don't even worry about it. You want me to be scarce that night. Not a problem. After dinner, I'll just head to my room. I've got some research I want to do on the culinary college in Twin. Christina's been telling me all about it, and I'm going to try to get in for January, at least part-time. I'll stay in my room and use the bathroom down the hall so I don't bother your guests. What's the second thing?"

Finn was the perfect houseguest. She was taking this better than Mia had expected. She looked at Abigail and held up her hand. She'd try to explain what was happening on Friday. "So, the event on Friday night might be a little strange. It's Halloween, and this group has a habit of going all out, including acting in character. This year's theme is witches. So they go a little over the top. I know you're working the event, so we didn't want you to get freaked out."

"Halloween parties are always cool. One of our neighbors set up a Frankenstein lab and everything in their house one year. It took them two months to build it in their garage." She took a bite of the sweet potato casserole that Abigail had made to go with their ham.

"We don't want you overwhelmed. If you see something weird or you don't understand, report it to Abigail or me, or anyone here at the table. We'll take care of the problem." Mia glanced around the room, and everyone nodded. "So the culinary program is calling to you? We were able to work around Christina's school schedule for her hours. I'm sure we can do the same for you if you want to keep working here."

"You're kidding, right? You guys are the best. If I was working fast food, I'd be sleeping in a shelter right now, trying to figure out how I could get to work every day. Magic Springs isn't set up for public transportation." She held up her fork. "And I wouldn't be eating like this. You all take your food seriously. Mom wasn't much of a cook, so I took over as soon as I could reach the stove. I'm great at making omelets."

Grans looked at her. "Did your mother ever talk about your father? You said she mentioned he was from Magic Springs?"

"Yes, him and my real, I mean, birth mom. My mom who raised me, she and Dad got married after I was born. I guess my birth mom didn't want a kid. Then my dad died in a car accident when I was three, and it was only Mom and me." Finn looked down at her plate. "Mom did the best she could, but she was young when she married Dad. She's still young, and her new husband is amazing."

"You're pretty young yourself to be out on your own." Mia didn't love how pained Finn looked as she talked about her past. Usually she was so positive, she shined, especially compared to Christina's more grumpy morning attitude.

"I graduated from high school. That's all she needed to do for me—get me through that. She needs a life now. Besides, I'm almost nineteen. I'm older than she was when she had a baby and a husband." Finn looked around the room, daring anyone to challenge her decision to leave home. "And I have a job, and I'm looking at school. No baby in tow for me."

"I don't know what I would have done at eighteen with a kid." Christina, who was sitting next to Finn, squeezed her shoulders. "I probably would have freaked out."

"Or lost it in your closet with your shoes." Levi didn't look at Christina but winced when she punched him in the shoulder. "Ouch, you need to stop taking boxing cardio."

"Or I need to take more classes so you stop saying stupid things." Christina sipped her wine. "I was trying to be sympathetic with Finn's mom."

"Poor little rich girl is getting feelings?" Levi said, then ducked. "Okay, I took that one a little too far."

Christina shook her head. "Levi is under the impression that if you live in a nice house and have wealthy parents, you are well taken care of. Ask Mia about what shape I was in when I came to live with her. My brother drove me up and dropped me off with a hundred dollars in my pocket. I'm glad Mia had a room for me."

"And thank goodness she did." Abigail smiled at the two women. "Having the two of you into my life has been an absolute joy. And you too, Finn. I didn't raise daughters, but somehow the Goddess granted me three."

Finn smiled, then Abigail's words sank in. "Who's the Goddess?"

Instead of answering, Mia tried to change the subject. "Well, before Abigail gets all weepy and starts hugging all of us, I want to make sure we're all on point for the next two days. Tomorrow we'll be doing a family dinner before the event, which will have desserts we'll need to prepare. Sarah Baldwin is bringing her chocolate cake and the baby."

As the conversation switched to all things dessert and baby, Mia met her grandmother's gaze. Hopefully, Finn would assume that Abigail had misspoken. They needed to find out who Finn's birth parents were so they could rule out any magical heritage. But if Finn was going to be around, maybe explaining the idea of being kitchen witches wouldn't be such a stretch for her. And maybe also share that the house was a little haunted still. At least she knew that her mother had adopted her. That was one less surprise that Mia wouldn't have to let her know.

Even as she thought it, she kicked herself. Normal people didn't accept witches and ghosts into their realities. She had a history with Christina, and she'd known Mia was a witch for years. Her mom had thought it was just Mia being weird, which made Christina love it even more.

Then there was the matter of Christina's adoption. When was the best time to tell a friend that her parents had lied to her for years?

Thursday morning, Mia woke to birds singing and sunshine flowing in her bedroom window. Trent had already left the room, and Mr. Darcy sat on the windowsill, watching outside. When she leaned up and tried to see what he was watching, Buddy's face filled the window.

Mr. Darcy was becoming friends with the baby dragon too.

"Good morning, Buddy." Mia went over and picked up the cat, stroking his gray fur. "Hey, Mr. Darcy. Today I become official. No more training wheels. So you're going to have to step up your game too. I'll let you know as soon as Grans gives me my first official assignment. We can figure it out together."

Mr. Darcy wiggled out of her arms and ran out of the room.

"So that's a no?" Mia called after him, laughing as she went to get ready for the day.

The smell of coffee and cinnamon rolls filled the kitchen when Mia entered the room. Abigail was alone for now. She smiled at Mia as she sat down at the table. "It's a big day for you. I thought you might sleep in."

"Buddy and Mr. Darcy were conversing at my window." Mia sipped the coffee Abigail gave her. "Have you seen Trent?"

"He and Levi went for a run this morning. We have specific instructions not to leave the house and . . ."

Mia held up a hand. "Don't take candy from strangers."

"Well, his exact words were, 'Don't let strangers in the house.' But you get the message." Abigail handed her a plate with a huge cinnamon roll. "I took coffee, orange juice, and two rolls down to Finn already. She's an early bird like us."

"She's a strong person for being so young." Mia considered the conversation they'd had about her family last night. "I hope Grans can find some living relatives for her in town."

"Doesn't she have a cousin?" Abigail sat and started eating a roll.

"I thought that was an excuse to get out of the house without us feeling sorry for her?" Mia glanced at Abigail. "Have you seen this cousin?"

"A man came to get her a few nights ago in a nicer car. I figured it was her cousin." Abigail sighed and put down her fork. "I messed up by mentioning the Goddess last night, didn't I?"

"It's fine. I'm sure she just thinks you're an emotional drunk." Mia smiled and waited for the reaction.

"I had two glasses of wine last night." Abigail snorted. "But her thinking that may be what's best. Anyway, I need to get baking. What do you want for dinner? It's your special day."

"I feel like I'm five, but I'd love your shrimp pasta. Do I get the red plate?" At home, Mia's mom had a red plate that declared the person eating off it was special. Funny, she hadn't thought about that plate for years.

"Oh, good idea. I'll ask Thomas to bring ours when he comes over for dinner. Do you want him and Steve at your ceremony?" Abigail asked, her tone casual.

Mia knew the question was less than casual. The Majors family was going to be her family if she and Trent got married. Or when they got married. She might not like Steve so far, but maybe he had a softer side that he showed when he wasn't trying to keep his brother out of jail. "Sure. That would be great."

"If you added a bit more enthusiasm, I might believe you. Think of it as practicing for all the family dinners we'll have together. And don't worry, all my kids fight at one time or another. Not liking Steve isn't uncommon at the table."

"I didn't say"—Mia stopped herself before she lied to Abigail. Not saying something was different from completely fibbing to save her feelings. "I still need one more for my circle."

"We can use Thomas or Steve if it comes to that. Don't worry, you'll have your seven. The Goddess will provide." She glanced at her watch. "I need to get

Christina up and going. We're going to have a busy day ahead. Finish your roll. Did you write your speech yet?"

"What? No one told me I'd have to give a speech. What am I supposed to say?" Mia asked to Abigail's back as she left to wake Christina.

"Nothing earth-shattering, believe me. You need to thank the Goddess for your gifts and pledge to always work toward the light. Think of it as an answer for a beauty queen contest. Working for world peace is always the right answer," Grans answered Mia's question as she walked in the kitchen and poured a cup of coffee. "I want you to come into the library with me today. Something's been off with the connection, and I need to see if I can fix it. I need you to watch my back."

"The ghosts giving you a bad time?" Mia asked.

"Maybe. They're messing with my notes." Grans waved her away as Mia's phone rang. "Go answer that, but you can't leave the house again until tomorrow morning. No excuses."

"You're kidding, right?" Mia stared at her grandmother as she answered the phone. "Good morning, Mark. What's going on?"

"Why do you sound stressed? Oh, never mind, it's that thing we're coming to tonight, right? Your launch? Or is it more of a debutante thing? Do you get to wear a poufy dress?" Mark teased.

"You're in a good mood." Mia stepped out of the kitchen so her grandmother could blend her shake. Somehow she was ignoring Abigail's cinnamon rolls.

"I have a lead." Mark was almost jubilant. "Do you want to go to the outdoor sports store with me in Sun

Valley today? We found a receipt for a bunch of swim-wear and hiking clothes in his room. None of it was there, of course. And a backpack was on the receipt, and it's not in his room or rental car. Trent didn't find one in the woods, did he?"

"Not that I know of, but I can ask. Can we go tomorrow?" Mia wasn't going to break Grans's trust. Not today.

"The guy who sold Howard the stuff is leaving for a rafting trip tomorrow. It's fine, I can go by myself. I just thought you might have more insight."

Mia translated Mark's words. "You wanted me to see if this guy was a witch so I could ask more pointed questions."

"Now, that sounds stupid, but yes." Mark chuckled. "Look at that, we're communicating."

"Sorry, I'm stuck at home today. Grans has forbidden me to leave the house. Something about the ceremony tonight. I'm vulnerable. And no, I don't think even the Magic Springs police chief could protect me if something went awry. Besides, I hate it when Grans says 'I told you so'."

"No worries. I'll call on my way back if I have cell service. Do you know a Harper Johns?"

"The name doesn't ring a bell, but I'll look him up and see if he's part of the coven. Did Sarah know him?"

"No. So, maybe he's just a normal guy who sold a half leprechaun a bunch of vacation gear." He chuckled. "I'm sure it happens all the time."

"Be safe, Mark." Mia ended the call, then grabbed her laptop and looked up Harper Johns. There was one link that showed he'd been featured as a local white-water specialist. It was his passion, according to the article. She texted Mark.

Be sure to ask who Howard was going rafting with. Had he hired a guide? Most newbies don't go down the River of No Return without a guide. Thomas had a no-show client that Friday, so we're thinking it's him, but that's a guess. And where did he rent his raft? Maybe this will lead us to the friend he was supposed to meet.

The answer came quickly. *Leaving now. All good questions. You have a knack for this if you ever want to leave the culinary field.*

She smiled and texted back. *That's the nicest thing you've ever said to me.*

Grans came into the living room. "Ready to go?"

"Sure, let me leave a note on the whiteboard for Abigail. Just in case." Mia made a note about going to the library and the time. She might as well stay busy since she couldn't leave the academy. She sent good thoughts to Mark and went to join her grandmother in the library.

Two hours later, Grans said she thought she was close to having the link fixed.

Mia sighed and walked around the table one more time, looking for even a strand of ectoplasm or fog. She'd missed the last one, and the link to the archives had snapped when the ghost attacked, pulling Grans out of the spirit world and back into her body.

Mia could see the effort this in-and-out-of-the-archives work was causing her grandmother. She'd have to nap soon so she could run the ceremony later. At least, Mia thought her grandmother would be running it. She'd never asked. One more thing that would be a total surprise to her if she was wrong. But at least, after tonight, she would have her life back. No more hiding in the school worried about what some deranged witch would do for more power. The one thing Mia didn't want to be when she grew up was someone's battery. Either metaphorically or in real life.

That's why she'd felt so comfortable in her relationship with Isaac. She'd thought their ability to have full lives outside of the relationship was a sign of maturity. Instead, it gave her ex-fiancé the time and space to cheat. She and Trent's lives were as intertwined as hers and Isaac's had been, but they were on the same page with the relationship. Sometimes a little too closely entwined, though, especially like tonight, when his dad and brother would be at her ceremony.

A flash of white brought her out of her thoughts, and she stepped in front of the materializing ghost, blocking her from affecting the archive connection. Mia swung the sage wand. She'd already burned through one wand. "Oh, no, you don't."

A moan, and the ghost disappeared. Another formed to her side. This was like the Whack-a-Mole game. She swung again, but the ghost dodged and went straight to the connection feed. Mia dove across the table and shoved the sage wand into the middle of the male ghost. He groaned and faded away.

Mia stood from the table. She rubbed her elbow, which she'd hit on the way down. She might have a bruise before long. The wand was burning down, and she didn't have the time to run to her potions lab to get another one. They'd thought Grans would be done before one burned out. The second one had been for backup. Life Lesson Number 498: Always be triple-prepared.

Maybe she should write these lessons down for future kitchen witches as they were going through their learning stages. She could even publish the book on Amazon. Humans would think it was satire, but the witching world might not find it as funny as she'd hoped.

"Get me the candy bar from my tote." Grans was out of the trance and watching her. She looked like she could sleep for a week. As she ate the chocolate, she told Mia what had happened. "A ghost must have gone through my connection during the last time or so I was connected. With him lost in the archive, I had to find him, trap him, and bring him back through. Did you see him?"

"I'm not sure. I've been fighting off a lot more ghosts than we'd planned for. I was almost out of sage." Mia wanted to make sure her grandmother knew she hadn't been just sitting around, waiting for her to come out of the archives. "Why were they trying to pass through?"

Grans finished her candy bar. "I don't think they wanted to go anywhere. I think they wanted to keep me from seeing something over there. Now I have to find out what that was."

"I have to ask. This isn't normal, right?" Mia ground the fire out of the sage wand and put it with the other in the cauldron they'd brought from the potions lab.

Grans gathered her things. "No, this isn't normal at all. Which is why it has me worried. I need to take a nap. Wake me up in two hours for lunch. Then we can dissect what happened this morning and why. Maybe you can see what I'm missing."

There seemed to be a lot happening that shouldn't be. Mia's spinning plates in her head clicked up to the next speed. Whatever was happening, Mia was going to crash when they figured this out.

Unless there was another crisis.

And it seemed like there was always another crisis.

CHAPTER 14

Dressed in a long white dress, her hair up on her head with a few curls drifting downward, Mia stared at herself in the mirror. She didn't feel beautiful every day. She didn't take the time to slather on make-up or curl her hair, just to put on sweats and work in the kitchen. Or, if it was her day off, jeans and a T-shirt to lounge around on the couch and watch reruns.

Jessica, Isaac's new wife, looked like she was walking the runway every time she'd seen her.

Tonight, though, Mia thought she might be able to give Jessica a run for her money. Dinner had been nice, but a little stilted, with Steve glowering in the corner and Finn quietly watching everyone. Mia assumed the girl was in fight-or-flight mode, waiting for something bad to happen. Mia wondered how much of her story Finn had decided not to share with her new employer and now, landlord. Even when Mia had been single, she hadn't been alone. She'd had a roommate or two, but she'd always known that if she needed anything, her parents or Grans would come to the rescue. Finn didn't appear to have any kind of safety net. She sent a prayer of guidance for Finn up to the Goddess. And protection.

Mia had just finished smoothing her dress when a knock alerted her it was time to go downstairs. They'd set up in the gym, using the decorations for tomorrow to their advantage. She thought it looked lovely. And if there was anywhere her life was going to change, she wanted her journey to start here. Here in the school that she'd saved from being demolished and rebuilt into a strip mall for a frozen yogurt shop, a coffee-house, and an axe-throwing bar. And probably a nail salon.

Instead, she'd used the commercial zoning for her cooking school, and her delivery and takeout business, but primarily, the academy was her home. For her and a few strays. A knock sounded again, but this time Trent called out, "Mia? Are you ready?"

She shook the thoughts and memories out of her head. No time to be waxing poetic about the building. She opened the door, and Trent's jaw dropped. "I'm ready."

"You sure are. I mean, you look amazing. You should wear that dress more often. At home. When we're alone." Trent held out his arm.

"You're a nut." She kissed his cheek, then wiped off the lipstick. "You clean up nice yourself."

"This old thing?" Trent smiled. "Thanks for notic-ing. Everyone's set up, so let's go make you official."

"And once we do, I can leave the house without worrying about being kidnapped for my powers?" Mia followed him to the apartment door.

"Most likely." Trent hugged her, and they headed downstairs.

They'd almost made it to the gym door when she realized what he'd said. "Wait, 'most likely'?"

"Just wanted to see if you were listening." He put his hand on the door handle. "If you're not ready, we can put it off."

She shook her head. "No, that would mean I'd have to go through the last week all over again. I want the threat gone."

He smiled as they walked down the stairs. "I told Mom and Dad that's what you'd say. Steve's trying to push the ceremony off. Something about you bothers him."

"Maybe it's because I see who he is now, not what a charming child he used to be?" Mia asked. She laughed at the look on Trent's face. "Don't even start. You all look at him like he's the golden child, and really, he's a bit of a jerk. Or at least he has been since he showed up here."

They were at the first-floor landing now. Trent leaned over and whispered in her ear, "I forgot you were so insightful on behavior. I'll tell him to cool it, as my almost-fiancée doesn't like the persona."

Mia wasn't sure it was a persona with Steve. She thought maybe his true colors were showing up. When people left home, they tried on a lot of different faces to find the one that matched their heart. Steve's heart was a little cold. Icy, in fact.

Three hard knocks on the front door made her jump. She looked at Trent. "Are we expecting someone else?"

"Everyone's accounted for. Stay here and I'll check it out." He grabbed a baseball bat that he kept in the umbrella stand and slowly opened the door. His shoulders dropped, then he bent down to pick up a package. "Another gift from your adoring public."

"Shut up," Mia walked over and took the brown paper–wrapped box from him. She peeked outside, but there was no one there. Then she took the package over to a chair with a table and lamp nearby. She turned it over in her hands, then pushed out some magic to check the interior of the box for any potions or spells. Nothing. "There's no address or writing at all. And it feels clean."

"I can't feel anything. And usually, I can." Trent sat across from her and looked at his watch. "They're waiting for us."

"I know, but I feel like I should open it. Maybe it's from the Goddess?" Mia met Trent's gaze. "She sent you Cerby."

"Maybe." Trent lifted his head and listened. "No comments from the peanut gallery, or, as you like to call her, Gloria."

Mia nodded. "She's been quiet since the incident in the library. So, should I open it?" Mia waited for his nod, then carefully took off the outer brown wrapping. Inside, the box was wrapped again with silver and blue paper and a big bow. A card was slipped inside the ribbon. She held it up and read it. " 'Congratulations on your big night. I always knew you were special.' "

"No name? Is it from your mom?" Trent took the paper and folded it.

Mia shook her head. "My parents sent me money. Five thousand. I'm putting it into my travel fund for someday."

She took a breath and unwrapped the paper. A carved wooden box sat on her lap. She warded the box, then opened it as well. A large opal, surrounded by what looked like diamonds set on a chain, was surrounded by blue velvet.

"Am I stupid in wanting to put this on?" She met Trent's gaze.

"We have a bunch of people on the other side of the door, waiting for us. If it goes bad, you have backup."

She smiled. "You're not going to be the guy who tries to talk me out of jumping off the cliff, are you?"

"I'll be the one jumping with you," he responded. "Touch it. If there's an issue, your grandmother's protection stone should cover you."

Mia reached out and felt a buzz, but it was positive and happy. No bad juju here. She lifted the necklace and put it on. It was made for the dress.

"Just another gift?" Mia handed Trent the wooden box. "Put that and the wrappings in the office, just in case."

"Okay, then we've got to go. They're going to come out and drag us inside if we don't." Trent came back from the office and pulled her up from the chair. "It looks beautiful on you."

As they opened the door, Mia was transported into a magical woods scene. Jeani had been busy in the old school gym while Mia had been trying to figure out who killed Howard. Fairy lights twinkled in the trees, and a rock path led them to a large opening that Mia would have sworn was under a real nighttime sky. The only thing that made her realize they were still in the gym was the fact that it was warm. If they were outside, even with the small bonfire in the middle of the scene, she'd be freezing in this dress.

Her grandmother came and took her other arm. "Way to make a—" She paused, looking at the necklace. "Where did you get that?"

"It was left at the front door just now." Mia reached up and touched the opal. "Isn't it beautiful?"

"It looks familiar." Grans shook her head and looked back at Mia. "And you look lovely. I'm so excited to be inviting you into my lineage tonight. When I pass on, my grimoire will find yours and meld into it. You will not only get my spells and knowledge, but you'll get everything that was handed down to me from my mother, and her mother, and so on, all the way to the beginning of time, when we began to work to protect the earth and all those who reside upon this soil."

She led Mia to a stone altar by the fire. A woman in silk stood there watching them approach. She looked familiar, but Mia didn't think they'd ever been introduced. She smiled at her.

"Mia Malone, I am Lilith Goldsman. I'm the most experienced—I don't use the word *old*—kitchen witch on this earth. There are so few of us now. I live in France, but I cover most of Europe. We have several others scattered over the continents. I'm so happy to invite a new voice to our group."

"Lilith, nice to meet you," Mia said. She didn't know

if she should curtsy or shake her hand. "I'm sure I have so much more to learn."

Lilith broke into a wide smile. "Mary Alice, you were right about this girl. She is extraordinary. Yes, there will be a welcome packet arriving tomorrow with your guidebook and a few initial assignments, but there is still a lot to learn. Tonight, though, is all about commitment and celebration."

The ceremony was mostly a promise to do no harm and to help build a positive energy shield around the planet. At least that's what Mia heard. She had to breathe to keep herself from falling over during Lilith's listing off of all the former kitchen witches from the archives list. One name hung in the air. Gloria Ann Lightfoot.

Mia heard the giggle from her kitchen witch doll and met Grans's shocked look. Grans hadn't been the only teacher for Mia's development. Mia's kitchen witch doll had been an actual person, once upon a time.

"You're going to do great things," Gloria said in Mia's head. *"I'm lucky to be on the journey with you."*

Mia decided that finding out more about Gloria would be her first entry into the research part of the archives. But that would have to wait until at least this weekend.

"Mia, are you ready to accept your new role as a kitchen witch?" Lilith smiled at her, and Mia wondered if she'd missed something while she was thinking about Gloria.

She took a deep breath and nodded. "I'm ready to

accept my new role, and I am grateful to accept my new position with your group."

A cheer went up, and Mia turned to greet her new circle. Grans, Abigail, Christina, Levi, Sarah, Thomas, and Trent. Seven people whom she could count on for advice as well as assistance. They were bound.

"Your circle of nine is very strong." Lilith hugged her. "I've got a late flight out of Boise, so I need to go. Come by the chateau sometime, and we can talk about your history. You've got a very interesting lineage. Thomas, are you driving me?"

"Steve is waiting in the car and will take you back to Boise. He's got to return to Denver now that Trent's situation is cleared up." Thomas kissed Lilith on the cheek. "It was nice to see you again."

Lilith said her goodbyes to everyone, and Mia found a chair. A glass of champagne appeared in front of her.

"That was beautiful. Do you feel any different?" Trent asked as he sat next to her.

Mia took the glass and downed it. "Different? I guess a little. I feel you all around me. It's kind of weird. Did this happen to you?"

"My initiation came with the coven. No circle of nine for me." He switched glasses with her. "It was overwhelming, but I don't think the attachment was quite as strong. Are you joining the coven tomorrow?"

"Still undecided. I don't want to inadvertently blow your cover by joining." Mia sipped from the new glass. Her dizziness was going away. "Wait, what did you say about the circle?"

"That the attachment was probably stronger." Trent

stood and grabbed a chocolate chip cookie off a tray. "You probably need some sugar after that."

"No, the number. I have seven in my circle, including Sarah and your dad." Mia looked around at the group mingling around her. They were giving her and Trent a minute. "You said nine."

"Lilith said nine. She must have felt two more witches attached to you. Any idea who they are?" Now Trent looked concerned.

"One was Gloria." Mia reached out to the connection and heard the giggle. "Gloria's not a familiar. She is an actual kitchen witch. She was listed on the rolls that Lilith read off."

Trent rolled his eyes. "I wasn't listening. It was a long ceremony. So, who's the other one?"

Mia closed her eyes and searched for another connection. She couldn't find it. There was a glimmer, then she felt a hand on her shoulder.

"Thank you for inviting us." Sarah smiled down at her. "I know you're exhausted. I've got to get this baby to bed. Too much energy floating around here. She's in heaven. I think one of your ghosts has been playing with her for the last hour. She keeps looking over and giggling."

Mia hugged Sarah. "Thank you for saying yes."

"My pleasure."

"This was interesting." Mark stood by his wife's side, holding the baby's car seat. "Weird, but interesting. I take it you're free to come talk to someone tomorrow about Howard? I think I found a lead on the rafting trip."

"If it's early. We're hosting the coven Halloween party, and there's still a lot to do," Mia explained.

"I'll pick you up at eight," Mark said, then he took his wife's arm and they made their way out of the gym.

"So now Mark's taking you on investigations?" Trent asked as they moved toward the treat table, where everyone had gathered.

"He's not supposed to be investigating, so I'm his cover." Mia took a sparkling water from the table, then looked around at her friends. Her family, really. She was still missing someone, but she'd figure it out.

"Here's to the best circle a kitchen witch could ever have!" Mia held up her glass. "Thank you all for being here tonight."

"To Mia!" the group responded, and as she sipped her water, she realized how happy she was at that moment.

Tomorrow would bring its own set of problems. But right now, right here, everything was good.

CHAPTER 15

Finn was at the table the next morning. Trent had found her downstairs, starting to microwave a bowl of instant oatmeal when he took Cerby and Muffy out. He smiled at Mia when she came out of the bedroom. "I saved her from a bad day. Breakfast is important for growing bones."

Finn shot him a dirty look. "I hope I'm not still growing."

"You may be an adult in the eyes of the law, but you're not twenty yet, so you're still a kid." Trent threw her a muffin. "Eat. You look like a scarecrow."

Mia laughed and poured coffee. "Face it, Finn. You're part of the family now. You get all the benefits, like being teased and worried about."

"And an endless supply of books to read. Your library is huge." Finn held up a paranormal mystery book. "I came up to leave the books I'd finished by the door to your apartment when I heard another door open. I thought someone was there, so I walked over and found the library. I can't believe you didn't mention it. And it's so well stocked. I found a whole series of a fantasy series I haven't read."

"You went into the library." Mia glanced around the table. Grans and Abigail were looking at each other, shock clearly registering.

"I'm sorry, should I have stayed out? Libraries were always my thing growing up. My mom would take off for work, and I'd go to the library and hang out all day." She set her fork down. "I broke a rule, didn't I? I can see it in your faces."

"No, it's just that we didn't think about telling you about the library since we didn't know how big a reader you were," Mia said, trying to make up some excuse.

"I don't think Christina's ever been inside," Abigail said, trying to support Mia's reasoning. "Young people don't seem to be readers anymore."

The security alarm went off, and Mia saw Mark Baldwin's truck entering the parking lot. "Sorry, I've got to go. I'll be back soon and help out with the party prep."

"No worries, I've got the guys here." Abigail smiled at her sons. "And someone needs to go wake up Christina."

Mia grabbed her jacket and purse. She kissed Trent, who was walking her to the door. "The library opened for Finn."

He looked back toward the apartment. "Maybe we found your extra circle member?"

"I'm sure Grans will be finishing her lineage soon.

That's unexpected." Mia pulled on her jacket when she reached the door.

"Not so unexpected. People find their way to Magic Springs for all kinds of reasons. Finn was drawn here. Who leaves one small Idaho town for an even smaller one in the mountains? Especially a young girl. She should have headed to the bright lights of California." He opened the door as Mark was coming up the path. "I'll see you later. Hi, Mark. She's all yours."

"Don't say such horrible things. I'll have her back in a couple of hours. We've got an appointment in Twin Falls at an outdoor adventure booking office. Hopefully, this guy didn't make the appointment online." Mark waved at Trent, then opened the truck door for Mia.

They were on the highway before Mark said anything else. "So your thing last night was nice. Not what I expected?"

"No chanting or calling to dark spirits to come inhabit my body?" Mia laughed. "You watch too much television."

"You have to realize I didn't grow up with this stuff. Sarah, she takes magic for granted, like it's another gift, like being smart or doing math without a calculator. You seem to question what's happening more." He shrugged. "Not that I don't love my wife, but sometimes, she can scare me."

"Which is how it should be." Mia relaxed into her seat. "We all need a little magic we keep to ourselves. I think more people have the potential for magic than we know."

"You've picked up another stray, I see." He glanced over at Mia. "Are you lonely now that Miss Adams has grown up and made a life for herself?"

"You think I like dealing with the teenage years?" Mia glanced out the window and saw a deer watching them drive past. She was far enough off the road not to be in danger. "Finn was Abigail's hire, but then she was living in her van. I have too many empty rooms to have an employee on the street. Besides, she's interesting."

"Sarah used the same word after she met the girl." Mark slowed down as they went past the deer. Mia hadn't thought he'd even seen her, but he had. "I hope she's not as interesting as Miss Adams was here in Magic Springs."

"Christina never did anything wrong. Even that arrest in Nevada was her friend's fault," Mia started, then realized Mark was grinning. "Stop doing that."

"I like seeing you riled up." Mark nodded to the notebook. "That's what I found out after interviewing the salesman yesterday. Howard bought clothes and supplies for a two-day rafting trip. And he asked about food. He said the guide was providing the meals, but he wanted to buy enough snacks for three people. He said his friend had paid for the trip. He wanted to contribute in some way."

Mia scanned the notes. His writing was horrible. "He didn't mention the friend's name."

"The clerk said he must have heard it wrong."

Mia looked up from the notes. "What did he hear?"

"Mortimer. He called him Mortimer and then Monty when the clerk asked again. Do you know a Mortimer?"

She shook her head. "Sorry, but we can announce his name at the party tonight and see if anyone comes to the front. Are you and Sarah going?"

He shook his head. "Nope. Sarah gave up her magic, remember? We don't need to have the coven thinking she is like Trent. Or messing with the baby. I don't want anyone telling us what Elisa Marie can and can't be when she grows up. If I have my way, she's going to be a princess or a college professor. Sarah's hoping for a novelist in the family."

Mia thought it must be nice to dream about your child's future. "She's lucky to have you two as parents."

"We're the lucky ones." Mark sniffed, then turned his head and wiped at his eyes. "Anyway, when we get there, I need you to do your magic stuff and see what you can learn."

"My 'magic stuff'." Mia chuckled. "I don't think it works that way. I'll keep my senses open to see what feels off. I can usually tell if someone is lying. Unless I'm close to them. Then my familiarity blinds me."

"I'm sure there's a story there," he commented as they drove on the suspension bridge over the canyon. "But I'm not asking."

"Good, because I'm not telling." Mia liked hanging out with Mark. She trusted him. They weren't quite friends yet, but she could see a path where they could get there. She pointed to an older strip mall on the right, painted blue. "Is that the business?"

He nodded and turned into the parking lot past the first light. Home Depot was on the other side of the street, and the parking lot there was busy, even this early on a Friday. This place looked deserted, but it had a neon-red *Open* sign in the window.

The sign painted on the window announced, *Out of This World Adventures*. River tours, hiking adventures, and woods to explore. Mia glanced at Mark as they got out of the car. "They seem to have it all covered."

"We're only interested in one customer, so don't get distracted. The owner is suspected of dealing in a few other out-of-this-world products." Mark got his badge out and opened the door. The overwhelming smell of incense failed to cover up the illegal weed that someone had smoked recently in the space. "Hello? Is anyone here?"

Mia watched as a man walked out of the back through a wall of hanging red beads. The beads must have also had bells at the end that softly tinkled as he moved through.

"Good morning, we weren't expecting customers this early." He took a deep breath, and his eyes widened.

Mia assumed he'd seen the badge. But instead of greeting Mark, the man came over and took Mia's hand. "Carter Johnson. I'm so honored to have you in my shop. What can I help you with? We have some amazing tours overseas that hit all the sacred stops, as well as introductions to the local covens."

"Okay, so you obviously know Miss Malone." Mark's voice was a little too cheerful for Mia's taste. "I'm Mark Baldwin, Magic Springs police chief. We're interested in a river tour you sold for last weekend. No one showed up for the tour."

"I think you mean the river tour for two for two days? They specifically asked for Thomas Majors to be the guide. It's hard to book a tour with Thomas. He's very popular, but they offered a bonus, and he took it. The tour was paid in advance. If they didn't show, they'd lose their entire payment." Carter walked back to the counter and pulled out a large red book.

Mia stepped closer. It was a calendar. The guy must not use anything electronic.

He pointed to that Friday. "Thomas called an hour after their meeting time to let me know the client hadn't shown up, so I told Thomas he was clear. Our no-show policies are very explicit. They even sign the contract explaining the penalty."

"Where were they meeting Thomas?" Mia asked, and Mark threw her a look. She'd forgotten about his direction to stay quiet.

"Thomas has all of his tours start at his house. He has a launching dock on his property. Then he uses a van he parks earlier at the other end to transport them back to his house. During the trip, the clients' cars are safe on his property. His wife cooks all the food for the trip. She's very talented." Carter leaned closer to the book. "You're probably looking for the client's information. It's not very informative. Edmund Pevensie. He came into the store and paid in cash last month. My assistant handled the transaction."

"No phone number, email, or address? Maybe a driver's license?" Mark asked, writing down the name.

"You don't need a driver's license to schedule a river tour." Carter shrugged. "The phone number he left had been disconnected. I was a little worried about the payment method, so I checked the records and saw he'd paid cash. So I figured he got a better offer for the weekend. It happens a lot nowadays. People throw away money like it was easy to make. Maybe for them, it is."

Mark asked a few more questions, then they left. He got in the truck and scribbled a note in his book. "At least we have a name. Would have been nice if it was Monty and had an address."

"You don't have a name. He left a fictional name." Mia was looking for something on her phone.

"How do you know that? It's odd, but people have odd names. It might just mean he's not local." Mark finished his notes, then started the engine. "Are you hungry? I could use a burger."

"Sure, but this is how I know it's fictional. Unless his mom was a big CHRONICLES OF NARNIA fan— Edmund Pevensie was the boy who chose the wrong side."

Mark turned off the car. "You're kidding me."

Mia showed him her phone. "The phone number was fake. The name was fake. And he paid in cash. I think we might be on to something. And yes, I'd love a burger."

"So you're telling me we're looking for a fictional character from a children's novel who killed a half leprechaun. It's never easy with you people." Mark started the car and headed into town. "Do you have a favorite fast-food place here?"

Mark dropped her off back at the school, but before he drove off, he asked her to check for both names—

Mortimer and Edmund Pevensie. She assured him that she would ask both Grans and Abigail, but she was certain the name left at the tour place had been intentionally fake. She wondered if it was a clue. Was there something in the CHRONICLES that would lead them to the killer? A hiding-in-plain-sight joke?

The academy was a madhouse. People were bringing in props, chairs, and tables. She ran into Jeani Langston in the foyer.

"Hey, there you are. I was worried that you were stuck at the Lodge working and would miss all the fun. How was your ceremony last night? Did you love the woodland scene I made?"

"It was so magical. Thank you!" Mia hugged the designer. "I don't know how you got the sky to twinkle like that. And what happened with the smoke from the fire?"

"Trade secret, sorry." Jeani laughed, then grabbed a deliveryman who was carrying a table toward the kitchen. "Wrong way. I'd love to chat, but I need to pay attention to these guys or we'll have things set up wrong all over."

"Okay, maybe we can sit down over coffee on Saturday when you come take this all down," Mia dodged another worker heading toward the stairs. They were fast.

"Coffee on Saturday sounds great. I'll need it after the party." Jeani threw air kisses and ran after the wayward delivery guy.

Mia decided to check in with Abigail and see where she was needed. The kitchen was busy, but calmer than the rest of the first floor. Abigail, Christina, and Finn were all at tables working, and the smell from the ovens promised something sweet. She made a beeline for Abigail, who was cutting out mini pumpkin cookies to go on top of cheesecake squares. "Hey, those look cute."

"I think so. The coven always goes so fancy with their desserts. I wanted to add a little fun to the occasion. How did it go with Mark?" Abigail lifted a cookie and moved it to the baking sheet.

"More questions than answers. Do you know a witch who uses the name either Mortimer or Edmund Pevensie? Maybe as a pen name or a joke?" She watched as Christina poured chocolate-cake batter into pans. Tonight's treats were going to be tasty.

"Not a witch, but there was an incubus that used to hang around here that loved using names of fictional villains. He was chased out about ten years ago. He liked to show up at the Harvest Queen Pageant and pretend to be from a talent agency. One year, it was modeling. One year, it was acting. Then musical. You get my drift. Anyway, the coven board figured him out and sent him packing. You don't think he attended this year's pageant, do you?"

"No, but it's a good lead. Blake, she asked if I'd heard of an incubus around the area too. It can't be a coincidence, can it?"

Abigail stopped cutting out cookies and looked back at Finn. "Attention, has anyone been approached by a man who offered you something you desperately wanted? Christina? Finn?"

"Besides Levi finally popping the question?" Christina shook her head. "No, but I've been out of the area for a few weeks."

"I don't know anyone except my cousin. And the only thing he's given me is gas money and dinner now and then." Finn grinned at Abigail. "Are you saying there's a genie running around town giving out three wishes? I'd love one of those expensive houses on the road to the ski lodge. And maybe a new car. I'm not sure what I'd ask for the third."

"You're going to need to ask for money to pay for the upkeep of the house, including taxes. And gas for the car. Don't get a sports car, though. Get something like mine. An SUV. Maybe a four-door Jeep?" Christina added to the fantasy. "Red, I'd get red."

"Fine, so no one's been approached. I get it." Abigail turned back to Mia, laughing. "I'll put some feelers out with the coven. I take it Blake's in hiding?"

"Hiding? No. Well, maybe." Mia wanted to kick herself. She'd outed her boss without meaning to. She dropped her voice. "She doesn't want anyone to know she's a witch. I shouldn't have said anything."

"You'd be surprised at how many of our Magic Springs residents are magical, come here to hide in plain sight. Don't worry, I recognized her the minute I saw her in the Lodge's dining room. I'm surprised you didn't."

Mia left the kitchen and went in search of Grans. Abigail's words haunted her. Who else in Magic Springs had power or wasn't quite human that Mia hadn't even noticed? Someone had said that people were drawn to the area before they even knew their own secret.

She felt like Dorothy on the start of her journey through Oz. She wasn't sure what she'd find next, and she was getting dizzy from all the turns. But right now, her focus was on solving Howard's murder. Just because Mark didn't think Trent or Cerby or Buddy had killed the man didn't mean the coven believed the same thing.

CHAPTER 16

Mia found Grans sitting in the library reviewing her notebook. Grans looked up when Mia came in the door. Peaches, an orange ghost cat who lived in the library, ran through Mia's legs, greeting her. "Just checking in with you. Any luck with Finn's heritage? I can't believe the library welcomed her."

"She definitely has some magical history for that to happen. I have her genealogy chart, but I don't think any of her close ancestors took on the mantle. They seem to be the magicless siblings of the family, as you know."

"Doesn't mean they're magicless. Why hasn't the coven figured this out yet?" Mia sat down across from her grandmother, and Peaches jumped on her lap and curled up, purring. Mia could feel the soft fur under her fingers as she petted her. "Mr. Darcy's going to be jealous."

"Probably. You know cats." Grans reached over and

grabbed another notebook. "Christina also comes from the non-magical side of a magical family. Her mom and dad got pregnant as high school seniors and put her up for adoption. She went with the Adams family as soon as she was born. Mr. Adams must have had a line on every adoptable healthy newborn in the area. Mother Adams gets what she wants. When she was done, she had a boy and a girl with no stretch marks."

"Wait, you're saying that Isaac is adopted as well?" Mia sat back in her chair, still rubbing the ghost cat's fur.

"Yep. They are three years apart, but Mother Adams has her perfect family. I think she must have been warned about Christina's heritage. That's why when she went goth, her mom had a fit." Grans smiled at Mia. "I'm so glad you didn't rebel during high school."

"I did. Mom wanted me to go pre-law. She kept pushing all the college prep classes, and all I wanted to do was cook. So we compromised. I got my degree and then did the culinary program. She's still mad that I didn't see the errors in my ways and go to U of I for law school after graduation." Mia smiled at the memory. "That might have been why Mrs. Adams wasn't surprised when Isaac told her I was a witch. I thought she took it too well. What about Christina's birth parents? Did you find them?"

"Both moved out of the area after high school and didn't look back, as far as I can see. When are you going to tell her?" Grans set her books down.

"Tomorrow. After the party tonight. I'll take her to lunch. Maybe she won't cause a scene." Mia hoped.

"Or she's going to be relieved that she's not related

to those awful people. I think Abigail should tell Finn. She has more of a relationship with her. And more to lose if Finn quits, because we're all crazy." Grans glanced at her watch. "I'm taking a nap before the event. I take it you haven't decided about joining the coven yet?"

"No. I'm going to ask for more time. I have so much still to learn. I don't want to commit more of my life than I already have from last night's ceremony." Mia looked down at the cat, who was now sleeping. "Anyway, I need to ask you about something."

She walked her grandmother through what she and Mark had found out and what Abigail had said about the names. She even told her about Blake's question about an incubus in the area.

When she was done, her grandmother didn't respond.

"So you don't know anything?" Mia prodded.

Grans turned off the archives and leaned forward. "Chatting about an incubus is like throwing up a neon sign alerting him to your presence. You need to be careful. If Blake is hiding from him and he's here, he'll know it. Incubi keep a trinket from each victim to track them. Especially if they're fairly close. I'd run now if I was Blake and even thought he might be here. As for the names, many magic folks like to use fictional names. They probably were muses for the authors when they were first writing the story. So it could be their true name. If Howard's killer is hiding his presence, you might not want to find him."

"So just let him get away with it?" Mia shook her head. "That's not right."

"You and Mark both have this morality thing deep

down in your core about right and wrong. Even as children, when I'd watch you, you two were always too easy. If you said you were going to the library, you went. Maybe this is one time Mark should let the coven's declaration of a natural death stand."

"You're saying we shouldn't go after him?" The cat woke and jumped off Mia's lap, feeling her anxiety.

Grans stared at her. "I'm saying it's dangerous."

The music was classic sixties and seventies with a fun, newer tune every once in a while. Mia loved the DJ. She'd have to make sure Abigail got his name for future parties. The food was a hit, too, as was the coven-sponsored open bar. Mia was starting to believe the party was a complete success when Sabrina Clayborn came up to her.

"Mia, darling, please tell me that Brandon misunderstood your message. You have to join our little family. Waiting another year won't change your final decision. I promise I won't give you any committee assignments for two years if you join tonight." Sabrina sipped her wine as she watched the party going on behind Mia.

"Sorry, I don't feel ready to commit. I want this to be mutually beneficial, and I don't have a lot to give right now." Mia nodded toward Abigail, who stepped into the gym. "I hate to cut this short, but duty calls."

She knew Sabrina hadn't seen Abigail come in, so she couldn't know Mia was lying, but the smile on her face told a different story. "We'll talk soon."

Mia met up with Abigail. "Everything okay?"

"I should be asking you that." Abigail nodded toward Sabrina, who was making her way toward Brandon Marshall. The two of them seemed close, and as Sabrina talked, Brandon's gaze searched the crowd until he found Mia.

"Great, she ratted me out." Mia smiled and waved. "Goddess, please help me get through this party."

Gloria's laugh echoed from above in the apartment. Mia rolled her eyes.

"Anyway, how's Finn doing? I see Christina and Levi making the rounds." Mia took a glass of champagne from one of the passing trays.

"As they should be. Levi marrying outside the coven is going to be gossip fodder for years. I'm sure the marriage department was already looking for a suitable match for him, even after I told them he wasn't ready." Abigail rolled her eyes. "They think they know what's best for people. Trent had a match as soon as he did his initiation."

"He did?" Now Mia turned toward Abigail. "Who was it?"

"Oh, I thought you knew." Abigail glanced at her watch. "I need to check the kitchen."

"Abigail, tell me." Mia blocked her from leaving to avoid the question.

"It's not my place to say, but since you already know they dated. It never developed into anything. It was Jeani Langston. She was his match."

Mia let Abigail flee as she thought about Trent and Jeani. She'd felt something between them, but no chemistry. More like two old friends. He hadn't pre-asked if he could propose to Jeani. He'd asked her. Time to tamp down any green jealousy.

Levi and Christina hurried over, and Christina grabbed Mia's arm, kissing her on both cheeks. "Thank you so much for moving here so I could meet my soul mate."

Christina was a little tipsy. Mia held her arms so she wouldn't fall over in her glass slippers. Yes, Christina had come as Cinderella and made Levi dress up as Prince Charming. Mia was in one of Christina's cast-off little black dresses. But she still felt like a princess, especially with her new necklace. It was a statement piece, and several people had commented on how lovely it looked on her. However, she saw some confusion on others' faces as they studied it. She'd been told many times it looked familiar and asked if it was a family heirloom. Maybe Mom had sent the gift. She'd call her tomorrow.

"You would have found Levi no matter what." Mia smiled at her friend. "I'm glad your mom is on board for the wedding."

"Oh, she's not. She even said that she'd brought me into this family and pulled me out of Magic Springs for a reason. And that marrying someone from here was beneath me." Christina rolled her eyes. "You'd think the woman was Mother Teresa for adopting rather than birthing her own children. Instead, she kept a slim waist and didn't have to deal with morning sickness."

"Wait, you know about the adoption?" Mia gasped.

"You didn't?" Christina shrugged. "That makes sense. Isaac wasn't as open about his origins. He didn't want to believe it, so I got into Mom's safe and showed him the court papers when he was in high school. He still wouldn't admit it, but he knew I knew."

"You are a complete mystery to me at times." Mia hugged her, then rolled her eyes when Levi brought back three glasses of champagne. "You should cut her off. She can't keep up with these people. They will magic away their hangovers. Christina's going to feel hers."

"Mom said she'd make her something. And since no one is driving anywhere, we're going to have fun celebrating our engagement and the move to Portland. I got a call today. I got hired on at a fire station, as long as I pass my physical. Trent and I are going running in the morning."

"Better you than me," Christina said as she sipped her drink. "Mia, I'm going to miss you so much."

"We can call and Facetime. Don't think you're going to get rid of me. Besides, Levi will drag you home for all the family holidays, and as long as I don't dump Trent, I'll be there too." Mia felt someone's arms around her. "Who is that?"

"You know who it is, or you wouldn't have been saying horrible things about dumping me." Trent kissed her neck. "Christina, you look beautiful."

"You're such a doll." Christina leaned on Levi's arm. "Let's go dance."

Mia and Trent took their glasses and set them on a nearby table. They watched as Christina and Levi slowly began to dance, their eyes only on each other.

"They look happy." Trent put his arm around Mia. "My brother finally met his match. I didn't think it would happen. I know Mom didn't. Did you know Steve's still single?"

"I'm shocked," Mia teased.

"Don't dog him. With Levi being the baby, Mom's been harping on Steve and me to get our lives started."

"Your lives are started. Your mom wants grand-children." Mia looked around the room. "Almost midnight. Soon the party will move outside for the coven meeting. Christina and Finn need to be kept inside."

"Mom already has a plan for Finn, and Christina will be poured into bed soon. There was a method to Levi's madness of letting her drink what she wanted." Trent nodded toward the backyard. "Are you going out or staying inside with me?"

"I'm staying inside. I'm not ready to join yet, and I told Brandon and Sabrina that tonight. Neither one is taking it well. Please don't let them drag me outside against my will, okay?"

"You've watched too many horror flicks. In real life, they would knock you out with Versed, then ask you to follow them out." Trent grinned. "That way, they can control you without having to carry you anywhere."

"That's horrible. Now I'm not taking any more drinks from strangers." She leaned against him. "Do you think anyone would notice if we snuck out now? I'm sure the pups need to be let outside. And how's Buddy hiding in all this?"

"He's in a tree, watching," Trent said. "Cerby and I have been checking on him off and on all night. They had quite the conversation the last time we went out. I think some of our guests are using their cars for a little hanky-panky."

"Now I really want to escape. What, do they think it's prom night?"

"For some of these people, it is. Come on, we'll let Mom know we're leaving, then head upstairs and watch a movie. That way you don't have to worry about being dragged out to the bonfire and inducted against your will." He smiled as he took her arm to lead her out of the gym.

"Sure, maybe a horror movie, since it's Halloween." Mia glanced around the party. It looked like everything was fine. She waved to Jeani, who was standing by the wall, watching them leave. Small towns were hard. Everyone knew everything about your past. Unless, like Mia, you were new in town. Was that what was bothering her? Or was it Trent's teasing about the coven? Something was making alarm bells go off in her head.

She hoped it wasn't something important that she was missing. She wanted tonight to be over so they could get back to normal life. Well, that and find a killer. She shivered as they left the gym.

"Are you cold?" Trent took off his suit jacket and draped it around her shoulders. "I was burning up in there. Maybe you're coming down with something."

"I got a chill." She nodded to the kitchen. "I'll wait here. You go tell your mom we're bailing. I don't want to see the judgment in her eyes."

"If we fooled around tonight and you got pregnant, that would make her happy." Trent kissed her, then headed to the kitchen.

"You're a dork," Mia called after him.

"Takes one to know one," he called back.

She reached down and slipped off her black pumps.

Her feet were killing her. Christina could stay in heels for days with no problem, but she was younger. Soon, Mia was going to be wearing flats all the time. They needed to do the wedding thing before she didn't want to wear the magic shoes anymore.

"Trent's a real catch." A voice came from the gym door.

Mia turned and saw Jeani watching her. "We're in a good place," Mia responded. She didn't want to catch Trent. Or have him catch her. She wanted a relationship built on love, mutual trust, and respect. But she wouldn't correct Jeani. Not tonight.

"I know. I hate it, but I know. Have a good evening." Jeani disappeared back into the gym.

Trent was coming out of the kitchen and saw the door closing. "Did you have company?"

Mia wasn't sure what to tell him, so she went with the truth. That couldn't hurt her later. "Jeani popped in. She was watching when we left. I think she still has feelings for you."

"We weren't a match, no matter what the number crunchers said. I felt more the first time I saw you than I ever felt for Jeani." He took Mia's hand. "Ready to go watch *Friday the 13th*?"

"Maybe *The Haunting of Hill House*? Shirley Jackson still scares the crap out of me, and I live in a real haunted house."

On the way to the stairs, they ran into Finn, who was taking sodas and cookies back into her room. "Hey, you two look amazing. I'm glad I stayed in the kitchen for this event. I didn't have to dress up at all."

"You look fine, but before Christina gets all packed

up, I'll see if she has some dress clothes she wants to get rid of." Mia saw the fear on the young woman's face. "Nothing crazy, like what she's wearing tonight. You need some mingle clothes for events. Like a little black dress and maybe a pantsuit."

"I'm a cook." Finn shook her head. "You guys are the figureheads of the company. I'm sure I don't need anything fancy."

Trent slapped his hand to his heart. "I never thought I'd see the day when someone turned down one of Christina's cast-offs. The girl has so many clothes she doesn't wear I think she could outfit every girl who wanted to attend prom this season in the local high schools. You must not have gotten the dress-up gene in your DNA. No playing with dolls growing up?"

Finn giggled. "I did have a Barbie with her dream house. It was a gift from one of my mother's friends. Sometimes I cut up old clothes and made her new dresses."

"A budding fashion designer." Mia watched as Finn relaxed in front of them. The girl liked Trent. Mia thought she might intimidate Finn a little. She wanted to fix that. "Do you want to come up to the apartment with us? We're watching a movie."

"I've got a game going with friends from home. But thanks. And if you think I need a dress, I'll take one. I just don't want to be a bother. You and Abigail have already done so much for me." She paused and looked around at the lobby area. "Funny, I heard that this used to be a school. If you didn't know about the gym or the classrooms upstairs, you'd never know it. Oh, and the library, of course."

As Mia and Trent walked upstairs, her thoughts stayed on Finn. She was a good fit for the company, and if they didn't become best friends immediately, she had to realize that she'd known Christina for years before their friendship grew into what it was today. She'd learned a lot today. She wondered if tomorrow would be as illuminating as she tried to put together a theory on Howard's death.

CHAPTER 17

Saturday was one of those warm, clear days in the fall when you think that maybe winter had been canceled for the year. Mia opened the window in the kitchen and waved at Trent, who was out playing with Cerby and Buddy. The two friends were enjoying their time together after they'd had to be separated last night.

Grans and Mia were alone at the kitchen table. Grans had packed her bags and would head back to her house today. Mia would be alone in the apartment, since Christina and Levi were staying with Abigail until the engagement party in a couple of weeks. Well, except for the week when they'd stay in Boise with the Adams family. Maybe she should move Finn upstairs into the apartment with her.

Even the thought of inviting one more person into her space made her hesitate. Grans got up and poured another cup of coffee. "Change isn't always a bad thing, Mia."

"Who was talking about change?" Mia grabbed a water pitcher that she'd put oranges and mint into yesterday to infuse. She poured a large glass and sat at the table. "So, who would want to kill Alfred Howard?"

"I could list off a few people." Grans held up her hand. "Not counting Trent or his familiar or Cerby's pet dragon. I'm beginning to wonder if Blake's incubus theory isn't in play here. There were several people at the party last night telling tales about strange goings-on. And Trent's investigation with Cerby wasn't even top on the list. There have been a few Buddy sightings, however, so I think Trent needs to move him back to his house. He's right on the National Forest. It's a great place for Buddy to grow rather than the backyard at the academy. You're too close to town for him to be here."

"I know. Buddy kind of forced my hand regarding moving in with Trent. I'm going to miss being here at the academy. I can't invite just anyone to rent the apartment. The library hasn't been dealt with yet. And I have my potions lab here. It would also have to be someone attached to the business, since people arrive at all times to do takeout." She paused. "Well, maybe that wouldn't be such an issue. We could make sure the front door is locked all the time or maybe set up a second entrance for the renter."

Mia realized she was thinking it out as she talked. "Anyway, I'll talk to Trent soon."

"And Abigail. Maybe she has someone in mind for

the apartment." Grans waved her hand to dismiss the subject. "We need to talk about Gloria. Since she is an actual elder, maybe her hanging in your kitchen is disrespectful to her?"

Gloria started to swing on her rope.

"I'd move her to my potions lab, but I don't want her to be by herself so much." Mia put a hand on the doll to stop the swinging. "Where I go, she goes. Her being an elder does add weight to the question of who gave her to me when I was a kid, though. You're sure it wasn't you?"

"No, but sometimes the Goddess uses people without their knowledge. I wonder if it was Adele? She was in the house all the time. She would have had access. There's no way to ask her now, though, since she's gone forward." Grans studied the doll.

"Grans, why didn't Gloria go forward?" Mia brushed the doll's raffia hair back as she talked.

"I don't know. I've sent a query to Lilith about the doll and Gloria's attachment, as well as asking about the doll's prior owner. No response yet." Grans stood and put her coffee cup in the sink. "She's probably still traveling. It was a blessing for her to come all this way for your ceremony."

"Should I send her a thank-you?" Mia had stopped getting flowers, or at least she thought she had. She'd reach out to the florist later today to make sure.

"That would be nice and she's already attached through the kitchen witch circle. I'll send you her address. Don't do it through email. That's too impersonal.

Buy a lovely card." She kissed Mia on the cheek. "Thank you for taking on your destiny. Call me when your guidebook and assignments arrive. We'll walk through the first one together. Now, I need to get home and finish packing up the house. I'm hoping to get it on the market before the end of the year."

"I'll get Trent to take your bags down." Mia stood and followed her.

Grans pulled on her jacket. "He's already packed them into my car, dear. Besides, I think there's someone downstairs who wants to talk to you."

Mia groaned. She'd forgotten about her coffee "date" with Jeani. But she needed to make sure everything was going well with the party tear-down process anyway. Abigail was home with Thomas and had taken the weekend off since they didn't have anything going on. Christina's Magic Springs engagement party was on Wednesday night. Then Friday they'd all head to Boise for the second party. Finally, Grans's engagement party was scheduled for Sunday. Then Thanksgiving would be here.

Mia knew her Lodge calendar was a complete madhouse starting next week. It was a good day to relax and actually take some time for herself, and maybe get some time to talk with Trent before the holidays blew up both their schedules.

She walked downstairs and said goodbye to her grandmother. The party supply van was parked near the entrance, and she saw Trent walking Muffy to Grans's car. She waved at him and then went to find Jeani.

The decorator was in the gym, clipboard in hand. She smiled as she saw Mia approaching. "You're in time to do a walk-through with me. I think I've got everything packed up and stored, but sometimes the guys get over productive and take a few things not on their list. So the gym's clear and clean." She used her pen and made a checkmark on the page. Mia saw she'd made one for the academy with *Mia's Morsels* listed on the top. "I already have the number of tables and chairs you own on my checklist, so we can go verify that your storage is still full right now."

Mia followed her to the small storage area. "Thanks for everything you've done this week. It was magical here both nights."

"I thought it worked out great." Jeani finished counting the tables and chairs. "My numbers match what we started with, so that's a good sign. We had to do some cleanup from the back, where the coven had their meeting, but I'll charge them for the damage."

Mia followed her outside to the backyard. It looked like it had on Thursday before the decorating for the party. "You did a great job."

"Thanks. It's all part of the service."

Mia groaned. They were both being so polite and not even mentioning the elephant in the room. Mia reached for Jeani's arm as she turned to go back inside. "Hey, can we sit a moment?"

Jeani froze, then nodded. "Of course. Look, I wanted to apologize for last night. I'd had one too many of the coven's witches' brew cocktails. Those things are powerful. Let me be clear. I am not in love with Trent. I might have seen a future for us once, but he never did. He was always waiting for you."

"I appreciate you saying that, but Jeani, I want to make sure we have a friendship. I work too closely with you and your sister for this to be a problem between us. And besides, I like talking to you." Mia waited, hoping Jeani would agree.

Instead, she pressed her lips together. "Mia, I like you, but right now, being around you makes me crazy. I can deal with a work relationship, but I'm not sure I can be friends. At least not yet. I'm so embarrassed by my actions last night. I need time to fix what's wrong up here. Or maybe stop drinking. I've been told I get sloppy and emotional, and not in a fun, Cameron Diaz way, like in *The Holiday*. I'm more of a Carrie, keying-your-car type."

Mia laughed and nodded. "I hope you can see your way to a friendship because I get you. Are you decorating for Christina's party on Wednesday?"

"Of course. I'll see you at the Lodge." She stood and held a hand out to pull Mia up off the bench. "Now, let's finish this up so I can get busy on the plans for that."

After Jeani and the delivery guys had left, Mia was locking up the gym when she ran into Finn. "What's on your schedule today?"

"My cousin is picking me up, and we're going driving. He wants to show me the area." Finn had on jeans and a sweatshirt. She carried a heavier coat. Her phone beeped, and she glanced at it. "He's here. I'll probably be back late, so don't freak out if you hear me coming in."

Mia had just finished locking up the gym doors when she realized she was missing an opportunity to actually meet the elusive cousin. She hurried out to the front door, in time to see a black Hummer pulling out of the drive.

Trent and Cerby were walking across the parking lot, so she waited for them. Trent kissed her.

"Good morning. Who did Finn drive off with?" He didn't move toward the front door, and Cerby sat near his feet.

"Her cousin. I missed the chance to meet him." She stepped back inside, but Trent didn't move. "Are you leaving?"

"Yeah, Cerby says Buddy needs to stretch his wings, so we're heading back to my place. Can I take you to dinner tonight?"

"'Cerby says'?" Mia looked down at the Maltese, who looked smug. "Dinner tonight would be great. We probably need to talk anyway."

"That doesn't sound good." He leaned over and kissed her. "I'll pick you up at seven. I'll have Christina and Levi come over and babysit the kids."

She was almost upstairs when she heard the security alarm alerting her that someone was in the parking lot. She went back down the stairs and opened the door. Mark was there, a pile of notebooks and a rolled-up flipchart in his arms.

"Are you alone?" He glanced around the foyer and saw Mr. Darcy sitting on the stairs. She must not have closed the apartment door all the way.

"I'm never all alone, not here, but yes. Everyone's gone." Mia stepped back as Mark pushed past her and into the foyer. "Come on in."

He looked like he hadn't slept. "Sorry. I need to talk this out with you. The mayor wants this case closed next week. I don't even know how Howard died." He hurried over to one of the tables. "I thought we could talk through a timeline."

"Don't you want to do this with one of your guys?" Mia closed the door and followed Mark into the reception area.

"And have it get back to the mayor? I like my job, Mia." He glanced around the room. "Do you have one of those portable whiteboards? Don't you do staff meetings in here?"

"Yes, sometimes. But Abigail's been dealing with that." His question made her think that maybe she should do a staff meeting with the group to set up a vision for the future. "I'll get a whiteboard."

When she came back into the room with the whiteboard, he set it up, then taped a chart he'd made. He turned and pointed to it. "This is a timeline of Howard's trip here. This dot is Wednesday, when he flew into Boise. I left some room at the front in case we have more data points to add or people he might have met who live in the area. Like Mortimer or Edmund, who, I'm thinking, are the same person."

"Trent got an email from the coven saying someone was coming to chat with him. I'll text him and see what date it had on it." Mia grabbed her phone as Mark continued.

"Anyway, here's the flight information I got from the airline. His flight originated in Boston." Mark stepped back to the table and threw a paper-clipped bundle of papers at her. "I've got his itinerary from the airline. And his rental car agreement. And his hotel information."

Mia read the pages he put in front of her as Mark added points to the chart. She finished the packet, then looked back up at the chart. "You're missing something."

He squinted at the points, then turned back. "No, here's when he left Boston. He hit Boise here, and then the Lodge here. You said he came to the academy on Thursday, right?"

Mia turned around the flight itinerary. "At first, I thought this was a layover. A change of planes, but on Tuesday, he went from Boston to Denver, then to LAX, where he stayed the night. He got back on a plane to Boise at ten on Wednesday. Who was he meeting in California?"

"I didn't see that layover. Of course, it's possible that there weren't flights from Denver to Boise, but that's a huge detour." Mark added a line to the timeline. "Good catch, Mia."

They went through the rest, but nothing else popped out to them. Mark sat down and put his head on the table. "This might be the one where I cave because I can't find anything to prove them wrong. Maybe the little man in the green suit just had a heart attack as the coven's autopsy said."

"From my reading about that type of person"—Mia avoided using the word *leprechaun*—"it's unlikely for him to die that young."

"He was in his late fifties. Sometimes that happens." Mark held up his coffee cup. "Thanks for the mojo juice."

"Hold on, don't give up yet. I need to show you something." Mia hurried upstairs and picked up the book she'd been reading about magical creatures. When she got downstairs, she opened it to the part talking about hybrids. "Read that."

He did, and as Mia watched, he blinked a few times, then reread what he'd completed. Finally he turned the book to the title page and wrote down the title, author's name, publisher, and the year published. "I take it this was published by a house owned by your group?"

"Again, still not 'my group', and I'm not sure. It was in my library upstairs. The books came with the property." She took the book and read the part she'd shown Mark again. There had to be a clue here. She wasn't seeing it.

While she read, he watched her.

"What?" She glared at him, finally unable to take the quiet.

"Nothing. It's just that Sarah thought you'd join the coven last night, especially after your test results came back. I guess all her friends are talking about your score. That you'll probably be part of the National

Board or whatever before too long." Mark blushed a little. Passing on gossip was not in his nature, but what Mia had said surprised him.

She carefully put her bookmark back, then closed the book. "I'm probably making a mistake, but I like my life now. I want my career, my legacy, to be this place. Mia's Morsels. Not some job where I can't tell half the people I love what I'm doing. Besides, I'm going to be busy with my new kitchen witch role. I'm getting a guidebook and assignments soon. I'm thinking it will be like going back to college."

"You're a nerd." He glanced around at the pile of papers. "You don't think he died of natural causes."

"No." Mia had always heard that "no" was a complete sentence. This time, it even felt right.

"I don't either. So if he didn't have a heart attack, and the death wasn't caused by magic, then what else looks like a heart attack? Can you ask your grandmother? I'll hit up my poison control contacts and see what they say. Maybe that will help." Mark's energy increased as he started listing off tasks.

"We need to follow up on what he did and who he saw in California too." Mia had a notebook and was writing down questions. "Oh, and who he had lunch with at the Lodge on his last day. Maybe that's our Edmund."

"I'm tracking down fictional characters to see who killed a mythical being. Sure, I can deal with that." Mark gathered up the loose reports and put them back in his briefcase.

Mia tapped on the leather. "I don't remember seeing this before."

"I use it to bring home reports and copies of evidence that I can't focus on during my normal workday. Sarah calls it my 'magic briefcase.' She's been helping me understand the coven hierarchy and regulations. Like how she and Trent aren't supposed to have magic or familiars." He clicked the case shut. "And with this, I can separate the parts of my job that I understand and lock up the parts I don't. Like who Alfred Howard was versus finding his killer. That way I don't say something stupid like 'leprechaun' or 'witch' during my staff briefings in the morning."

Mia giggled as she gathered up the cups and plates from their work session. "I think you'd be surprised how easy that statement would go over in Magic Springs. I'm sure some of your staff are coven members or at least come from a magical family and understand the language."

"I don't want to know," Mark said as he walked toward the door. "Oh, someone dropped off a puppy at the house. It looks like it has Saint Bernard blood. Sarah thinks it's for the baby. A protector?"

"I would say yes, but Sarah would know best." Mia thought about the kittens she'd had dropped off on her doorstep. They hadn't been familiars, but she hadn't realized that until the owner came to collect them. Now she knew she had one familiar, Mr. Darcy. Gloria had been an elder all along. Sent to watch over the newest kitchen witch. Even before her mother had refused the assignment.

She held the door for him and watched Mark leave. "Or the puppy could be just a puppy. You never know until you know."

"That's less than helpful," Mark replied as he got into his truck. "It's like saying you're a weatherman because you walked out and found out it was raining."

It might not be raining, but both Grans and Trent thought a storm was coming. Maybe Elisa Marie's new protector was another sign from the Goddess of the upcoming conflict.

CHAPTER 18

Mia headed up to her potions lab after calling her grandmother and not getting any answer. According to Trent, the autopsy had traces of a drug that would make someone compliant. She didn't know if the potion cookbooks she had would have a recipe for such a potion. Kitchen witches were around to help people, not to help people hurt others.

She thought there might be a need for such a drug if it was carefully protected. That kind of potion wouldn't be in a beginner's potion cookbook. But she'd found random books in her lab before. Books that had to have come from the library. At first, she'd asked Grans and Abigail if they'd stocked the lab library for her, but they'd laughed.

"You'll find what you need when you need it," Grans had said, letting the cryptic message stand.

Mia realized she'd done that a lot recently. Or the library would throw the book at her.

She wasn't surprised when she found an old textbook on her shelves. *Advanced Potion Making*. The ancient book's cover was about to come off, and there were notes all over on the pages. It was hard to read the faded ink, but soon, she found the page she'd been looking for. The Emerald Potion. She took a picture of it and sent it to Mark.

Then she texted. *Did the lab find any of these ingredients in Howard's blood sample?*

She didn't get an answer back right away, so she tucked her phone into her jeans pocket and started reading about the "class" of spells and potions that were restricted for use. According to the textbook, students caught making any of these potions outside the official class lab times would face immediate suspension. Now she grabbed the laptop she kept in the lab.

She pulled up the coven's website, and then, using her visitor login, she looked up a list of restricted spells and potions.

There were a lot. She ran her finger down the list and finally found the potion from the book. It had a star next to it. When she found the notation, it said that special permission to acquire the ingredients and make the potion had to go through the coven's board. Brandon Maxwell would know if anyone had made the potion here. And, according to the potions book, the effect only lasted twelve hours from its creation.

If this was what had killed Howard, it had to have been made sometime Friday morning.

But the coven had already said this death wasn't magical. So it wasn't the potion. Or maybe it was the ingredients and not an official potion? Or, maybe, the coven had lied. She went to her herb supplies and checked off all the ingredients. She had them all, except as she picked up the last bottle, it felt lighter than the others. She opened it up and found it empty. There were bits of the herb at the bottom, so she could tell it had been full at some point. She looked at the label: *Foxglove*. She'd run into this poison before; it was called "digitalis" in the modern world. Had the killer gotten into her supply at the potions lab?

She looked at the clock. She'd wasted the day on a lead that might or might not be the cause of death. She closed up her laptop and the potions lab, making sure she locked the door as she left.

When she went upstairs to get ready for her date, she fed Mr. Darcy. He'd been sitting at the apartment door waiting when she came inside. Being alone for the first time in months, she hadn't even thought about the need to feed her cat. Before Dorian left, Mr. Darcy had been mostly self-sufficient, as the witch spirit inside him would levitate and open his food when he was hungry. After that, either Abigail, Christina, or Trent had been in the apartment when it was time to feed him. Now Mr. Darcy had to rely on her.

And he let her know she was falling behind on her duties.

"Sorry, I'll set an alarm on my phone for five," she told him as she dished up the wet food. At least it would give her a good excuse for leaving work on time.

A book of herbs sat on her counter. *Thanks, library.* Once she was ready for her date, she opened the book and started reading. By the time Trent showed up to take her to dinner, she'd sent Mark several options of possible mixtures that might have caused Howard's death. She wasn't even close to finding out who had killed him, but if she could help Mark figure out how it happened, that might lead them to the killer.

As they drove to the Lodge for dinner, she stared out the window. Winter would arrive soon. In her experience, one day it would be a beautiful fall day, then the next, it would turn ugly and stay that way until spring started.

"Should we have ordered pizza instead?" Trent asked as they arrived at the Lodge. "You seem a little lost in your thoughts."

"Sorry, big events like last night's party suck the life out of me. I thought it was the work of them, but now I believe it's being around the mass of people." She straightened her leather jacket as she slid out of the truck, then held out her phone. "Do you mind if I text your mom real quick? I'm probably overthinking something, but I can't get it out of my mind."

"Go ahead, I'll wait."

Mia asked Abigail about the foxglove. Abigail responded back that the bottle had been full on the day she'd helped her and Grans stock the potions lab.

Mia sighed and texted Grans to ask her opinion. She didn't expect an answer. Her grandmother was probably out with Robert, but she wanted it off her mind. "Okay, I'm ready. I'm glad it's just the two of us tonight."

"And everyone else in the dining room. Seriously, we can cancel and go back home." Trent took her arm and pulled her close, tucking a swirl of hair back behind her ears. "I want to have some time with you."

"Let's have a quiet dinner here, then go home and see if we can find a movie. And we need to talk about our living arrangements. The apartment was way too quiet for me today." She leaned on him, and they strolled to the main entrance.

"Are you saying you're considering moving in with me?" Trent's smile was way too large.

"Don't be thinking you won. I'm thinking about Cerby and Buddy. If he hadn't brought home a dragon friend from camp, my place would still be a contender. As it is, though, I'm not sure what to do with it. The school doesn't like being empty. And I can't rent out the apartment to anyone." She paused as she thought about Mr. Darcy. "Besides, I need help remembering to feed my cat."

"I'm sure there's someone around with a connection to the coven who needs a reasonably priced place to live." Trent waved toward a couple in the lobby.

"That's the problem." Mia smiled and waved too. "I can't have a coven spy in the school. There are too many secrets. And the library would have to agree with my choice."

"So you want someone magical, but not in the coven." Trent smiled. "Got it. So this discussion was just a way to make me feel like you're considering moving in?"

"No, that's not—" Mia didn't get to finish her words before Blake descended on them.

"Mia, I'm so glad you're here. I need to talk to you for a minute." She grabbed Mia's jacket sleeve and started to drag her to an alcove. As Blake did, she called out, "We'll be right back, Trent."

When they were alone, Mia turned to her boss. "What's wrong? Did I forget about an event? Why are you sweating?"

Blake's hair around her face was wet, and sweat was dripping off her. She looked like she'd run a marathon. She pulled out some tissues and started dabbing her face. "I'm a little worked up."

"I can see that." Mia pulled out a package of tissues she kept in her purse, just in case. "Here. So, what's wrong?"

"The coven's here." Blake's eyes widened.

"You mean, people from the coven are eating here? I suspect they are still dealing with the hangovers from last night. The party went long. I'm sure they didn't want to cook tonight." Mia was trying to explain, but inwardly, she wished she'd taken Trent up on the pizza night.

"No. Every member of the coven who's in an active leadership role is here. The only ones missing are Abigail, Thomas, and Levi Majors." Blake waved away Mia's look. "Okay, so I have a list, and I keep track of their whereabouts. I have a tracking spell set on the Lodge just in case Morty shows up."

"Your ex." Mia let out the breath. "That's understandable. I don't think they're here for you, Blake. I think this is an intervention for me. Thanks for warning us. I think I'm going home to have pizza. You can release our reservation."

Blake was staring out at where Trent was now talking to Brandon Maxwell in the lobby. "Sorry, you've already been spotted. At least I tried to warn you. I'm heading to my apartment upstairs and locking the doors. Please don't blow up my hotel. And no mention of my secret, okay?"

Before Mia could stop her, Blake had disappeared into the employees-only section of the hotel. There were several staff apartments there, and Blake had grabbed the largest one when she'd taken over for Frank. Alone, Mia took a breath, then headed out to join Trent.

"Good evening. I hope your boss didn't ruin your night with a work assignment?" Brandon leaned in for a quick hug and cheek kisses. He prided himself on his European ancestry.

"No, she was filling me in on some changes for next week's schedule. My best friend is having her engagement party here on Wednesday. We're swamped this month with parties. You know, the holidays." Mia stepped into Trent's arm as she spoke, appreciating the support she felt almost immediately. "I take it you're still recovering from last night?"

"I'm aware of the Majors/Adams party. I got my invitation last week." A frown came over Brandon's too-handsome face, then disappeared. "As far as tonight, we're not hung over. On the contrary, we're still celebrating. There are some people I'd love to introduce you to here. I asked Trent for you two to join me and Sabrina at our table. We've got so much to talk about with your future."

Mia tried to keep her laugh light. "Trent and I are here to do the same thing. Talking about our future as a couple. I'm probably feeling all the warm fuzzies from Christina and Levi's upcoming nuptials, but he's being very persuasive. I'm sorry we can't join you tonight. Maybe another time."

She leaned her head on Trent's shoulder and looked up at him, hoping he'd get the message.

"You have to strike when the iron's hot," Trent added, smiling down at her. "Thanks again for the offer, Brandon. I'm sure we can get together soon."

As they walked away from Brandon and toward the dining room, she snuck a peek back. Brandon was on his phone but still staring at them. "The entire coven, according to Blake, is in the dining room. Any way that we can still get pizza?"

"Sorry, but at least your acting skills are spot-on. Impromptu presentations were never my strong point in drama class." He paused at the hostess stand. "A reservation for two for Majors? A private table, if you have one?"

The woman, a young girl actually, smiled at him. "My boss, James, had me hold back the alcove for you two. It's the most private table we have. Come this way."

As they walked through the dining room toward the back, Mia felt all eyes on them. She leaned close and whispered, "This is because of that darn exam score, isn't it?"

"Or you saying no last night. Or both." Trent helped her into the booth, then slid in next to her.

"Kat will be your waitress," the young hostess said as she disappeared.

"All I can say is, thank the Goddess for James." Mia scanned the menu and peeked over the top. Blake was right. Every person she knew from the coven was here. Trent would probably know the rest. "Anyone looking out of place or guilty?"

"You're still looking for Howard's killer?" He glanced around the room. "Everyone here I've known for years. Most of them were at my initiation."

"I figured, but I was hoping it might be easy." She sipped her water as their waitress came and put a basket of bread on the table.

"One of our tables sent you a bottle of champagne." Kat set it down and wrestled to open the bottle.

"Is this from James's wine cellar?" Mia asked, watching the woman fill their glasses.

She nodded and looked up, surprise widening her eyes. "Oh, Miss Malone, I didn't realize it was you. Yes, he and I ran down and got it. Mr. Holder has a great collection, but I should have asked you if this vintage was fine. I can get something else. Should I tell him you're here?"

"This is lovely, Kat. Tell him I said hi, but if he's busy, not to bother coming out. I'll chat with him on Monday." Mia saw Brandon lifting a glass to them, and Trent responded, then turned back to look at her. "I think we're ready to order. And if anyone else tries to buy us a drink, please turn them down. I've got so much work to do this weekend."

Kat laughed. "Tell me about it. I've got to get my laundry done on Monday. It's the first day I've been off for ten days. And then I come back on schedule Tuesday. But at least I'm getting hours."

After taking their orders, Kat left.

"Good call on the upfront drink refusal." Trent held up his glass. "I'm assuming this is safe?"

"No one can get into James's wine cellar. Even on busy nights like this, he goes down with the waitresses.

It's his rule. When he's not here, he leaves a limited selection upstairs and takes his keys with him. It used to drive Frank crazy." She sipped the champagne, glancing around the room. "They want me to join. If this show of support wasn't so creepy, it would be heartwarming."

"The coven survives by adding new, powerful talents to their roles. I suspect, having you as part of the Magic Springs group would move them up on the national ranking system. They're concerned they aren't relevant in today's anything-goes society." He broke a roll and buttered it. "Tell James I love the way they salt their butter. And the tops of the rolls."

"Tell him yourself." Mia smiled at her friend who had come out of the kitchen. "He's here."

"Can you believe that I was supposed to be out of here at five? Then all these reservations hit, and Blake told me to stay until closing. Told me, not asked. I see she just ordered room service, so I'll give it a couple of hours, then leave the night shift to finish up." He leaned on the empty side of the booth. "Everyone is saying your party last night was off the hook. Thanks for inviting me, by the way."

"It wasn't my party. It was held at the academy. Mia's Morsels was catering, but if you want to work the next one, I'm sure Abigail would love a prep chef." Mia broke open a still-steaming roll. "And Trent loves the bread."

"Everyone does. It's full of salt." James adjusted a fork that wasn't straight. "I don't need a second job, but if you do have a party, you should invite me."

"Come to Christina's engagement party on Wednesday. She'd love to see you. Mia's Morsels is catering, but we're having it here. Mother Adams has a little bit of pull with the corporation."

"Mother Adams has a friend on the board. Maybe she can get Blake to change her rules for contract catering," James corrected her. He refilled their wineglasses. "Someone has expensive taste in wine. We've only sold two of these bottles since I bought the case last year."

"It's nice, thank you." Mia wondered if James was starting to figure out the coven's power. Sometimes their actions were obvious, even to humans. "Blake's been acting weird lately, don't you think?"

"How can you tell with the Queen of Cold?" James asked as he reached for his beeping pager. "Sorry, I'm needed in the kitchen. I hope you didn't order the pasta. The girl I have cooking on that station tonight is a total airhead. Some days she's great, others, well, pasta. If I didn't feel so sorry for her, I would have fired her weeks ago."

After James left, their dinners were delivered, and except for making sure they were okay, Kat left them alone. The dining room had begun to empty. Brandon had clearly passed on the message that Mia wasn't in a talking mood. Mia set her fork down and took a sip of water. "I need to learn more about the coven administration side. I don't understand why they're so set on getting me to join."

"Mom used to be a board member," Trent said as he cut into his steak. "You could ask her for a quick tutorial. She'd be glad to talk about it. I think she misses the work. Or she did, before you asked her to run Mia's

Morsels. She quit when Levi took over the inherited power."

Mia knew what Trent wasn't saying. She'd quit when the power didn't totally transfer to Levi. She didn't want to put her sons in danger by exposing what she knew to the coven board. Mia leaned closer. "Have you ever talked to Steve about what happened to him when he transferred power to you?"

Trent set his fork down, picked up his phone, and texted someone. Then he gathered his fork back up and continued eating. "No, but I'm going to talk to him tomorrow."

"He's back in town?" Mia had thought the oldest brother had left midweek.

Trent nodded. "His business issues got settled, so he came back Thursday night. He's staying with the folks. He doesn't think this thing with Howard is done yet."

Mia thought Steve Majors was right on that front. She didn't want to be thinking this, but if she didn't ask, she'd be wondering anyway.

She took a breath, then asked, "Trent, when did Steve come into town? And who told him about Alfred Howard?"

CHAPTER 19

"You can't think my brother killed Howard? That's ludicrous." Trent's eyes flared, and Mia felt the energy surge from Cerby, trying to figure out if Trent was safe.

"You need to calm down and let Cerby know you're okay." Mia pointed out. The last thing they needed was a dragon and a hellhound bursting into the Lodge, looking for their master.

He stared at her for a long minute, then took a deep breath. His heart rate dropped, and Mia could see that he was telepathically chatting with his dog. Then he squeezed her hand. "Sorry, that came out of nowhere."

Mia wondered if that was true. If Steve shared the same talents as the other two brothers, it would be reasonable to guess that he might also have a trigger set in his brother's mind, just in case Steve's loyalty or actions were questioned. "Do you know when Steve arrived?"

Mia's phone rang.

Frowning, she checked the incoming number. "I don't know the number. It must be spam."

She went to set it down when Trent said, "Answer it. Steve is calling you. And yes, I need to talk to my brother."

Mia didn't want to be a fly on the wall during that discussion. She accepted the call. "Hi, Steve. So, when did you arrive in Magic Springs, and did you know about Howard before you got here?"

"Of course I knew about Howard. That's why I flew in. To save my family. I know that Trent didn't kill the guy, but sometimes innocence isn't enough to keep you out of jail." He paused. "I'm not happy you disclosed my attachment to Trent. It was an easy way to keep track of the family without the long plane ride. You know, the folks are going to ream me for this. And especially for not disclosing our connection. Mom asked a few years ago, and I lied. I'm going to pay for that now."

"You shouldn't lie to your mom." Mia didn't feel sorry for Steve. He'd set himself up for this years ago when he handed Trent his powers. He should have mentioned it then. Abigail had been aware of Trent's non-limitations for years now. Which was probably when she asked Steve and took his word. "Please answer my questions. Your brother and I are trying to enjoy a lovely meal together, but other things keep getting in the way."

"Oh, yeah? Like what? Trent has his wards up, so I can't hear anything."

"None of your business." Mia rolled her eyes, and Trent laughed. "The questions?"

"I got here on Tuesday. I knew Howard was coming because I have a friend in the national office. Apparently, they've been watching Magic Springs for a while. Things are happening here that should happen. Like the witch and werewolf wedding you were a part of last year."

"And Cerby's arrival." Mia felt the chill going through her. Brandon and Sabrina were still here, but most of the coven had left. "So the national office is involved in this?"

"Someone from the local coven is feeding them the information. I don't think the rest of the coven is even aware that there's a divide. The National Board has been split on this subject for years. It's kind of a Hogwarts pureblood debate. Most witches know we're growing and that the strict, one-magic-user-per-generation policy is stupid. Of course, we're considered the rebels out to destroy the old guard."

Trent must have let his wards down because he was hearing all of this at the same time. His eyes were worried, but she could tell he was holding it together mostly to keep Cerby calm. She mouthed the name *Levi*, and he nodded. So, both brothers and probably the entire Majors family was hearing Steve's confession of sorts. "This has to be the conflict that Grans has been seeing in her dreams. Why she wants Trent and me together before it happens."

Mia heard a sigh from Steve. "Probably. There have been signs that the Goddess is involved, trying to stop the war, but anyway, that's a discussion for another day. I want to be clear here. I had lunch with Howard on Thursday, trying to figure out what his game plan was. Which side he was on, so to speak. He seemed to be sympathetic to our side when I talked with him. And then he visited you and Trent that same day. I was shocked he was continuing the investigation."

"Maybe he needed to," Mia said, thinking about that day. "If he'd turned down the assignment, the national office would have sent someone else. Howard might have been the rebels' best chance for a peaceful settlement of the argument."

"Whatever. I'm not sure there is a peaceful outcome, but I didn't kill anyone, including Alfred Howard. Tell Trent he owes me breakfast tomorrow if he wants to meet that early. We'll go to the Sunrise Village in Sun Valley. Less chance of being overheard."

And with that, Steve hung up on her.

She put the phone away and waited for a long minute before picking up her utensils. "Even if he didn't kill Howard, I need to tell Mark about the lunch meeting, and he can clear Steve since he was with your dad that night, right?"

"Just tell Mark. Let the chips fall where they may. I'm done covering for Steve." Trent tossed his fork onto his plate. His older brother had used him as a listening device without telling him. He threw his napkin on the table. "We can leave whenever you're ready. I'm not hungry anymore."

*   *   *

Sunday morning, Mia was still alone in the apartment. Trent had gone home to be with Cerby and Buddy. She had Mr. Darcy and Gloria, but for some reason, the apartment didn't feel like home right now. Mia poured herself a coffee. "I guess I've gotten used to living with a lot of other people around."

Mr. Darcy lifted his head, seeming to agree.

"And I bet it's been hard on you with losing Dorian." She sat next to him on the window seat. "Do you miss your buddy?"

He rubbed his head against her hand.

"Well, I wanted to ask you and Gloria what you thought about moving in with Trent. It will be a little busy since Cerby now has Buddy, but I think it's the right time." She looked around her little kitchen. She'd been on her own since she'd left Isaac. The school had been her refuge when she'd bought it. Way too big for her, but she'd managed not only to fill it with Mia's Morsels, but also to make it a home. A home where her newfound family, plus Grans, could gather and protect each other.

It might be needed for that again, but for now, Mia thought she'd start spending more time at Trent's house and see how it felt. "Of course, you'll need to come with me," she said as she kissed Mr. Darcy on the head.

He jumped down and ran to the apartment's front door, meowing. Someone was outside.

Mia followed, wondering who had come inside the building. She opened the door and found Finn coming up the stairs, books in her arms.

She looked surprised to see Mia. As Mr. Darcy wound

around her feet once she was on the landing, she reached down to rub his head. "I hope I didn't wake you up. I thought maybe the building was empty. I came in late last night."

"You didn't wake me." Mia looked at the books. "Are you already done with those?"

"I don't do much lately but read, sleep, and work." Finn made an *L* with her thumb and forefinger and put it on her forehead. She laughed and said, "Nerd alert on the third floor."

"You're not a nerd, and sometimes life goes that way," Mia answered as she grabbed the key to the library. It was probably already open since the house knew she was coming. But just in case. "Besides, you spend time with your cousin, right? That must be fun."

Finn's eyes widened, and she nodded. "Oh, yes. I should have said that too."

Something was off about her response. Mia tried the library door, and as she'd suspected, it was already open. "Well, you don't need me here. Why don't you come up for lunch and we can talk? I'd like to hear how you're settling in. Remember, if you need a reference for admission to the culinary program, I'm more than willing to write one."

Finn set her books on the first table. Mr. Darcy hissed at a corner, then left the room. Mia saw Peaches return the not-so-friendly greeting.

"I wonder what he saw?" Finn asked, looking in the corner too.

Mia wondered why she'd focused on the exact corner that held the orange ghost cat, but maybe it was a coincidence. Or more likely, Finn's heritage was starting to wake up now that she was in the academy. Mia would have to ask Grans about that. If it was true, they might have to gently ease Finn into her new worldview so she didn't go screaming out into the night if a ghost decided to talk to her.

Mia ignored the question. "I'll see you at lunch, then. Soup and sandwiches okay?"

"Sounds great. My cousin is coming to get me at three. We'll be done by then, right?" She looked up at Mia, hope shining on her face.

"Of course." Mia nodded to the shelves. "Good luck finding your next read. Sometimes the library can be a little shy on bestsellers."

"Not even close. I've found several fantasy series that I've been meaning to read. I need to get as much reading done as possible before January, just in case I get into school." She beamed as she started reshelving the books she'd brought up.

As Mia left, she thought about how comfortable Finn was in the academy. She'd fit in since Abigail hired her.

That couldn't be just luck. The last perfect hire had wound up to be a plant for a bad guy. Mia needed to find out more about Finn's cousin. Maybe she'd go down and meet him at three.

When she got back into the apartment, her phone was ringing. She hurried to answer it. "Hello?"

"I knew you were in the library. I could sense it off your tracker necklace, but why was it so calm in there? I thought maybe something had happened." Grans didn't bother to say hello most of the time. Or goodbye. She just ended the call when she was done talking.

"It's playing nice with Finn." Mia glanced toward

the joint wall that separated her apartment from the library. "She almost saw Peaches."

"The cat?" Grans was silent for a while. "We need to talk to her if she's staying around. She needs to be aware of what might occur."

"I was thinking the same thing. Maybe next weekend?"

"My engagement party is next Sunday—or did you forget?"

Mia groaned. She had forgotten. "And Christina's are Wednesday and Friday. So I guess we'll be worn out and busy cooking on Saturday. I hope Abigail has shared the catering schedule with Finn. We're going to need her. And maybe I should invite her to ride with Trent and me to Boise for Friday's event."

"Have Abigail take her. You and Trent need time to talk logistics if you're moving in together soon."

Mia stared at Gloria. "And where exactly did you hear that bit of gossip?"

"I didn't hear it, I can feel it. Besides, I had a dream last night that you were living in Trent's house and helping to raise Buddy. However, I wouldn't wish that chore on anyone. Make sure you ask the library for dragon-raising books."

"As soon as Finn goes downstairs, that will be the first thing I do." Mia was teasing, but Grans did have a point. Reading about hellhounds had helped her understand Cerby's unique talents. Maybe reading about dragons would do the same.

She heard a book drop in the living room. Walking in from the kitchen, she realized the library had been listening. Or the ghosts of the library. Whatever, it was confusing. She picked up the book: *Dragons in the Modern Era*. "Well, scratch that. The library has provided already."

Grans chuckled. "You need to start trusting in your new world."

"Oh, did you get my text about the foxglove?"

Her grandmother *tsk*ed. "I dumped that bottle. It's against coven law to have it in an open potions lab without specific permission from the coven. Abigail should have known better. Don't worry, I went back through everything you have and made sure there wasn't any other contraband in the supplies. Sometimes that woman doesn't realize rules are there for a reason. That stuff can kill a person."

Mia grabbed some frozen soup and put it in a pot to warm it, then sat down with the book. She'd make sandwiches before lunchtime. Now she had some light reading to do. The book must have weighed five pounds, which told Mia all she needed to know. Dragons were real and hanging around in the world today. Maybe they could find Buddy a group to live with?

Cerby flashed into her head. The dog would be heartbroken if they sent his friend away, even if it was better for the dragon. She guessed the mountains of Idaho wasn't such a bad place to raise creatures. The werewolves had been here for centuries.

Mark called after she finished the long, first chapter. Someone loved the sound of their voice. She closed her eyes to refocus, then answered. "Hey, thanks for the break."

"You're welcome? But I thought you'd be chilling after Friday night. Or are you still cleaning up?"

"Nope, the academy is all back in order. The coven doesn't leave a trace. I don't know if it's habit or paranoia. I'm reading some industry stuff." She set the book on the table. It was true, she hadn't said what industry. "What can I help you with?"

"I wanted to thank you for convincing Steve to come in and give a statement. He appears to have an alibi, but I'll need to verify it. I suspect you know that he was Howard's lunch companion on Thursday." He paused. "Steve says that Howard wasn't going to turn Trent in to the national office for his unregistered magic."

"Yeah, Steve told me that too. This brings up the question of who would have wanted Trent turned in. Is that our motive? To get another investigator here? Killing Howard doesn't stop the investigation. It might delay the inquiry, but it puts someone else in charge."

"All good questions, and ones that I'll need your help with. Is there any way you can get into the local coven building and their records? Sarah says the request for an investigation will be filed in the library. She said Cleo would know where."

"I'll try to get over there on Monday." Mia stood and found her planner on a shelf in the kitchen. Having Sarah and Mark talking was working out well. "I have a few meetings, including one for Christina's engagement party. Are you and Sarah coming?"

"Yes. She's so excited. We have a babysitter, and she says it's dress-up time. I'm afraid I'll be in a suit."

Mia laughed at his discomfort. "Well, you won't be

the only one. Be happy you're not going to the Boise event. It's black tie."

"I'm not wearing another tuxedo until the baby gets married, if the gods are with me." He signed off, leaving Mia alone with the book.

Instead of continuing her reading, she went into the kitchen to make cookies before lunch. The apartment would smell like sugar and soup for the rest of the day—and she'd probably be snacking all afternoon. But baking helped her think.

She played with Mark's timeline in her head. Howard had arrived on Wednesday. He'd had lunch with Steve on Thursday, and then he came over to the apartment that night. Somewhere in there, he'd talked to Blake.

She turned the mixer on to cream the sugar with the butter. Why did he talk to Blake? Did he immediately sense her special talent? Something Mia hadn't seen after months of working with her since Frank had left. She turned off the mixer and went to the living room. She pulled the magical-creatures book off her small bookcase and flipped to the section on leprechauns.

Yep, one of their known talents was seeing magical creatures, even when they were in another form. So Blake's secret hadn't been a secret to Howard. She closed the book.

Who else was hiding in Magic Springs? Steve and Trent, but Steve had to have known that Howard would see through him—especially since he was focusing on Trent's transfer of magic to Levi.

Blake's question about her ex made Mia pause a moment. If Blake had been upfront with Mia about hiding from her ex, maybe she'd told Howard the same thing. She wouldn't want him telling the national office where she was if she was in hiding. But she had to know that if Howard could see her, he should be able to help her make sure her ex wasn't here.

And if he was, maybe that was who had killed Howard?

Maybes, ifs, and more magical reasons. Mia stood and put the book back on the shelf along with the one on dragons. She had company coming for lunch. No time to research magical creatures and their characteristics. Especially when the company was showing signs of being part of Mia's secret world herself.

Mia had a plan for at least the next hour. Bake cookies, make sandwiches, and then lightly grill her newest employee to find out if she'd ever displayed any magical abilities. Should be a walk in the park.

Except nothing worthwhile ever came easy.

She hated motivational sayings. Especially when they meant she was going to have to work for what she needed to know.

CHAPTER 20

When Finn knocked, Mia swung open the apartment door. "Come on in, lunch is ready. And I made oatmeal cookies."

"It smells amazing in here." Finn stepped in and reached out a hand to steady herself.

"Are you alright?" Mia saw the fatigue in the girl's face that hadn't been there even a few hours ago.

"I'm not sure what's happening to me, but all of a sudden—" She lurched to a chair and sat. "Sorry, I thought I was going to faint. Anyway, I'm worn out."

Mia recognized the signs. There was no doubt in her mind about Finn's magical connection now. She was a witch, and she had dragon breath. She must have been around Buddy too much. She needed to call Grans and Abigail. "I'm going to get you a cookie and some milk."

Grans called before she could find her phone. "What's happening? Your aura's going all over the place. You realize I have a lot of things to do here, right? Your tracker can't be going off like this all the time. Are you sick?"

"No, but Finn is. She needs that shot I got for dragon breath." Mia stacked cookies on a plate, then poured a glass of milk.

"So she is coming into her talents," Grans said thoughtfully.

"Not the most important part of this conversation, but yes. How do we get that shot?" She held the phone between her shoulder and ear, stacked the glass and plate, and headed to the living room.

Finn lay passed out on the floor.

"She's out. What do I do?" Mia set down the cookies and put her grandmother's call on speaker. She felt for a pulse and checked for breathing. Finn was still alive, but Mia wondered for how long.

"Take her to my room. I'll call Abigail, and someone will be there in a few minutes," Grans said and ended the call.

"Sure, pick her up and carry her to your room," Mia grumbled, then saw Trent's truck pull into the driveway on the security camera. "Thank the Goddess."

She hurried down and waved him in. "Hurry, we need to move Finn!"

He ran from the truck. "I was reading in the den. Then Cerby started barking at my keys. He dragged over that blanket you made him. I tried to call, but you were on the line. I'm glad I didn't misunderstand his warning. What's wrong with Finn?"

"Dragon breath." Mia held the door open, then followed him upstairs. As she did, the alarm for the parking lot went off again. "Put her in Grans's room. I'm checking to see who's here. It might be her cousin."

A car Mia didn't recognize pulled into the lot, and as she stood at the front door, a woman got out. It was Cleo from the coven headquarters.

"Miss Malone, nice to see you again. Abigail Majors called regarding a situation?" Cleo came to the door, a black bag in her hand.

"You're a doctor?" They went in the house, and Mia shut the door behind them, leaving it unlocked just in case someone else showed up. "She's upstairs. We moved her to a bed. It looks like dragon breath. I had it last week."

"I remember, but you must not remember me being here." Cleo smiled as Mia's face reddened. "I'm not quite a doctor, at least not by AMA rules, but I'm aware of the situation. No worries, I've been friends with Abigail for years, and I'm very discreet. Who knew we'd have a dragon breath problem in our lifetime? The good news is, the coven is very faithful to their vaccination schedule. It's all these outliers who are being affected this week. Your dragon is getting around."

"I guess we didn't think about that." Mia wondered if Christina needed a shot as well. "I have a friend . . ."

"Miss Adams has been vaccinated. I did it myself on Friday before the party. Didn't you notice how oddly she was behaving? Or did you think she was drunk? For some people, like you and this Finn girl, it knocks them out. For others, they want to run and play. Levi had quite a night keeping her from doing anything dangerous on Friday." Cleo paused in the living room.

"Very cute. Let me know when you're ready to rent it out. I might have someone who would be perfect."

Mia was past asking how people knew things in Magic Springs. "She's in the first room on your left."

"I will just be a minute, then she'll sleep until tomorrow morning and this will be all taken care of, unless she reacts badly to the medicine. Which we should know in a few minutes."

Mia followed Cleo into the room, where Trent was sitting in a chair, watching Finn. He stood and greeted Cleo with a kiss on the cheek.

"Give me a few minutes, and she'll be as good as new." Cleo waved them out of the room, and they went to the kitchen.

Trent stirred the soup. "Do you mind? I haven't had lunch yet."

"Please. I made food for me and Finn. Now it will be just me. Unless Cleo's hungry."

Trent looked at her oddly, then let it go. "I'm glad she was here and not out with her cousin somewhere hiking. I feel bad that Buddy's causing this."

"Your dragon isn't causing this. Coven policy is to blame." Cleo came into the kitchen. "Your soup smells divine."

"Do you want to stay for lunch?" Mia asked.

Gloria giggled, and Cleo shot the doll a withering glance. "No, dear, I don't usually eat. But it doesn't mean I can't enjoy the way food tantalizes our senses. Your friend is asleep. No reaction. She's taking the shot like a full-blood. This leads me to believe that she must have a sibling who took the wand, so to speak. Do you know her family?"

"Her stepmom lives in Nampa. I'm not sure about her birth mother. Her dad's dead." Mia updated Cleo on what Finn had told them. "She was led here to Magic Springs. A pull."

"She might be from another coven. Maybe Dad had another family before he died. Whatever it is, she's coming into her magic. And according to coven law, that shouldn't be happening."

"One witch per generation," Mia repeated what she'd learned.

"Exactly. I'm afraid the things the coven knows to be true may not be inclusive enough. I'll keep my promise not to tell anyone, but you all need to find out what's happening. Why are the laws dissolving?" She glanced at her watch. "Mia, I'll be in the office at eight a.m. sharp. Please don't be late. Blake will have a cow if I keep you and you don't arrive at work in time for the meeting."

"Eight a.m., I'll be there." Mia set the table while Trent walked Cleo out. Then she realized she hadn't told Cleo she needed to look up the reports. She'd known. And she'd known Mia's work schedule.

After Cleo had left and Trent had come upstairs after seeing her out and locking the front door, Mia dished up soup in two bowls. "There are sandwiches in the fridge if you want to get them out."

As they were eating, Mia pulled out her planner again. Now she had an actual time to go to the coven headquarters. "Mark, well, Sarah thinks that if we find who requested the investigation, that might tell us who wanted Howard out of here."

He took a bite of the sandwich, then set it down. "Wait, what?"

She told him about her conversation with Mark and then how Cleo knew she was visiting. She mentioned Gloria's giggle about Cleo but didn't mention his silence. "So Cleo's not just a coven member, is she?"

He shrugged, picking his sandwich back up after Mia cleared his confusion. "Not my story to tell. But rumor has it, she was one of the original coven members. We've been here almost two hundred years now. You do the math."

She decided to leave that puzzle alone. She had enough going on with a sick teenager who didn't know she was a witch sleeping in her apartment. "I guess we're going to have to tell Finn about all this."

"I don't know who you mean by 'we'," Trent said as he looked up at the security monitor. "Are you expecting someone?"

"No, but Finn was. That's her cousin. I'll go down and tell him she's not feeling well. Hopefully he won't want to check on her."

"All he'll see is a sleeping girl. Don't worry so much." Trent refilled his soup bowl. "Want me to go down with you?"

She shook her head. "I'll be right back up."

Hurrying down the stairs, she opened the door, then when no one got out of the car, she walked over and opened the passenger-side door. James Holder sat in the front seat, looking at his phone. "Get in. I'm late for a meeting."

"James, what are you doing here? Are you Finn's cousin?" she asked, confusion clouding her mind.

He looked up and saw her. "I think we're busted. Where's Finn? She's going to be late for her shift."

"She's cooking for you at the Lodge," Mia stated, understanding. "But she didn't want us to know because she was afraid we'd fire her."

"That's what she told me. She's a whiz in the kitchen. She only works shifts that don't interfere with Mia's Morsels work. But she's good enough that I'll deal with working around her other job." He tucked his phone in his pocket. "Sorry, she asked me not to tell you."

"One, we wouldn't have fired her, and you should have known that." She squatted down to be face-to-face with James. "And two, she's sick today. What's her next shift?"

"Tomorrow dinner." James took his phone out again. "I need to find someone to cover her, then. I've got a date."

"She'll be back tomorrow, but I'm telling her that I know. She can work at McDonald's from midnight to eight, I don't care, as long as it doesn't interfere with what we have going. I know Abigail can't give her full-time hours yet."

"I knew you were a good kid." He finished a text message. "I'll see you tomorrow. Tell Finn she still has tomorrow's shift. I hope she feels better."

"See you at the staff meeting on Monday. I've got an appointment at eight, so I'll be running in hot. Pour me some coffee, will ya?"

Upstairs, Trent was still eating. Mia finished her soup and told him about James being Finn's fictional cousin.

"Well, he's not related. She was just saying that so we wouldn't know she's cooking at the Lodge."

"Secrets always get you in trouble." Trent finished his lunch and leaned back. "Levi and Christina said they'd stay at the house to babysit if you want some company this afternoon. Maybe we could watch a movie while Sleeping Beauty gets better?"

Mia thought that sounded like a wonderful idea.

The next morning, Mia was up and ready for work early. She had to visit Cleo, then get to the Lodge by nine. She sliced the zucchini bread she'd made as soon as she'd gotten into the kitchen.

Finn came out of the bedroom. "What happened to me? I feel like I've slept for days."

"It's only Monday. Sit down and eat. We need to talk. Coffee?" Mia held up the pot. Finn nodded and slipped into a chair.

"I'm sorry, I don't know what happened. I was reading in one of those comfy chairs in the library. A cat was there and jumped on my lap. I must have fallen asleep, because the next thing I knew, it was lunchtime. I came over here, and you let me in, then nothing. Did I pass out?" Finn's eyes widened. "I missed my shift—I mean, seeing my cousin."

"I talked to James and told him you weren't feeling well. He said you still have your shift tonight if you're better." Mia paused. "You didn't have to hide the fact that you were working at the Lodge. It's your life, and I know you want to save up money."

"I should have told you, but I didn't want to lose this job." Finn sipped her coffee after she'd added milk and four tablespoons of sugar. "Is that what you wanted to tell me?"

Mia shook her head. "No, I think I'm going to say something hard to understand, and I don't want to scare you. So can you have an open mind for a minute?"

Finn took a bite of her bread. "Of course."

"Finn, I think you come from people who, I mean, a family with witch's power." Mia nodded. "I think you're a witch."

Finn finished her bread, then sipped her coffee as she considered what Mia was saying. Finally, she nodded and said, "Cool."

"That's all you have to say?"

Finn shrugged. When she finally spoke, she chose her words carefully. "I've felt different all my life. My mom said my dad was special. I thought she meant I had Asperger's or something like that. The cat in the library—she's not real, is she?"

"Peaches is real, but she's a ghost. We have ghosts in the building too. I'm what they call a kitchen witch. And so is my grandmother." Mia decided that Abigail and her family needed to decide on when to tell Finn themselves.

"She felt strange. I could feel her weight, then it would disappear and I'd think she'd jumped down, but when I'd look, she'd be there, purring." Finn got a second slice of bread. "Did she make me sick yesterday?"

Great, now I have to tell her about dragons too. Mia took a deep breath. "Not quite."

The alarm she'd set on her watch went off as Abigail pulled into the parking lot. "Sorry, I have to run. Abigail's here. I'll have her come upstairs. We can finish this talk tonight when you get back from the Lodge."

"Cool." Finn pulled a bride's magazine over and started flipping through it. Then she paused and looked over at Mia. "Does Abigail know about you and the ghost cat?"

Mia smiled as she answered. "Abigail knows everything."

Downstairs, she filled Abigail in on what they'd talked about. "I left out your status. I thought I'd let you make the decision about telling her that."

"Dear, we're in for a penny, we're in for a pound. But thank you. I'll talk to her about the situation she finds herself in and what happened yesterday. And I'll tell her about Buddy and Cerby. If she's going to stay here, she needs to know to take care of herself." Abigail held the door open for Mia. "Tell Cleo hi for me."

Mia was halfway to the coven headquarters when she realized she hadn't told Abigail where she was heading. Maybe Trent had mentioned it or Cleo. Probably not, but thinking that kept her from worrying about Abigail reading her mind too. Having Trent there before she found out felt weird enough. Having his mother able to hear her thoughts, well, that just felt icky. Oh, the joy of living in the witchy world.

She parked in a two-hour-free space and grabbed her purse. She hurried up the stairs and found herself back inside the large rotunda. She took a deep breath. This place made her happy. Probably something they pumped into the ventilation system, but right now, she didn't care. She walked over to the desk, where Cleo was on the phone.

When she got off, she smiled and nodded toward the clock. "Five minutes early. I knew I liked you. Come this way."

Mia followed Cleo past the doorway that had *Examination Room* etched on the frosted glass. The hallway looked like they were at Harvard or any Ivy League school. Finally, they stopped at a door labeled *Summons and Requests*. Cleo opened the door and they walked into a room filled with wooden file cabinets. A table with a pen and paper sat in the middle. There was no attendant.

Cleo indicated that Mia should sit. She pushed the pen and paper closer to her. "So this is based on a simple request system. Write down what you want to know, and the room will provide any file that has at least some of that information. Be as specific as possible. One witch was hurt by falling files one year for requesting all information on illegal spell work. Way too general."

"Okay, write down what I want, then what? Where do I put the note?" Mia looked around at the file cabinets. "Is there a slot or something?"

"Just write the question and wait. All will be clear soon enough." Cleo turned and walked toward the door. "I'll be back to get you in forty-five minutes, so you won't miss your meeting."

CHAPTER 21

Mia sat and thought for a few minutes, then wrote *Trent Majors and familiar reports to the national office* on the page. As she set down her pen, one piece of paper materialized on the table. She tentatively pulled it toward her and read the paragraph. She wrote down the date and the person who filed the report, *Marsha Fieldstone, coven familiar coordinator*, then tried to summarize the report. It confirmed what she and Trent had assumed. The Goddess had sent Trent, listed as inactive, a familiar named Cerby, whose breed was listed as Maltese, followed by a question mark.

Mia glanced at the back of the page, but there was nothing else there. She took the paper and pen that Cleo had given her. It was now blank. "Okay, then, more specific."

She wrote, *An investigation request into Trent Majors into why a familiar was provided to an inactive witch.* Maybe using their terminology would give her more information. She set the pen down. She'd been right. This time four more pages appeared.

Mia took her pen and wrote a number one on the report she'd read, then numbered the others consecutively. She picked up the page she'd labeled with a two. It was also from Ms. Fieldstone. *Cerby, Trent Majors's familiar, has been invited to hellhound training with McMann Hellhound Training and Boarding.* She questioned why the Goddess would send a hellhound to an inactive member of the coven.

Again, Ms. Fieldstone's report had been short and factual.

The next request came from Brandon Marshall. As the board president, it made sense that he would have asked for an investigation. He probably read all of Ms. Fieldstone's reports. Or he had someone in his office read them. The request was short and to the point. It requested an investigator to establish whether Cerby had been placed correctly and determine the possibility of a delivery error. That made Mia blink. Even if Cerby should have been sent to Levi, there would be no way Trent would give up the little guy willingly. He loved his pocket puppy.

She wrote down Brandon's name and the date of the request in her notebook. This wasn't telling her anything she couldn't have guessed herself.

Finally, she read the correspondence she'd marked as number five. *The investigator will arrive next week.*

One line. No signature. The header said, *The Department of Magical Creatures, Familiar Division.*

It was maddening. She wrote down the date and the information from the header in her notebook. As she thought about asking the archives another question, a new page emerged. She picked it up and wrote a number six on the top. It was dated today and had a time stamp of 8:15.

She read the missive aloud. "The investigator we sent has passed on to another life. There will be no replacement. The situation is too chaotic to risk more personnel. The request is closed."

Mia heard the door open behind her. She'd wanted to ask one more question about her own skills and her test score, but Cleo was already waiting to walk her to the front door. She tucked the responses and her notebook into her tote, then stood. "Thanks for making time for me."

"Anytime, my dear. Please tell Gloria I said hello." She glanced at her watch. "You'd better hurry or you'll miss your staff meeting. I suppose Blake is challenging to work for."

Mia smiled as she opened the door. "You should have met my last boss. He was horrible to work with. Blake's a breeze."

As she went through her day, Mia thought about the reports she'd read. Brandon had instigated the investigation, but he hadn't seemed that worried about it. It was more like he was passing on the question from the familiar coordinator.

She closed her office door and called Grans.

"What's wrong?" her grandmother asked as she answered.

Direct and to the point. Mia had to smile. "Nothing. I'm wondering if you know a Marsha Fieldstone."

"Yes, and you do as well. She runs the coffee shop

here in town. Magic Brews? She's the tall woman with her hair in a bun?"

Mia tried to picture her and came up with a vague image. "Oh, okay."

"She kind of blends into her surroundings. One of her talents. She should color her hair. It's been gray since she turned thirty. An unfortunate encounter with a rogue hellhound she was trying to round up."

That made sense as to why she was focused on Cerby. Maybe she thought Trent couldn't handle him. She decided to go talk to her after work.

"Sorry, dear, I need to run. I'm making up a batch of love potions for a neighbor. She's looking for a new husband. If you let it burn, the potion will curdle and ruin. And so will the relationship."

Mia heard the line disconnect in her ear, and she set down her phone. She hoped Grans hadn't used a love potion to catch Robert. Or worse, one on her to catch Trent's eye. But she wouldn't put it past her.

She finished up the last few emails. The big event on Wednesday had mostly been handled by Mother Adams already. Jeani would be coming tomorrow to decorate the ballroom at the lodge. And Abigail was handling the food. All Mia needed to do was keep all the balls in the air. And maybe help with the cooking on Wednesday. She didn't want Christina to have to prepare the appetizers for her own engagement party.

She checked her project management spreadsheet, sent off a few emails, and decided to call it a day. Maybe she'd do some baking tonight to get ahead of the game. And get out of her own head.

First, instead of heading home, she went to get a

coffee and talk to Marsha Fieldstone. When she got to Magic Brews, the coffee shop was almost empty. Two booths had people working on laptops, and one person was in line in front of her, waiting for a to-go coffee.

She studied the menu. Something sweet would be great. Maybe a Mountain Goat Caramel Mocha. As long as it didn't have goat milk. Two-percent regular dairy would be fine.

She stepped up to the counter, and a woman came to take her order. Mia had been lucky. Marsha was the name on her apron, and she looked like the woman Grans had described. She asked about the milk source and then ordered the large, to-go specialty drink. Then she met the woman's gaze as she handed her a credit card. "Marsha, can we talk for a minute? I'll even buy you a coffee?"

The woman glanced at her card, then handed it back to her without charging her for the coffee. "Sure, Mia, let me get your drink and one for myself. I'll buy. It's one of the few perks of owning your own business, free coffee, right?"

Mia took a seat across the shop from the laptop owners and waited. She wasn't sure what she wanted to ask. She might be poking the bear, but she thought maybe the woman cared about animals and simply needed to know that Cerby was well taken care of by Trent. Well, Trent and their village.

Like they said, it took a village to raise a child, or in this case, a hellhound and a dragon.

Marsha came over with a tray holding the coffee as well as a plate with two dog-shaped cookies. "I thought you might need a little pick-me-up. I know you were busy last week. Congratulations on the exam. You're all anyone wants to talk about. And you want to talk to me? I think I can guess what the subject matter is. A small white dog with a big personality?"

Mia laughed as she took her coffee. "That's a good description of Cerby. He's such a sweetheart. I understand you were concerned about his placement?"

"I was until your scores came out. Then the Goddess's plans seemed a little more apparent. He's here as a bodyguard, right? It's horrible that we're still dealing with these things at this time, but what are you going to do? All you can affect is your little corner of the world."

Mia sipped her coffee. She could let Marsha think that she'd stumbled onto why the Goddess had sent Cerby, but that might not be the whole story. "I'm actually not sure why Cerby is here. But I wanted you to know that he's well cared for and loved by many people in our family. He'll never be a problem to others."

Marsha rubbed her neck, and Mia saw a faint scar. "I appreciate your concern. His appearance indeed gave me a bit of a fright. Especially here in Magic Springs. The werewolves being close by make me a little nervous as well. But mostly, it's a good town with good people." She pushed the cookies closer. "Try one."

Mia held up her hand. "Sorry. I've put myself on a strict no-sweets diet. At least until the sugar from Halloween drains from my body. Marsha, I wanted to ask about the investigation request to the National Office on Cerby. Did you ask Brandon to make it? Because of your concern?"

Marsha shook her head. "I didn't ask him to do that.

When I filed the report, he called me and asked my professional opinion of Cerby's arrival. Well, my unofficial opinion. He already had my report."

"Brandon initiated the contact?"

"I didn't know that Alfred Howard was here until my book showed him arriving on Tuesday." She smiled at Mia's confused look. "I also monitor the book that shows every magical creature and their arrival and departure from Magic Springs. Like your friend, Christina. I knew she'd come back for her engagement parties before anyone else even knew she was coming. Besides you, that is."

Another piece of magic that Mia had known nothing about. Or maybe it was only a need-to-know type of thing. She stood and adjusted her purse over her shoulder. "Thanks for the coffee. I need to get home and start baking for the party. You should come. We're going to have a lot of fun."

"Thanks, but I'm running the coffee shop on Wednesday. It's nice to be invited, though." Marsha stood and walked back to the counter. As soon as she did, the door opened, and a customer stepped inside.

The woman had an uncanny ability to see when she was going to get traffic in the shop.

Mia was almost home when she realized that Marsha Fieldstone had said that Alfred Howard had arrived on Tuesday. But the flight records had said Wednesday. Where had he been for a night, and how did he get here on Tuesday? Or was Marsha remembering wrong?

It happened—people get dates mixed up all the time. Mia wondered if Howard's early arrival said more than they'd thought. She decided she needed to find out if Howard had stayed the night in Los Angeles or if Marsha's book was right.

She decided to check the Lodge records again, this time without Carol's help. She put it on her to-do list for tomorrow. She had access to hotel records, check-ins, and check-outs, which allowed her to credit clients with room stays and give them a discount on their events. Maybe Howard had had more than one off-the-books meeting in Magic Springs.

It was beginning to look like Alfred Howard was a bit of a mystery himself. This could be why the coven didn't want anyone snooping into his death.

When she got home, she took out the notebook she'd used during her meetings with Mark. There had to be someone they were overlooking. She found the note about Howard's unknown lunch partner and wrote in Steve's name.

Mark had taken him off the suspect list because he had been with most of the Majors family during the time Howard was killed. But what if Howard was given a poison and he consumed it later? She saw she still had questions on what substance had actually killed Howard. She texted Mark regarding the new toxicology report.

Abigail would never forgive her if she was the one to find evidence that her firstborn was a killer. Besides, unless one of the restricted ingredients showed up in Howard's toxicology report, the mixture that killed Howard wasn't a magical potion. Or at least not one tracked by the coven. So why wouldn't Steve use his powers to get rid of a problem?

The short answer was, he wouldn't.

So now she was back to looking for someone who was a human or had a human motive to kill someone. She sighed and wrote down several more items. Why did people kill? The big four reasons were love, money, revenge, and fear.

If she looked at fear, that motive would point to Trent and his need to keep Cerby and Buddy off the coven's books. But she knew he didn't kill Howard. And Howard's death had made it more apparent that the coven actually already knew about the hellhound and the dragon.

Money? She didn't see anything that brought up that idea. She wondered if the legends were true about leprechauns and pots of gold. Maybe there was a treasure hidden near the river where he was supposed to go rafting? That would put Thomas Majors in the spotlight as a potential suspect. But Thomas had been down that river way too many times before. If there was a treasure, he would have found it.

Treasure. Rafting trip. If someone had told Howard there was a treasure to find, he might have been more willing to spend more time here in remote Idaho than to talk to Trent about Cerby.

Love didn't seem to be a factor, so Mia checked it off her list. But revenge. That could be something.

Mia looked up Edmund Pevensie and found two hits. One, as expected, was the fictional character in the CHRONICLES OF NARNIA books. But the second one made her blink.

There was a land deed registered in that name right here in Magic Springs, and the plot was near Trent's place. She wrote down the address and called Trent. Maybe there would be a clue on the property.

If not, she'd still have a nice visit with her boyfriend and his menagerie of creatures. Maybe he'd even cook dinner.

She finished reading through her notes about Howard's death, made a new plan, then tucked the notebook back away in the apartment. As she was making her way downstairs, she looked guiltily at the kitchen. She'd planned on getting a start on the baking for Christina's party tonight.

There never seemed to be enough time. She'd come home early tomorrow after making sure the decorating was going well and everything was in place. Then she could start baking. The fact that it would limit her time around Jeani and her sister was an unforeseen bonus in her eyes.

At least she knew that no one had gotten into her potions lab and used the foxglove to kill Howard.

She'd told Trent she'd be at the house at six, so that gave her time to stop by the address for the Pevensie property. When she got there, a dirt driveway was marked by an old mailbox that looked like it hadn't been used for years. She hated lying, especially to Trent, so she made a quick decision and texted him. She said she was stopping to check out the property—and she even gave him the address.

Mia had seen too many movies where she'd yelled at the too-stupid-to-live character for not leaving bread crumbs so they could at least find her body later. "Wow, that turned dark," she said to herself as she tucked her phone away and turned the car to go up the drive.

Worst-case scenario, she would find a pot farm where a group of armed men would send her on her way. Or at least she hoped they would. She felt for the amethyst necklace under her shirt. Grans had infused it with a protection spell, but she didn't know if it shielded her from human bad guys or only magical ones. She probably needed to find out before her next nosy adventure.

It was a little too late for this one.

She continued up the narrow dirt road that now was winding up a mountainside. Whoever lived here liked being remote. If she hadn't been looking for the property, she would have missed the road and the mailbox.

Then the road turned, and suddenly, she was in a clearing with a view of the Magic Mountains behind the old cabin that sat on the lot.

She turned off the engine and noticed smoke coming out of the chimney.

Edmund Pevensie must be home.

CHAPTER 22

For the first time since she'd turned off the highway, Mia felt a twinge of fear. Maybe this had been a bad idea. Maybe she should start the car, drive back down the dirt road, and head to Trent's. Cerby would keep her safe. She knew now that he was sent for her protection.

And yet, here she was, at a remote cabin in the woods, getting ready to see if the guy who had set up Howard's rafting trip lived there.

She was living out the too-stupid-to-live scenario.

The door opened, and a tall man stepped out.

It was too late to run and hide. If the man meant her harm, he had already seen her face. And probably her license plate. People who built rural cabins like this tended to have security cameras everywhere.

She took a breath and stepped out of the car. She paused for a second, then shut the door and stepped closer. "Edmund Pevensie, I presume?"

"I'm not hiding in the jungles of Africa, but yes, I use that name, or I do at times. You're Mia Malone, the surprisingly talented kitchen witch." He stepped off the porch and came closer. "I'd shake your hand, but I seem to have somewhat of a Midas touch, at least when it comes to females. I don't want your boyfriend to come looking for me." He smiled, and Mia noticed his eyes were kind.

"You're the incubus." Mia almost had called him "Blake's incubus," but she'd stopped herself in time.

"Guilty as charged, but seriously, we get a bad rap. Come in and have a cup of tea with me. I promise I'll keep my hands off you." He held out a hand, motioning toward the cabin.

Mia looked down at her necklace. It hadn't turned from purple to red, which was her sign that danger was near. She'd come here for answers. It was stupid to walk, or run, away without them. "That would be nice, thank you."

She followed him into the cabin, which, for all of its rustic flavor outside, looked like it had just been set up and photographed for a magazine shoot. Luxury furniture; a large eighty-inch flat screen; and a walnut desk with a computer on the top. A notebook and pens were also on the desk. A bookshelf overflowing with books was next to it.

She stepped closer to the bookshelves to examine the titles. "You must be a big reader."

"I am, but most of those are mine. I'm J.C. Hart, or at least that's my pen name. I'm currently writing what they call historical romance. Mostly for me, it's a memoir. I'm in love with love, what can I say?" He walked over with a tray service for the tea. "I've been expecting a visit from you. Or your police officer friend."

"So you knew Alfred Howard." Mia sat on the couch, watching him.

"Al and I were friends for years. Centuries, actually. We had some fun years. He was the money guy, and I . . . well, I brought the female companionship to the party. But that was years ago. We've both mellowed with age. Well, I should say Al had mellowed." He stood and picked up a photo from the bookshelf. "This is us in New Orleans. We stayed for years. The party never stopped."

Mia looked at a much-younger Edmund with a shorter man who was clearly Howard. She smiled at the way the men had their arms around each other and were grinning like fools into the camera. "You made the arrangements for the rafting trip. Were you looking for treasure?"

"What?" Edmund took the frame from Mia and put it back on the shelf. "No, there's no treasure on that stretch of the river. Unless you count the heartbreaking beauty of the scenery as treasure. We were going to enjoy the rafting. Al was looking forward to it. He took the assignment to look into your boyfriend, his hell-hound, and his dragon so we could go on the trip and use the coven's dime for the costs. Alfred Howard was a rich man. He stayed that way by not paying for anything that he could get someone else to finance."

"You're saying he was cheap." Mia sipped her tea.

Edmund grinned. "Rich men always are. But Al was

so kind and generous, at least when it came to giving of his talents."

"You didn't kill him," Mia stated, knowing in her heart she was right.

Edmund sipped his tea, then set down the cup. "No, but I'm afraid I might have been partly responsible for his death."

"In what way?" Mia set her own cup down. It didn't feel laced with anything, but she was new enough that she might not know.

"I was the one who nudged Marsha to have questions about Cerby. She would have let it go—she's friends with the Majors family—but I gave her a push because I knew they'd send Al. We'd been looking for an opportunity to do this for years, but he wouldn't come unless someone paid him to be here. Like I said, he was all about making the money." He leaned back and closed his eyes. "I wish I had the power to turn back time. My friend would still be around."

"Why did Howard show up at Trent's house rather than his dad's? Was he coming here?" Mia was trying to think through Howard's last days and make sense of them.

Edmund leaned forward, his eyes widening as he heard something Mia couldn't. "Sorry, I believe we have guests. Your baby dragon is near your car, and a truck is coming up the driveway."

"Trent." Mia stood and nodded to the door. "I'd better go head him off. It was nice to meet you. I hope we can talk more about this."

"I'm probably leaving for my villa in France soon.

Al's death has made this place too tender in memories." He followed her to the door and held it open.

As they walked outside to the porch, Buddy made his presence known with a puff of fire. Mia stepped off the porch and headed over to her car, where the dragon was now sitting on the ground, staring at Edmund. Steam was coming out of his nose.

"Buddy, be nice. He didn't hurt me." Mia reached out and rubbed the dragon's nose as he smelled her body. Satisfied that Mia wasn't under the incubus's spell, Buddy flew up to the tree by the house and settled on a branch as Trent drove up. When he opened the door to the truck, Cerby jumped out and ran to her, barking.

She picked him up, and he licked her face. Then he curled up in her arms, also satisfied she was safe.

Trent walked over. "Apparently the rescue wasn't needed?"

"Not in the least, but I'm glad you stopped by." Mia nodded to Edmund. "Have you met your neighbor?"

Trent made eye contact with Edmund. "Sorry, I haven't had the pleasure. I thought this place was abandoned until Mia mentioned coming up to check it out. Cerby got a little protective."

Edmund shrugged in return. "He's a hellhound, what do you expect? I have to admit, I haven't had the best reputation over my lifetime. I am an almost-changed man. I can control my desires much better than I could when I was younger. Even though some people don't believe in redemption."

Mia wondered if he was referring to Blake. And

what was Mia going to tell her boss? *Hey, I met your ex—he seems to be a nice guy. Or at least he was to me.* That would go over like a lead balloon. "Well, thank you for the tea and conversation. I'll let Mark know we've talked, but he might try to reach you."

Edmund's eyes sparkled. "Your law man will have to find me first."

As the incubus went inside, Trent turned to her and took Cerby. "I feel like an idiot. But Cerby went crazy, and then Buddy took off. I thought you needed help."

"You know, at first, I thought I did. Maybe they were reacting to that? I'd rather them overreact than not alert you at all." Mia rubbed Cerby's nose. "Are you still making me dinner?"

"I've already got the baked potatoes in the oven. I'll follow you out. Buddy? Get out of that tree and head home, okay?" Trent looked over to where it appeared the dragon was sleeping.

A beat of his wings, and he shot up in the air. He must have just been resting his eyes. Mia climbed into her car and started it. Then she drove past Trent's truck and down the hill to the main road. Edmund Pevensie was an interesting guy. And he was heartbroken at the loss of his friend.

Mia didn't need magic to see that.

Tuesday morning, Mia was surprised to find Blake in her office. She sat in a visitor's chair on her phone, reading.

"Well, good morning. I'm glad you're here. I wanted

to let you know I'll be working from home most of tomorrow and leaving early today to start working on the Adams–Majors engagement party." Mia set her tote down and took off her jacket. The weather had turned cold. The ski lodge was expecting snow any day. Mia hoped it stayed away until after Grans's party on Sunday.

"Whatever you need. Your friends and family are paying enough for the use of the Lodge over the next week." Blake put her phone away. "I wanted to ask about the incubus. Have you heard anything? My alarm spell keeps ringing, but it's softly, like he's in the area, but not focused on me. Maybe I should leave before something bad happens again."

"'Again'?" Now Mia's attention was on Blake's face. "What do you mean, 'again'?"

"He's an incubus. What do you think I mean?" Blake said as she jumped up from the chair. "Anyway, let me know if you need any signatures or anything else for Wednesday's event. Jeani's doing an amazing job in the ballroom. You should check it out."

Mia watched her boss almost run out of her office. For someone who'd been waiting for her to show up this morning, she'd sure left in a hurry.

James poked his head into her office. "Why do you look like you're trying to solve the ancient mysteries like where Atlantis disappeared to?"

She laughed and softened her face. She didn't need James getting suspicious of what she knew about their boss. He had a knack for getting stuff out of her, even when she didn't want to tell him. "That's oddly specific. But not correct. Blake stopped in, and she was nice."

"That *is* weird. Maybe more of a mystery than Atlantis. I was watching a new documentary last night. Oh, so good. And there's missing gold. Maybe I should take up deep-sea diving for a hobby. I might get rich. And lucky. Or lucky, then rich."

Mia tried to listen as he started talking about the show he'd seen and fallen in love with. When he took a breath, she smiled and added, "There's one problem with your plan. Idaho is a landlocked state. And you can't leave the Lodge before I do. We have a deal."

"You always put a damper on my dreams. Now, I wanted to talk to you about Mary Alice's party. She wants our kitchen to do the dinner but Mia's Morsels to make the desserts. I have the menu here if you want to preapprove it before I call your grandmother. I want her to think I'm a genius."

"Everyone thinks you're a genius," Mia responded, taking the piece of paper away. Now that she'd dodged Blake's question, she needed to get things done so she could get out of the Lodge before she ran into her again.

After she approved the menu, she checked her email and responded to several items that also needed her approval. Then she opened the hotel guest log. Howard might have stayed Tuesday night with Edmund, but she didn't want to assume anything.

She scrolled through the names and finally found three possibilities. Each reservation was for one night. And had a male name. They were paid by a corporate credit card.

Maybe Edmund was right. Maybe Howard had found another source of income to pay for his vacation time here in Magic Springs. She printed off the list and tucked it into her tote.

Then she went to see the ballroom.

As soon as she stepped inside, she knew that Christina was going to be ecstatic. It was a Cinderella fairy tale wrapped in shimmering silver and blue tones. The dance floor area was all old-castle charm with the sides mixing castle and woodland. There were even birds and butterflies set around the edges.

"Oh, Mia, I'm so glad you're here." An excited Jeani grabbed her arm. "I didn't see it on the outline, but we're doing passed trays for appetizers, correct? I put small tables out for extras and a drinks station on this side. The bar's closer to the side door, where they can restock. I'm going a little more male-centric on that side. I know, old-fashioned, but this is an engagement party."

"It looks beautiful. She's going to be so pleased." Mia hoped Christina wouldn't come to check out the ballroom. She needed to see it fresh when she walked in for the party. "You're talented."

"Well, I figured since it was Magic Springs, I could go a little crazy. Her mom has already asked me to do the Friday-night event in Boise. I told her I'd have to upcharge since it was last minute, and she said she didn't care. She fired her designer, and I'll be heading there tomorrow after this is set to start the planning." She paused and looked at Mia. "Her folks are normals, right?"

"Yes. Very, very normal. Lawyer and old-money types." Mia turned away from a tree where fairies were playing in the branches.

"I was afraid you'd say that." Jeani sighed and took in her creation. "Here, if I can imagine it, I can make it. In real life, I need to tone down my, and my client's expectations. I already told Mrs. Adams that I'd been working on this for weeks. I can't pull this off down in the valley for several reasons."

Mia laughed. "At least you have a valid excuse. As long as the party looks expensive and upscale, you'll be fine with Mrs. Adams. Think modern *Great Gatsby*."

"What a great idea!" Jeani hugged Mia, surprising her. She held on as she whispered, "I'm so glad you're here. We work well together. I like you."

Mia patted Jeani on the back. Not what she'd been expecting after the last encounter with Trent's ex. As she let her go, she said, "I like you, too."

"Sorry about the over-the-top emotions. It's my creative process. I tend to say what I mean without a filter. Sometimes it's good, sometimes not." Jeani peered at a branch that covered part of a table. "That won't do. I guess I'd better get going. Thanks to you, I need to start playing with 1920s glam."

Mia watched the decorating crew for a little longer. The champagne fountain was going to be beautiful. Mother Adams would be pleased. She turned around and ran into her almost-future mother-in-law. "Mrs. Adams, I'm so glad to see you."

"Now, dear, you know we're past that stage, call me

Roxanne? Even Jessica calls me by my first name. She's such a delight. Isaac's a lucky man." Evil glinted in Mother Adams's eyes as she brought up Mia's ex's new bride.

"Of course, Roxanne." Mia put on her client smile, the one she saved for customers she didn't like. "How is the new couple doing? Christina said they went to Europe for their honeymoon."

"Very well. Jessica's fitting in nicely as a member of my charity groups, and they're already trying for a baby. I told her that adoption was the way to go, but she wanted to make one of her own. I'm sure she'll change her mind after the first one ruins her tiny waist." She looked at Mia. "You look comfortable here in the backwoods. I'm sure you're going to miss Christina."

Mia breathed past all the pokes at how she wouldn't have made a perfect wife for Mother Adams's son. And how she was a hick. Smiling, she focused on the one true statement the woman had made. "I am going to miss having her around all the time. She's a joy to work with and live with, but of course, you already know that, since you raised her. The good thing is, Portland isn't that far away. I'm sure I'll see her often at the Majorses' holiday events, since I'm dating another one of their sons."

The color drained from the woman's face. "If she can get away from her new job. You know how intense the hospitality business can be."

"If she can't come here, then we'll pack up the festivities and take them to her and Levi." Mia paused for effect. "It's what family does. Oh, look at the time. I'd better get home. Those tasty bits aren't going to make themselves."

Mia turned to leave, then stopped. She might as well ask. She'd probably burned a bridge here anyway. "Roxanne, do you know who Christina's birth parents are? Is there any chance they were from Magic Springs? She seems to fit in here so well, you know what I mean?"

CHAPTER 23

Mia started another batch of cheesecake bites, this recipe with a huckleberry topping, while she thought about Mother Adams's answer. She had known what Mia was implying, so somehow, she'd known about Christina's magical heritage. As long as she wasn't a baby whom Abigail had given up, or any of her or Thomas's siblings, it wasn't an issue with her marrying Levi.

Besides, Abigail knew about Christina's heritage. Mia thought she might have suspected a few years ago now, looking at the way she treated Levi's girlfriend. Abigail had brought both Mia and Christina in as more than her son's girlfriends. She already treated them like family.

Mia wondered if any of Trent's past girlfriends had gotten Abigail's seal of approval that quickly. Moving in together would even up the ante as far as being part of the Majors family. She didn't like Steve, but right now, Trent didn't either. Thomas could go hot or cold depending on the day.

She guessed his family was like any other.

Tired of trying to see into her future, she focused instead on Alfred Howard. She needed to follow up on the three names she had gotten from the reservation desk. But if he'd come in early, why not adjust his reservation? Why use an alias?

That was if he even came in early. The thing was, **mag**ical sensors usually were spot-on. They didn't have human intervention to count or not count an arrival. That's why the coven had set them up and had someone who was not on the board monitor and report on who entered the area. It kept everyone honest.

Assuming that Marsha's count was right, then why did Alfred Howard come into town on Tuesday undercover?

"I can't believe you're here cooking." Abigail came through the back door with a few empty totes in her hands. "I told Finn we needed to get unloaded and start baking, and yet here you are, making light work of the event."

Mia held up Abigail's prep list. "You left this out on the table, so I started when I got home. I wanted to get away from a few people."

Abigail set the totes by the sink. "Okay, I'll guess Mother Adams and Blake."

"Close, Mother Adams, Blake, and Jeani." Mia turned the mixer off and went to the fridge. "She was acting strange at the Halloween party."

"Mia, she was drunk at the Halloween party. Don't worry about her, she was never really a part of Trent's life. I think she might have had a hand in why he decided to hand off his magic. He hated the idea that his entire life including who he was to marry was being planned for him by the coven. Jeani's nice, but she's not you." Abigail hugged Mia, then turned to see Finn coming in. "Finn, can you finish unloading, then clean the van's shelves? Lock it up when you're done and bring in the keys. I'm going to start baking cakes."

"Okay. Oh, hi, Mia. We had a lot of deliveries today, and almost everyone wanted us to tell you hi." Finn put the totes by the ones Abigail had brought in. They'd wash them and then put them away for next week's deliveries.

Mia met Abigail's gaze, shrugging.

"You're a celebrity, my dear. Don't worry, it will go away." Abigail patted her shoulder, then went to wash her hands and put on an apron.

"What if it doesn't?" Mia asked after Finn had gone back outside.

Abigail grabbed a container of sugar from the cabinet and set it on her worktable. "Then we'll deal with that when it happens. Don't borrow tomorrow's problems for today."

And with that, she turned up the music, and they spent the rest of the day cooking.

At six, Trent poked his head around the kitchen door. "Find a stopping point," he said as he looked around at the women baking. "We've got pizza."

Mia scratched off an item on Abigail's list. She'd put the last pan of double-chocolate brownies in the oven. They needed thirty minutes to bake, then she'd let it cool until tomorrow, when she'd cut them into mini squares and put a chocolate-covered cherry on top of each. A local chocolate shop made them in their store on Main Street, and they were amazing.

She grabbed all of her dirty bowls and set them in the sink. "I'm ready to eat. I'll need to come back and get the brownies out of the oven and clean up, but I'm starving."

Finn was cleaning her station. She'd finished her cookies, and Abigail had stopped her from starting to work on the hot appetizers. "I'm good. I can help to-night if you want. I'm not working at the Lodge until Thursday."

Abigail collected all their prep sheets. "If we put in another hour after pizza, I think we'll be in good shape for tomorrow."

Mia loved Abigail's organizational process. At first, her changes had bugged her. It was *Mia's* Morsels, right? But she had to admit, things ran smoother with Abigail at the helm.

"Finn and I will clean up, and you can do your prep sheet work," Mia said as they walked out to the reception area, which smelled like pepperoni, tomato sauce, cheese, and fresh bread. There was nothing better than the smell of pizza when you were hungry.

She grabbed a plate and put three slices on it. Trent tossed her a bottle of water, and she sat down with a groan. "You guys are the best."

Christina dabbed at her eyes.

"Now you've done it." Levi handed her a box of tis-sues. "My girl has been crying about leaving Magic Springs all day. She's a wreck."

Mia took a bite of the pizza and perked up. She'd

forgotten to eat lunch. "Your mother thinks I'll be heart-broken with you out of the boonies. She's sure you're going to love Portland much more than Magic Springs."

"Uh-oh. You had a run-in with Mom today? That must have been when I got the ton of texts from her. I ignored them. She's not ruining my mood. I want to celebrate getting engaged to my knight in shining armor without her digging at every choice I made for the party. Tell me that Jeani did a good job. I asked Mom to hire her for the Boise event."

"She did an excellent job," Mia said between bites. "You're going to *love* it. And don't ask, because I'm not telling you what it looks like. I didn't even take pictures, but I wanted to. Even your mom was impressed."

Trent looked over at Mia but didn't say anything. It was like the guy could read her mind. Well, he could, but she thought she'd blocked him out. He knew she'd been concerned about Jeani and that she didn't like Mother Adams. As a result, he knew she'd had a stress-ful afternoon.

"How's the cooking going? Are you going to need help tomorrow?" Christina asked. "I've got a spa day planned with Mom and Jessica, but if you need me in the kitchen, I'll dump them."

"You will not." Abigail shook her head. "Like I told you this morning, you're not needed. Go have a mas-sage and a facial and get those nails done. You look practically homeless."

Finn burst into giggles. There was no way Christina looked anything but polished and perfect.

"Oh, don't you laugh, missy. I have a slot for you at the hair salon at five. All of you are expected there at that time. Finn, I left an outfit in your bedroom. Dress, shoes, and the necessary underthings. I hope you like it." Christina grabbed another slice of pizza. "Although, if I don't stop eating like this, I'm not going to fit into my gown. And it's designer."

Mia was wearing another one of Christina's castoffs. Before she packed for Portland, she had brought several dresses out of her storage room on the second floor. Mother Adams had told Christina to get her bedroom cleared out when it became clear she wasn't coming home to live. So Mia had let her put her furniture and the ton of boxes filled with clothes and shoes in an empty classroom.

There was still stuff there, but Mia wasn't going to make Christina pack up everything. She wanted her friend to know she always had a home here in Magic Springs, just in case.

Mia grabbed a fourth slice and ate it a little slower. "Christina, you look amazing. The dress is going to fit like a glove. You have a second one for Friday night?"

"Of course, and so do you and Finn. Thanks for ruining the surprise." Christina smiled as Finn almost dropped her slice of pizza.

"I get to come on Friday? But I don't have a car. I work at the Lodge that night." Finn set the slice on the plate.

"I already talked to James, and you can ride with me and Trent. We're driving back after the party."

Trent held up his hand. "Mia always volunteers me to be the designated driver," he grumbled.

"No need for you kids to come back, Thomas and I will be coming back. Finn can ride with us," Abigail announced. "Besides, I reserved both couples a room at the Owyhee. We'll see you Saturday midday. You need to be back for Mary Alice's party."

Mia winced. She didn't want to stay in Boise, especially not at the hotel where she used to work with Isaac, but giving Finn a ride home had been her only excuse. Christina was watching, so she smiled at Abigail. "Oh, what a surprise. Thank you so much."

After everyone had left and the kitchen was cleaned up, Trent walked her upstairs. He'd sent Cerby home with Christina and Levi. Buddy would follow them back to the house. The two were inseparable. Finn had disappeared into her bedroom as soon as the kitchen was closed up, and Mia had heard the screams of joy when she'd found Christina's gifts.

"Everyone seemed like they were having fun tonight. How has it been having Levi and Christina staying with you?" Mia asked as she unlocked the apartment door. Mr. Darcy looked up from where he'd been sleeping and yawned. But when he saw they were without Cerby, he laid his head down and went back to sleep.

"Interesting. Mostly quiet, but when she starts talking, she doesn't stop. They're planning a cruise to Alaska next summer and want us to come along." He sat on the couch, apparently not ready to leave her yet.

"That might be nice. Depending on Cerby and Buddy." Mia headed to the kitchen. "Do you want a soda or a glass of wine?"

"Soda, please," he called back. "I think wine would put me out right here on the couch."

She brought out two cans and a plate of cookies. Then she curled up next to him. "I haven't figured out why Howard was here a day early. And why the National Office blew off sending someone else to do the investigation. But I wondered, do you think it was because of my score on the exam? Since you're my boyfriend?"

"I've been wondering that too." He rubbed her arm gently. "You freaked me out by visiting Edmund Pevensie yesterday. I should have trusted your gut."

"Probably. But my 'innate talent' is going to take some getting used to for both of us. You don't think they made a mistake? Maybe I'm not the genius they think I am." She laid her head on his shoulder. "I don't believe Edmund killed Howard. They were too close, and he was so sad at losing his friend."

"Emotion isn't a valid alibi in a court case. I think Mark needs more than that." He sipped his soda. "Like an actual killer to take the blame."

"Too bad." Mia leaned away from him. "Hey, you didn't answer my other question. Do you think they made a mistake on my test?"

"I will never question your ability or what level the examination process gave you. My mother taught me better than that."

She slugged him in his arm.

Mark texted just as she'd finished the first appetizer on her prep list the next morning.

She washed her hands, then opened his text. It only was two words long. *Call me*.

Mia held her phone up for Abigail to see. "I'll be right back."

When she got to the sofa, she sat down and called him. "What's up?"

"Don't be mad. I know you have Christina's party tonight, but can you come with me to Twin for lunch? I found someone who might have seen our victim the day he was killed."

Mia thought about her prep list. She was almost done. She thought Abigail had made hers a little lighter just in case she needed to help Finn. But the girl was doing fine. And from the excited chatter about the party and her dress, she was in a great mood. "What time can you pick me up?"

As Mia settled into Mark's truck thirty minutes later, she pulled on her seat belt. "People are going to talk if you keep asking me out to meals."

"I feel bad taking up your time. Besides, Sarah knows every step I make and with whom. She'll shut any rumors down, believe me." He glanced over at her. "Trent's not upset I'm involving you in the investigation, is he?"

Mia laughed as she watched the trees go by while they drove. "Not in the least. He's more upset when I'm solo investigating." Mia explained her visit to Edmund Pevensie and what she'd learned. When Mark didn't respond, she looked over at him. He was rubbing his temples. "Do you have a headache?"

"I do now," he responded. "I'm trying to think how I'm going to write up the statement of an incubus in the official file."

"Maybe you just call him Edmund?" Mia turned and looked at him. "I think you're looking at this wrong. If you treat people as people and stop labeling them, you won't have this problem. I've already told you that magic wasn't involved in Howard's killing. So now it's either money, love, fear, or revenge. It's that simple."

When he didn't respond, she worried she'd upset him. "Mark, I'm sorry. I've got a lot on my mind. I didn't mean to question your methods."

He shook his head, focusing on the road. "Sometimes I forget that. You're right, people are people. I've been focusing so long on what makes us different, I've failed to see what makes us alike. Elise Marie is going to have to grow up in this world. Good or bad, we have to accept the life we've been given and stop hoping for a different one. It's the only way we'll move forward."

Mia didn't respond. She knew Mark had had a huge paradigm shift when his daughter was born with witch powers. Then to find out his wife and his mother had hidden the coven and their involvement in it for years. Maybe Mia was asking him to go one step too far.

After a few minutes of silence in the truck, he looked over at her. "What, do we sing 'Kumbaya' now and clasp hands together?"

Mia burst out laughing. "How should I know? I'm a newbie to this world too. Mark, I think we do what we can."

"Well, I have you investigating with me. Who would have thought that would happen two, three years ago?" He looked sharply at her. "And don't think this is an ongoing situation. One and done, and you don't tell anyone about it."

"I think I've already broken that last rule." Mia relaxed into the seat. The fall sun was shining brightly, warming the truck cab. Soon, rays of sun wouldn't be able to shine brightly enough to break through the blanket of cold they'd have this winter. And this road would at times be a sheet of ice.

Another reason Mia liked living in Magic Springs. Especially with her old car. Maybe she should replace the tires this year.

They came up to the freeway, then crossed it and the bridge over the Snake River. As they started coming into town, she turned to Mark. "So, where are we going?"

"The pancake house. The cook is a friend of Sarah's and swears she saw Alfred Howard there on Wednesday morning. With a friend. She wouldn't talk on the phone. She thinks people are listening to her conversations. So she mailed a letter to Sarah. A letter." Mark shook his head. "I'd be more afraid that the post office was reading my mail if I had paranoia."

CHAPTER 24

Mia followed Mark into the log cabin–style restaurant and immediately was overtaken by the smell of warm maple syrup and pancakes. And maybe sausage or bacon. Mia's stomach rumbled, and Mark laughed at her warming face.

"I told you I'd buy lunch. If you don't mind brunch, we can eat here." He approached the hostess stand. "Two in that booth in the corner, and we need to see Patty."

"She's cooking, but I'll tell her. Name?" The girl grabbed two menus and two sets of silverware rolled in paper napkins.

"Chief Baldwin. She's expecting us." He motioned Mia into a seat and took the one that put his back against the wall. Old cop trick. She'd noticed he'd done the same thing at the school. He didn't want to be blindsided.

At least not by a person.

"The caramel-apple topping is homemade and pretty amazing," he said as they studied their menus.

After the waitress took their order and brought coffee, a woman in kitchen whites came out and approached their table. She hugged Mark, then smiled at Mia. "This isn't your lovely wife, Mark. I'm Patty. Chief cook and bottle washer around here."

Mia liked the woman immediately. Some people had that glow around them that told you they were fun. "Mia Malone. I own a delivery and catering business in Magic Springs and work at the Lodge."

"Oh, I've heard of you. Good food coming out of your kitchen. My mom lives in town and gets her meals delivered." Patty nodded at Mia, then looked at the clock. "Sorry, I don't have a lot of time, so I'll get right to it. That leprechaun guy was here with a woman. She handed him an envelope. I have my staff watch for those things around here—too many drug deals since we're so close to the Nevada border. Anyway, she never took anything back. So, Janie, your waitress, she was confused. She almost didn't tell me, but she's a good girl, and she listens."

Mia glanced at Mark. "Do you have a picture of Howard?" She was hoping it wasn't the one from the morgue.

"I got one from Brandon last week." Mark opened his phone and showed Patty. "This was the guy?"

She narrowed her eyes. "I know a leprechaun when I see one, Mark. But yes, that was him. The woman paid the bill in cash and wore a hat and coat. It was one of those gorgeous, warm fall days here, and she wore a coat. Talk about standing out. Anyway, I came out and visited the couple in the next booth. They're regulars. I heard her talking about an incubus in town. I thought maybe she was talking about Halloween outfits. You don't see one of those guys around much. I don't think I've even heard of one being out this far west. Unless you're in Nevada."

An idea was beginning to form in Mia's head. Where had Blake been on Wednesday? Had she hired the leprechaun to take care of the incubus without knowing that he and Edmund were friends?

It was crazy enough to be true. Mia didn't have a picture of Blake in her phone.

Their meal arrived, and Patty returned to the kitchen. She'd added bacon to both of their orders, because it was the best bacon in town.

As they started eating, Mia waved a strip at Mark. "You're right. This place is so good. Is Patty involved in the local group?"

He nodded as he ate a bite of the pancakes. "Sarah and Patty went to school together. Patty moved to Twin to open this place, and Sarah quit the group so she could marry me."

"Connections, it's always about connections," Mia said as she focused on her food. "Do you mind dropping me off at the Lodge? I'll have Trent come and get me when I'm done."

"You think you know something." He studied her over his coffee cup. "Are you going to let me in on what you've found?"

She shook her head. With this connection, maybe Blake had killed Howard because he'd taken her money to scare off his friend. "It might be nothing, but if I find out who paid for Howard's first night at the Lodge—if he was even there—I think it might turn into something. Especially with what Patty just told us."

"Okay, but I don't want you to put yourself in danger." Mark raised his hand to indicate they were ready for a check.

When Mark dropped her off at the lodge, he repeated his warning. "Call me if you get in over your head."

"If I'm in over my head, I'm probably not going to be able to call," Mia pointed out. When Mark stared at her, she shook her head. "Don't worry so much. I'm not doing anything dangerous. Just looking at some accounting records."

Mark's phone beeped. "That's Sarah, seeing when I'm coming home so I can get ready for this shindig. Miss Adams had better appreciate all the dolling up I'm doing to attend."

"I'll make sure to point out how nice you look in your suit. See you soon." Mia closed his truck door, and as she walked through the lobby to her office, she texted Trent to pick her up in thirty minutes. Hopefully, that would give her enough time.

James caught her in the staff hallway. "What are you doing here?"

"Just a little work. I'll be gone in a few minutes. How's the day going?" Mia unlocked her office door. Or she thought she did. She pushed on it, but the door didn't move.

"Did the boss change the locks?" James teased as he leaned against the doorway.

"One could only hope." Mia turned the key again, and this time the door opened. "Did Abigail and Finn drop off the food?"

"About thirty minutes ago. You missed them. Abigail walked our kitchen staff through the final prep steps. That woman could lead an army brigade of cooks. She had a system for everything."

"I know, she's organized and prepared. I've learned a lot from working with her." Mia dropped her tote and logged on to her computer. "Huh."

"What's up?" James now leaned in the doorway. He leaned on everything.

"My mouse was in the wrong place. Maybe the cleaners wiped off the top of my desk." She pushed away the thought and tried to find the file she'd been looking at. It wasn't there. "I thought I put that file on my desktop."

"Check the trash. I always seem to find stuff there I didn't delete. Or I thought I didn't. Anyway, it looks like you're busy, so I'll chat you up tonight. You're going to love my tux," he said, closing the door behind him as he left.

Mia found the file in the trash, just like James had predicted, but she never threw anything away. She checked the first reservation and then went to the payment method. Edmund had said that Howard didn't pay for anything he didn't have to, so when the name of the credit card matched the reservation, she made a note on the spreadsheet she'd created, then went to the next name. When she started looking at the third name, a knock on her door distracted her.

This file had a Lodge credit on the room. Now she had to find where the credit came from. She glanced at her watch. Maybe she could ignore whoever was out there. But it was probably about the event tonight, and there was no reason for the person to call Abigail and bother her while she was getting ready. She let the computer do its work and called out, "Come in."

Carol Hathaway, from the front desk, stepped into the office and closed the door behind her. "I'm so glad I caught you. The rooms are disappearing fast for Sunday night, and I wanted to know if you wanted me to save you a room."

Mia shook her head. "Trent and I will be heading home after the party. Between Cerby and Mr. Darcy, we can't leave them alone, and all my usual babysitters will be here at the party. But thanks for thinking about us."

"I'm sure it's hard to leave a hellhound alone for any amount of time." Carol walked over and looked at Mia's screen. "I can't believe you're working right before Christina's big party. Don't you want to head home and get ready? I can finish whatever it is you are working on."

Mia frowned. Carol wasn't usually this pushy, and did everyone in the coven know about Cerby's secret? And if so, did they also know about Buddy? "I'm fine. I am just matching up some rooms with events so we can make sure we charge correctly for the ballroom."

"That's not what you're doing."

Mia felt the change in the woman's demeanor. From helpful coworker to predator in thirty seconds. Her gut tightened as she glanced at the clock on the computer screen. Trent wouldn't be here for another nineteen minutes. Could she stall that long? "Of course it's what I'm doing. You know Blake and her reports. I need to get last week's numbers to her before I go home to get ready for the party. She'll come find me and drag me back to the office if I don't."

"That's not last week's numbers. That room reservation was from two weeks ago. You're looking to see who paid for Alfred Howard's room on Tuesday." Carol's voice had turned to steel. "I'm sorry you got involved in this, but it's one more body count that Blake will have to deal with."

"Blake killed Howard?" Mia now knew that wasn't the right answer, but keeping Carol talking could keep her alive. And hopefully, Trent would hear the cry for backup she'd tried to send him telepathically.

"You and I both know that she didn't, but everyone else will think she did. It's a good thing he couldn't resist cookies. And I know how to bake." Carol giggled a little. "Frank was a better boss. He kept his nose out of my business. Now I'll have to train a new boss when your friend arrests Blake."

"I'll tell Mark she didn't do it." Mia sounded a lot more confident than she felt.

Carol reached out and stroked Mia's hair. "No, you won't. You'll be dead. And unless you believe in vengeful ghosts, you'll be the only one who will think that. Besides, Mark Baldwin doesn't believe in ghosts or witches, not even when they're right under his nose. I wonder how Sarah's been keeping him ignorant all these years. Maybe her cooking, or maybe her other talents?"

She pulled a vial out of her jacket. "Grab one of those water bottles out of your mini fridge, and I'll get this mixed for you."

"You think I'm going to sit here and help you murder me?"

"If you don't, I'll kill you, and then your friends. How sad for Christina to die at her very own engagement party." Carol let the vial dance between her fingers. "The one thing I'm good at is poisons. Howard had warded himself against potions and spells, but he didn't realize that a human mixture of poisons could be so lethal. And since I hid the foxglove in the cookies, he didn't expect a thing. Besides, if he'd just killed Edmund Pevensie as he promised, he'd still be alive."

"You killed him because he wouldn't kill his friend?"

Carol's eyes went dark. "How was I supposed to know they were friends? These things live forever. And that incubus, he changes names every time he comes back to Magic Springs. When Marsha told me an incubus was living here, I knew it was the same one who had attacked me after my Harvest Festival Queen Pageant. He feeds on us. Then I heard Blake telling you about her ex—well, I figured she would be the perfect scapegoat. I sent an email to the National Office about Cerby, knowing that Howard would most likely be the investigator they sent. And he has a talent for gathering rogue creatures, so I offered him a contract."

"Then he told you that he couldn't kill Edmund."

"He laughed at me. Said I was overreacting. If we hadn't been at that pancake house, I would have shown him overreacting, but Polly has it warded so you can't do magic there." Carol rolled her eyes and pointed to the mini fridge on Mia's right. "Get your water, please."

Mia groaned but followed Carol's direction. At least her murderer was polite. She tried the cap on the water bottle, but like all of this brand, the seal was too tight. Mia held it toward her as she saw a shape behind the frosted glass of her door. Trent must already be here. It was now or never. "I can never get these open."

"Are you kidding me?" Carol reached for the water, then Mia squeezed the bottle, shooting water up into the woman's face. Pushing her away, she stood and ran to the door as Mark Baldwin came inside, his gun drawn.

"Stay right where you are," Mark called out to Carol, who was now blindly reaching out to try to find Mia.

"You ruined my contacts," Carol screamed. "How can I see now?"

Mark pulled Mia out of her office and nodded to two hotel security guards who were behind him in the hallway. "Take her and put her in the cell in Zander's office. I'll be right there."

As they dragged out a still-yelling Carol, her hands now handcuffed behind her back, one guard handed Mark a vial he'd placed in a plastic bag.

"That's what killed Howard, and she was going to use it on me." Mia leaned against the wall, her adrenaline level dropping. She wasn't sure she could even stand anymore.

Mark must have recognized the look, because he pulled a chair from her office and sat her down in the hallway. "Didn't I tell you to call if you got in over your head?"

"I was sitting in my office, looking up some reservations. I think I found evidence that links her to Howard. I don't know how much of her confession you heard. She used her employee discount code to get a cheap room for Howard. I suspect she was going to change it to Blake's code to frame her, but she hadn't gotten around to it before I pulled the records of everyone who came to town that week."

Trent came running down the hallway. "What happened?"

"Long story, but Mia jumped in front of a moving car to find a killer," Mark groused.

Trent's face crumpled. "In the staff hallway?"

"Not literally. But your girlfriend has a knack for being exactly where she shouldn't be at the exact wrong time." Mark looked at her. "I got to thinking about Mia's tendency and thought I was probably needed here. I turned back around to double-check. I was sure I was being overly cautious, but I found her door shut and someone yelling at her. She's alive because of me."

"You're so attention-needy." Mia stood and leaned into Trent's arms. "If you don't need me right now, I should get home to get dressed. The information is on my computer screen. Just hit the *print* button. My printer is on top of the mini fridge."

"How in the world did you figure out it was Carol?" Trent asked as they walked out to his truck.

"I thought it was Blake, but we all have our own, separate employee codes to get cheaper rates at the Lodge. When I looked up the code, I saw Carol hadn't changed it. Her cheapness put her in jail."

Once they were in the truck, Mia leaned back and closed her eyes. "She threatened to kill all of you. She knew about Cerby. Does everyone in the coven know about his talents?"

"Not that I'm aware of. I'm going to ask Mom to dig into that. Tomorrow. Tonight, Christina needs you at this party. You have time for a short bath if you hurry. I've got my suit already at the apartment." He reached over and squeezed her hand. "How in the world do you always wind up in the middle of these things? Mark is right, you have a talent."

"Sarah's going to be mad at me because now he has an excuse not to come to the party." Mia groaned. "Even when I'm right, I'm wrong."

Trent laughed as he pulled into the parking lot for the academy. "I don't think she'll blame you, but Mark had better hurry and get Carol processed so he can get changed. Sarah doesn't like to be kept waiting."

Mia hurried upstairs, where a worried Mr. Darcy followed her straight into the bathroom. She turned on the hot water, then rubbed his head. "I'm fine, but I'm glad it's all over."

Trent brought her a glass of wine to calm her nerves as she filled her tub. "I talked to your grandmother. Your phone must still be in your office. I'll come get you in thirty minutes. I'll get dressed, then I need to call Mom and let her know what happened."

As Mia sank into the tub, she closed her eyes and thought about butterflies and rainbows. Anything to take away the taste of what she assumed poison water would have felt like in her mouth.

Even her wine tasted a little off right now.

CHAPTER 25

At the party, Mia walked in to see Christina and Levi already on the dance floor. She wore a sparkling white pouf of a dress, and she looked like a diamond and snowflake storm. Levi was in a black tuxedo and only had eyes for his fiancée.

Mia and Trent walked over to where Abigail and Grans were sitting. Mia sat between them, and her grandmother touched the necklace Mia had received for her induction ceremony. "You may want to keep your protection amulet on for a while. The world is shifting."

"I've got it tucked away in a pocket inside the dress," Mia admitted. "After today, there's no way I'm going anywhere without it. But I thought this necklace was perfect for the event and the dress."

"You still don't know who sent it?" Grans leaned back in her chair, studying the room.

"I've been a little busy the last two weeks. I'll figure it out." Mia glanced around the room. "Where are Thomas and Robert?"

"Robert had a prior engagement he couldn't get out of," Grans said, but Mia heard the anger in her tone.

Abigail jumped in. "Thomas went to get us more drinks."

"I'll go help him, then." Trent stood and kissed Mia's shoulder. "Don't move, okay? White wine?"

"That will work," Mia replied. She would have said something sharp, like she didn't need to be coddled, but right now, maybe she did. At least for a minute. Carol had scared her.

"Trent and Abigail filled me in. The protection alarm from your necklace was going crazy, and I was trying to call you. I can't believe Carol did all of this. I know she was terrorized after the attack during the competition, but that was years ago. The coven sent in counselors, and even they thought she was better. I guess some things never go away." Grans emptied her glass and reached for another one off a passing tray. "I'm worried all this is only the beginning. Maybe it's not a good time for Christina to be leaving the area. We may need to quarantine together before this is all over."

Mia tried not to roll her eyes. Her grandmother had been talking about her dreams for years now. A war between paranormal forces. Us against them. "Grans, maybe all of this is only a dream."

"Mia, you know that's not true. Just because the Goddess is communicating through dream works, doesn't mean it's not a real message." Grans sipped her champagne. Then she gasped and dropped the almost-full glass. It bounced on the carpet, spilling, but didn't break.

"Grans, are you okay?" Mia stood and stepped in front of her chair. She turned her grandmother's head toward her, looking for changes in her eyes. "Are you having pain anywhere? Any numbness?" *Please don't be a stroke*, she said over and over in her head.

"Stop pushing me around and get out of my way." Grans moved Mia out from in front of her with a force that convinced Mia it hadn't been a stroke. "I thought I saw . . ."

Grans stopped talking, and Mia turned back to see what she was looking at.

There, walking toward them, was Dorian Alexander, decked out in a tuxedo that made him a James Bond lookalike. His salt-and-pepper hair was accented by a dark tan. The man looked better than he did when he was alive. Well, his golem looked better. It all got confusing.

The band had taken a break. Dorian moved through the crowd, and everyone who was connected with Magic Springs stared, those in the coven and out. Everyone knew that Dorian Alexander had been killed. And yet, he was here, at Christina and Levi's engagement party.

Mia heard Mrs. Adams's voice over the now-quiet crowd. "Who is that man?"

Dorian greeted Mia first. "You look lovely, my dear. And that necklace is perfect. Consider it a gift from Mr. Darcy with a little help from me. Your cat loves you very much."

Mia's hand flew to the necklace. "You sent this? Why?"

"Mr. Darcy always talked about giving you something for your induction. If I was still there, we would have done it together. So, please, accept it in the manner it was intended. No strings. Just a lot of love." He stepped around Mia to take Grans's hand and kiss it. "You're looking well, Mary Alice."

"You, as well, Dorian. You seem to be fitting into your golem. So, why are you here? You know your being in Magic Springs is not allowed."

He nodded toward Christina and Levi, who had joined the table sometime in the confusion. The music had started up again. "I wanted to toast the happy couple. I'm so glad you two lovebirds made it."

"So you did, and now you have to leave. The humans won't understand," Abigail said, stepping closer to Mia.

"Oh, I'm not leaving. Not until you agree to stop this nonsense about a wedding." Dorian stared at Grans.

"Why do you want to stop my wedding?" Christina asked, her voice choked with tears.

He looked up and smiled at her. "Not your wedding, dear heart. Mary Alice's wedding. I'm here to fight for our relationship. Marry me, Mary Alice." He dropped to one knee and held out an open ring box.

The crowds parted, and a different man walked toward them. "I'm finally through with that horrible meeting. What's all the commotion?" Robert saw Dorian with the ring pointed toward Grans. "Mary Alice, tell this creature that you already have a ring and have made promises—to me."

Grans reached out and closed the box. "Get up," she whispered to Dorian. "This is not the time or the place. We'll meet you at the academy after this party is over."

Dorian stood, tucking the ring box in his pocket. "You will meet me?"

Grans nodded. "Yes, I promise. Just go. Please."

Dorian made his way out of the ballroom, and the crowd seemed to dissipate around them. Mia reached out and rubbed her grandmother's arm. "Are you okay?"

When Grans raised her head to look at her, tiredness ebbed from her face. "I'm fine. I'm sorry I scared you."

"That man had no right to come here." Robert sat next to Grans. "I should file a complaint with the coven."

"Let's change the subject, please?" Grans took Robert's hand in hers. "This is Christina's party."

Levi met his mom's gaze, then took Christina's hand. "Let's go dance. Now that Mia's here, we'll be starting the toasts soon."

Christina nodded and let him guide her away to the dance floor.

"That was weird," she said to Grans.

"We'll talk about it later," Grans said, then turned to Robert. "Please be a dear and find out what happened to Thomas and our drinks. I'm feeling a bit parched."

Mia wasn't sure whether Grans needed a drink because she'd spilled the last one, or if she, like Mia, was freaking out.

Dorian being back in Magic Springs changed up everything, including the arrival of Cerby and Buddy. Now that the group was all together again, did that mean Grans's dreams were real? Whatever was going on, Mia wasn't ready for a war. No matter how many supplies her grandmother had stockpiled in her second-floor classroom. No, she wasn't ready for war.

Especially a war that maybe no one could win.

RECIPE

I think the best recipes are those handed down from friend to friend or generation to generation—usually on the back of a piece of paper. My hairdresser gave me this recipe when she heard I had bought a bushel of South Carolina peaches this summer. It's as good as she predicted.

Stacy's Southern Peach Cobbler

Mix together:
   1 cup self-rising flour
   1 cup sugar
   1 cup milk
   1 teaspoon salt

Melt 1 stick of butter in a 9x13-inch baking pan. Pour mixture over butter.

Add 1 quart of peaches with a little of the peach juice on top.

Bake for 30–45 minutes at 350 degrees.

Take out of the oven and let set for 10 minutes. Serve warm with vanilla ice cream.

Hungry for more Lynn Cahoon? Turn the page to enjoy the first chapter of *Merry Murder Season*, a holiday-spirited Tourist Trap Mystery coming soon from Kensington Publishing Corp.

Merry Murder Season

CHAPTER 1

As I took in the angry faces gathered around the tables in Coffee, Books, and More, my coffee shop and bookstore, I regretted signing my "Jill King" to a new ten-year contract to host and sponsor the Business-to-Business meetings. Usually the meetings went smoothly. Darla Taylor, owner of South Cove Winery, ran the meeting with an iron fist. Since it was the holidays, you would think that everyone would be in a festive mood. But there was no peace on earth, goodwill to men, I mean, mankind, feeling today.

No, Mayor Baylor and his wife, Tina, had shown up to press the flesh because there was an election coming soon. He usually only showed up around election time. They didn't care about the huge Christmas bazaar or Santa's Village. They just wanted the votes to keep the smarmy Mayor Baylor in office. And the mayor had news for the group.

I'd broken the report that the mayor's office had

planned to close Main Street for the holiday season last year, but like all things that we don't want to deal with, people had already forgotten the warning. So no one had petitioned the city council to rethink their idea.

No one except for one business, whose owner didn't even attend the monthly business-to-business meetings. Chip's Bar had asked for an exemption for motorcycles to use the street during the closure. With Diamond Lille's owner, Lille Stanley, adding in her support, the council's decision to grant the exception had been made in August. And a motorcycle parking lot would take up part of the closed-off Main Street.

On Thanksgiving morning, which was two days away, the barriers would go up, and cars and trucks would be banned from 9 a.m. to midnight. Then the street would reopen to vehicles, allowing businesses to restock. Most of the businesses, like mine, had an alley behind our shops for deliveries anyway.

Darla banged the gavel on the lectern. "Folks, you knew this was coming. If it doesn't work, I'm sure the mayor and city council will be glad to discuss next year's plan."

Josh Thomas stood. "No one told us that there could be exceptions. My delivery truck needs to be loaded and unloaded in front of the store. What am I supposed to do? Unload in the dark?"

"There are streetlights . . ." Mayor Baylor interrupted what we all knew would be a long tirade from Josh. He was notorious for them, even when he was wrong. I thought this time, though, he might just have a point. Instead of continuing, another voice interrupted the mayor.

"And why are motorcycles allowed on the street? Those things are death traps. And they're so loud. If you're allowing motorcycles, you should just reverse the entire thing." Matty Leaven, who owned a jewelry store and, since she'd joined our business council, always seemed to be on Josh's side, pointed out. "Maybe there needs to be new blood in City Hall. People who stand up for the little guy."

Josh looked at Matty like she'd just won a Nobel Prize for standing with him. It was a new experience to have someone agree with his ideas, and he wasn't used to it yet. Mandy, his wife, who came in a lot for coffee, often laughed about Josh's infatuation with the jewelry designer. I thought he was playing with fire.

"This isn't about the upcoming election. We are a bipartisan group, and our mandate doesn't allow electioneering during the meeting." Darla met my gaze and rolled her eyes. "Anyway, if we could get back on the subject, Main Street is closing. Any further comments can go to the mayor's office or any member of our city council. Their names are on the city website with an email address. We'll talk more about the Holiday Festival next meeting, but Jill wanted to bring up our annual charity event. This year, we're partnering with Chip's Bar for a dart tournament. The entry fee will be in cash and a new toy. Then the donations and the toys will be donated to the California Central Coast Family Project for kids who won't be on Santa's delivery route this year. Jill, do you want to give us the details?"

I stood up. I had a list of talking points, and none of them dealt with the closed road or the motorcycle exemption. I introduced myself, even though most of the people already knew me. "Thanks, Darla. I'm Jill Gardner, I mean, Jill King. I own the coffee shop–slash–bookstore you're sitting in, and I'm your council liaison for the next ten years. Wow, that sounds like a long time. Anyway, I wanted to let you know that the dart tournament is also being sponsored by Coffee, Books, and More, and it is the brainchild of Chris Aquilla and Carrie Jones. It was at Carrie's suggestion that we start the book club last year."

I could see people starting to put their notes away. I was talking too much and needed to get to the point, quickly. "Anyway, it's this Saturday night at the community center across from Chip's. The entry fee is ten dollars, and the bar is kicking in the money for the players' winnings so every dollar from entries goes to the charity. They're also kicking in fifty percent of that night's profits." I handed out flyers. "Please have these available for people to take. I believe Chris and Carrie have already stopped by your business and given you a stash, but just in case you've already handed those out, here's more. Both Greg and I are playing, and I hope to see the rest of you there as well."

"It's Thanksgiving weekend. We might have family at the house," a woman from my right side mumbled. She probably didn't think I'd heard, but I had.

"Bring them along! We have family in town as well. The more, the merrier." I pasted a smile on my face, hoping it didn't look as fake as it felt. Greg didn't want to go. He worried that having the presence of law enforcement there might dampen the mood. He also didn't want to go out when his family would be in town. I was hoping they'd tag along, at least for the charity part of the night. This hadn't been my idea, but I was supporting it like it had been. Besides, it was for the kids.

"Matt and I are coming too, but if you already have plans that night"—Darla looked pointedly at Marvin and Tina Baylor—"just drop a donation check off with Amy Newman-Cole at City Hall or at Coffee, Books, and More. We don't want any child to go without a merry Christmas."

Josh glowered at Darla but didn't object. I knew that Mandy had already committed to coming on Saturday night, so he couldn't say anything against the event. But you could tell he wanted to.

Darla ended the meeting, and everyone scattered before Mayor Baylor could corner them. Tina had reached the exit first and was blocking the exit and handing out *Baylor for Mayor* buttons as people left. I noticed that Matty Leaven snuck out while Tina was handing a button to another member. The girl was smart, that was for sure.

After everyone was gone, I moved tables back in order with my barista on deck, Deek Kerr. He seemed quiet, distracted, and not his usual chatty self. Deek was a writer, so it wasn't unusual for him to be in his own world. I took the rag away where he'd cleaned the same spot for the last few minutes. "What's got you up in your head? Plotting another book?"

He glanced toward the door. Everyone had left the coffee shop, and it was just the two of us. "I'm not thinking about a book. What do you think about Matty Leaven?"

"I don't know her very well. She seems to think like Josh a lot, though." I wiped the last table and went to the sink to rinse the rag. "Why?"

"I can't figure out her aura. It changes colors based on what she's saying. And I don't think she agrees with Josh. I think she likes stirring up trouble." He poured himself a cup of coffee. "I'm probably just overanalyzing the situation."

"I don't like her at all. She's nice to your face, then I overhear her saying mean things about people, like Josh and Mandy. She says awful things about Josh all the time to her friends while they're getting coffee. And she's one of those who don't think baristas or whoever is serving her is even around." Tilly North, my newest barista, filled the treat display case. "I worked with people like that when I was at the hospital. They think you can't hear them when they're talking right outside your room."

Tilly had been in a car accident and had lost a lot of her long-term memories, like the fact that she and Toby Killian, another one of my baristas, had dated in high school. When she'd come to work for me, she'd been dating someone new. Now that relationship was over, but Tilly had stayed in the area. She was a great addition to the bookstore team. And usually very perceptive about people.

"I'll watch her more carefully." I hoped that Josh wouldn't figure out that Matty was messing with him. He had enough self-esteem issues. He didn't need to know that Matty was only pretending to like him. I poured myself a fresh cup of coffee. I had back-of-the-house work to do, namely, accounting and scheduling, since Evie was in the city, visiting her cousin, Sasha, and her daughter this week for the Thanksgiving holiday.

Toby had also dated Sasha. The boy did get around.

"Just be careful around her, Jill." Deek was staring out the window again. "I have a feeling. And it's not good."

Now I was worried. Deek Kerr liked everyone. He could read auras, or at least he thought he could. Sometimes he told me things that, when I looked them up, didn't match the aura lore published on the internet. But when you're talking about magic and seeing things that aren't there, maybe the internet didn't have all the information. Deek was a good guy, and he saw people clearly, which made him an excellent barista and bookseller.

I decided to change the subject. "Are you coming to Thanksgiving at the house? I haven't heard from either of you."

"Mom's out of town, so I thought I'd just hang in the apartment." Deek moved back behind the coffee bar. "I'll grab the boxes of books that need to be shelved."

"Deek Kerr, you stay right there." I didn't use my boss voice often, but this was going to be one of those times. When he froze and turned to me, I continued. "There is no way you're not coming for dinner now that I know your mom's not home. So, what are you bringing?"

"Jill, it's your first family dinner since you've been married. You don't need strays hanging around." He blushed as he glanced over at Tilly, who now had her hands on her hips.

"Oh, so you don't think I should go either?" she challenged him. "I don't appreciate being called a stray."

"I didn't say that." Deek stumbled over his words. Finally, he let his shoulders drop. "Look, I don't want you to invite me because I'm some loser who doesn't have family here for Thanksgiving. Mom's just not into those traditions, so she's going on a cruise. I'm used to this."

"Which is why you're coming. My family isn't made up of just those people who are related to Greg or me. You should know that by now. I won't have you sitting around the apartment eating ramen while we're having a turkey dinner. Besides, I think Harrold is bringing Lille, so I'll need some of my people to watch my back."

Lille Stanley, the owner of Diamond Lille's, was one of my uncle Harrold's favorite people. Lille liked Greg and my aunt Jackie too. She just hated me. Thanksgiving should be fun. I'd say Lille would have Jim to chat with since he used to hate me too, but since he started dating Beth, he'd been more open. Besides, since Greg and I were married now, Greg's first wife, Sherry, was out of the picture.

"She hates you?" Tilly's eyes widened. She was such a nice young woman she didn't understand the concept. "Well, I'll be there to watch your back. I don't have the money to go visit my folks now that they've moved to Tennessee, and I don't want to be in the house all by myself. I love the holidays. Mom left me all the old Christmas decorations, so I've been working on getting the house decorated for weeks."

"My mom never decorated," Deek admitted. "I hated

the holidays growing up, because we were always the one family who didn't have a tree or lights on the house."

"Well, Greg is going to get everyone to help string lights outside the house, and we'll be decorating the tree after dinner. It's one of the King family traditions." I was looking forward to celebrating Thanksgiving this year. "Aunt Jackie and Harrold are leaving for a cruise on Friday. So you won't see her for two weeks if you don't come."

Deek stared at me. "I thought you wanted me to come?"

"Stop it." I started laughing. "You love Aunt Jackie, I know you do."

"Did I tell you she updated my author questionnaire last week for people who want to schedule book events here? She thinks we should charge an event fee if they don't hit a certain amount of sales." Deek threw a clean towel over his shoulder as he talked.

I groaned. Aunt Jackie had been harping on that for a while. And she hated the Cove Connection book club. She thought they should be required to buy the book from the store to participate. I didn't care where they bought or borrowed the book from, I just wanted people to be reading more. Besides, we worked closely with our local library on author events. "I'll talk to her. Just file away the changed copy and don't make any drastic movements. We're doing fine on author events. Some are just more popular than others. Everyone needs a shot in the arm every once in a while."

"Thanks. I'd rather not tell my newly published authors I don't think they're big enough to bother with."

Deek nodded to the back door. "Am I excused? Those books aren't going to shelve themselves."

"Are you coming to Thanksgiving?" I stared him down.

He blinked first. "I'll bring focaccia bread. I've been working on my recipe."

Tilly watched him head to the back room. "He reads, he's cute, *and* he bakes? How on earth is he still single?"

Greg came into the shop just before my shift ended at eleven. "Do you have time for lunch at Diamond Lille's?"

"I'd love to." I nodded to Deek. "You have the helm, good sir."

Deek laughed and pointed to Tilly. "This one thinks she's in charge. If I didn't know better, I would think I was working with your aunt. She loves the checklists."

Tilly playfully slapped him on his arm. "There's nothing wrong with a little organization now and then. With my sieve of a brain, writing things down is the only way I know I'll remember to do something. By the way, I'm going to bring pumpkin cheesecake on Thanksgiving if that's okay."

I was a little thrown by the change of subject, but that was how Tilly thought. And anything she thought came out of her mouth. Mostly. "Sounds great. I'll see you both on Thursday. Call if you need anything."

As Greg and I started down the street toward Diamond Lille's, he glanced back at the bookstore. "Are both of them coming to Thanksgiving?"

"Yes. Judith is going out of town. Toby, of course, will be there, and Evie's already gone to see Sasha. Anyone from the station?" I ticked off my staff members as I listed them off.

"Your friends Amy and Justin are heading to see his folks. Esmeralda is going to New Orleans to be with her family. And the rest of them are otherwise committed. I'd hoped that Tim and Dona might come and bring the baby, but they're going to her folks' place in Sacramento." He nodded to the antique store. "Josh and Mandy are going to her family's farm. He's not looking forward to it."

"He hates being around people." I knew there was more to the story, but at least Josh was trying to forgive Mandy's family for a few things that had happened before they were married.

"And, I might as well tell you now, Jim and Beth are fighting." He checked the road, then we jaywalked across the street to the restaurant. It was good being married to the head detective, although jaywalking was about all Greg did to skirt the law. He was a rule follower.

"Oh, no. What did he do now?" I liked Beth. Probably a lot more than I liked Greg's brother, Jim.

"He's being a pill about her working once they're married. She's standing up for herself. Mom thinks it will blow over, but they may not want to go to this fundraiser thing on Saturday. You know Jim and bars. Or she might want to go, and he would want me to stay behind with him." He held the door open for me. "I might just offer to take Mom and them to dinner while you do this. I'll give you a check for the entrance fees we aren't paying."

"No way. You and your family are coming. I've already bought the toys to get us inside." I was going to say more, but then Lille walked up to seat us.

"Hi, Greg, I've got a booth just for you." She smiled at my husband, grabbed two menus, and walked us to the table. "Carrie will be right with you."

Then she disappeared. Without even looking at me.

I slipped onto the red leather bench seat. I rolled my eyes before holding up the menu so I could see what I'd read at least once a week for five years. "Some things never change. I'm so glad she's coming for our family dinner on Thursday."

"Jill, I'm sure it will be fine. She was probably just—" Greg's phone rang. From the ringtone, I knew it was his brother, Jim. "Look, I need to take this. I'll try to keep it short."

He walked out of the restaurant. I could see him pacing as he talked to his brother. I had a bad feeling that Beth wasn't going to make it for dinner on Thursday.

ACKNOWLEDGMENTS

As I write this, I'm at a writers' conference. It's one of the big ones, so you see all kinds of writers here. Those just starting out and the big names, all milling around Gaylord's Opryland Hotel's conference center. As I people-watch—my favorite activity—I'm always in awe of all the things that must happen to bring a book or a series to the hands of a reader. All the people involved in the process, including the muse who's standing behind me laughing as I write. I think she's related to Gloria from the story.

So thank you for reading the KITCHEN WITCH books, if this is your first or if you're following the series. I am humbled and honored you chose this book over all the other books out there calling your name.

Thanks to my Kensington team—Michaela Hamilton, Cassidy, Larissa, Alex, Rebecca, and so many others who treat the books with so much care. Thanks also to my agent, who gently guides me in my career, keeping me from coloring outside the lines of my contracts.

Finally, thanks to my friends and family, especially the Cowboy and the pups, Dexter and Quinn, who keep me laughing.

Visit our website at
KensingtonBooks.com
to sign up for our newsletters, read
more from your favorite authors, see
books by series, view reading group
guides, and more!

BOOK CLUB
BETWEEN THE CHAPTERS

Become a Part of Our
Between the Chapters Book Club
Community and Join the Conversation

Betweenthechapters.net